SECOND CHANCE

A RYAN LOCK NOVEL

SEAN BLACK

D1089532

SBD

SECOND CHANCE

An SBD Book

Copyright © Sean Black 2017

For my friend, David Seidler, and in memory of the late David Shaber, two brilliant Hollywood screenwriters, who, in their own way, and at different times, kept me going when the going was tough.

ABOUT THE BOOK

Over the years, former military bodyguard Ryan Lock has made more than his fair share of enemies. It was only a matter of time before one of them came looking for payback . . .

A serial rapist brutally murdered *inside* California's highest-security prison for women. A frantic gun battle in the middle of downtown Los Angeles. A beautiful, young defense attorney violently abducted from her office.

A series of apparently random events that are anything but.

Someone is hell bent on revenge, and their target's name is Ryan Lock.

~

Praise for the Ryan Lock series:

"Readers, meet Ryan Lock – a tough-guy hero for the new age." Gregg Hurwitz

AUTHOR'S NOTE

This is the eight novel featuring military veterans turned private security operatives, Ryan Lock and Ty Johnson. You can read each novel in the series by itself, or read the entire series.

If you're new to Ryan and Ty you can get three Lock ebooks (one novel and two novellas) by signing up to my mailing list at www.seanblackauthor.com/subscribe

Your email won't be shared, you won't be spammed, and you can unsubscribe at any time.

You can also contact me via the website. I love hearing from readers, and I do my best to reply to every email.

I hope you enjoy Second Chance.

Best wishes,

Sean Black

1

Manhattan Beach, California

ALICIA HALLIS DIDN'T like the way this guy was looking at her son. She didn't like it one little bit. She nudged her husband, who was busy replying to a work-related email on his iPhone. "That guy over there's been staring at Jackson for, like, the past five minutes."

Jim Hallis looked up from the screen with a nonchalance that made Alicia want to scream. "What guy?"

"Over there. Standing next to the bench. With the black ball cap and the red and black shorts."

Jim lowered his sunglasses from where they were perched atop his head, and looked over toward the bench. He picked out the man his wife had just described. She'd missed out on a few details. Like the dude being well over six feet tall, two hundred pounds, with a thick black beard and covered with tattoos. And not your usual hipster Manhattan Beach-type ink either. He was sporting a huge eagle across his chest, lightning bolts that ran all the way up his neck, and a couple of teardrops. Jim was sure he'd heard somewhere that tear-drops signified you'd killed someone.

The guy saw Jim looking at him. He didn't blink. He didn't break eye contact. He stared straight back.

Jim Hallis quickly turned back to his wife. "Where is Jackson anyway?"

Wrong question. Alicia immediately went into panic mode.

"Oh, my God! I can't see him. Where *is* he?" she said, grabbing her bag.

Jim quickly scanned the kids weaving their skateboards through the crowds. He picked out Jackson, who was talking to a group of slightly older girls. "Chill out. I see him. He's right over there," he said, with a nod.

Alicia shifted back down from completely panicked to mildly uptight. Jim wondered if her obsession with keeping tabs on Jackson's every waking move would ever pass. He got that some moms could be over-protective, but Alicia took it way too far. She'd even gone so far as installing a hidden tracking app on Jackson's phone so she'd know where he was when he was out of the house.

Alicia was heading over to their son. Jim hurried to keep up with her. The work email would have to wait. "Hey, don't go cramping his style," he said, trying to lighten her mood.

"What style? He's eight."

"Yeah, and those girls are at least eleven. Wish I'd had that kind of confidence when I was his age. I couldn't even look at a girl without blushing."

Alicia slowed up. He walked next to her.

"Anyway, the dude's gone."

"Can you not say 'dude'? It makes you sound like a moron."

Alicia looked back over at the bench. Jim was right. He wasn't there. She scanned the crowds but the man with the tattoos was nowhere to be seen. "He really was staring at Jackson. You believe me, right?"

"Of course," Jim lied. The truth was that ever since they'd welcomed Jackson into their home Alicia had never fully accepted that he wouldn't be taken back again. That his being there was permanent. That they were Jackson's parents. She'd wanted a child so badly, and they'd been so lucky to get a baby that she seemed to believe their good fortune could evaporate at any moment.

Jim was worried that as their son grew older he'd begin to resent Alicia's overbearing behavior. Kids had to be allowed some space to grow up. To make their own mistakes.

Jackson broke away from the group and wandered back to them.

"Who were those girls?" Alicia asked.

Jackson blushed. "I don't know. They wanted to know where I got my board. Where I went to school. That sort of junk," he said, glancing down at the brightly colored skateboard tucked under his arm.

Jim slapped Jackson on the back. "That's my boy."

Jackson shot him a sheepish smile from under a tangled blond fringe.

"Jim!" Alicia scolded.

"Hey, when you got it, you got it." He put a hand on his son's shoulders. "Tell you what, why don't we all head down to Tomboy's? Grab ourselves a chili burger. Mom can have a salad if she's still on that dumb diet."

Alicia glared at him. "I'm not on a diet. I just like to look after myself."

He smiled at her. "I'm teasing. You look great, honey. Jackson, why don't you go on ahead?"

Jackson dropped his board, and took the opportunity to skate away from his parents' bickering.

"It's a beautiful day. Whoever that weird guy was, he's gone. Let's just enjoy ourselves."

Something about the way Jim said it seemed to break the tension. Alicia smiled back at him. "Okay."

He took her hand and together they threaded their way through the crowds toward the restaurant, Jackson skillfully carving out a path on his skateboard.

THE THREE GIRLS turned the corner and ran straight into the man with the tattoos and the thick black beard. They took a step back, exchanging nervous glances.

"So?" the man said.

"He's really cool," the oldest of the three said. She was twelve.

"For a little kid," one of the others added. She had found the whole thing too creepy for words. Some guy paying them to go talk to a boy like that.

"I didn't ask you to find out if he was cool. What school does he go to?"

The older of the girls shrugged. "Pacific."

"Grade?"

"Third."

"His teacher?"

The girl's hand shot out, palm facing up. "Where's that twenty?"

The guy dug into his pocket and pulled out a roll of notes. He peeled off a twenty and slapped it into her hand. Her fingers closed around it.

"Miss Parsons. I think that was what he said."

"You think?"

"That was it. I'm sure."

It didn't matter. That would be easy enough to verify. And this had saved him a lot of time and hanging about. Manhattan Beach wasn't exactly the kind of place where a man like Padre blended in. The last thing he needed was to be bounced back to the joint on some bullshit PV (parole violation) because a neighbor called the cops.

2

C entral California Women's Facility
Chowchilla, California
TV satellite trucks lined either side of the road leading
to the Central California Women's Facility. It was home to the state's
female death-row prisoners, and others who offered a particular
security challenge.

Up near the gatehouse, a perfectly made-up blond television
reporter was delivering a breathless piece to camera. Behind her, a
small group of protestors holding an assortment of handmade plac-
ards were pushed back into a small fenced-off area by a half-dozen
members of local law enforcement. The reporter took in the
protestors with a sweep of her hand, then looked back down the
barrel of the camera lens to finish her piece to camera.

"As you can see, Brad, the transfer of serial rapist Gerard, now
Ginny, Browell to this women's facility has drawn a small crowd of
protestors. Some of them have family members inside here, and are
concerned about their safety. As for California's Department of
Corrections and Rehabilitation, they say that the latest court ruling
has left them with no alternative but to move Browell to a women's
facility, regardless of their own concerns. And the nature of this indi-

vidual's crime has meant that advocates for the rights of transgender people have been remarkably silent on the issue. But in less than one hour, it's our understanding that one of America's most notorious and prolific serial rapists will be placed inside this women's correctional facility."

~

CHANCE, whose real name was Freya Vaden, sat in her usual spot as the other inmates in the unit clucked around her, like hens who'd just spotted a fox digging its way under the coop fence. Except this fox hadn't needed to dig: the California Supreme Court had done the spade work.

Clarissa Thoms, a thin meth-addict, with frizzy red hair, who was serving life without possibility for parole for drowning her twin sons, shoved in next to her. "What we gonna do, Chance? That's what I want to know."

Chance leaned in and brushed away a stray strand of hair from over Clarissa's eye. "Calm yourself, honey. I have it all under control."

That served to set off a fresh round of clucking from the others in the group.

"Under control? This is a monster coming into our house."

"It ain't a woman, that's for sure. I don't care what no doctor says."

"I heard he only claimed he was trans so he could get a transfer and keep raping."

"How's he gonna rape without a dick, huh?"

"Shows what you know. I heard he uses a shank. Shoves it up inside you so you'll be hoping it was his pecker."

Chance had heard enough. She slammed down two open palms on the plastic table top. "Hush now. All of you. If they put him in this here unit with us then I said I'm going to deal with it."

That brought more questions.

"How?"

"What you gonna do, Chance?"

"He's strong, Chance. You won't be able to take him on your own."

Chance smiled at them. "Whoever said anything about doing it on my own?" She turned so that she was facing Clarissa. "Ol' Ginny Browell's gonna kick and scream more than your two little 'uns. You think you can handle that, Clarissa?"

Clarissa's smile fell away, and tears blossomed in her eyes. "That ain't a nice thing to say, Chance. I didn't mean to do what I did to those boys."

Chance got up from the table with a shrug. "I'll do it myself if I have to. Makes no difference to me."

As a couple of the hens huddled around Clarissa, Chance walked over to the stairs that led to the upper level of cells and climbed them. At the top she passed a guard. She didn't look at him. He didn't look at her.

As she passed him, he palmed a small phone to her. Without breaking stride, she took it and headed for her cell. She stepped inside, closed the door, powered up the phone and began to scroll through the messages that rolled in.

She stopped at the third, tapped on an image that had been attached. The picture filled the screen. It showed a couple standing on the curb outside a coffee shop. Freya was already familiar with the woman but seeing the man with her made her heart leap into her throat. Every feature of his face had been etched into her memory.

"No way," she muttered to herself. "No freaking way."

What were the odds? After all these years?

Oh, this was going to be even better than she'd imagined in her wildest dreams. Way better.

3

Santa Monica, California

Ryan Lock didn't believe in second chances. Or, perhaps more accurately, he had chosen not to believe in them. When things went bad—really bad—you had one opportunity to avert disaster. And, if you wanted to live to see another sunrise, you'd better take it.

If you didn't, or if your aim was off, you wouldn't get another. The other side would make their move, and you'd be so much road kill, lying squashed on the verge.

In Lock's line of work, close-protection security—what the general public thought of as bodyguarding—there were rarely do-overs. There was no reset button. There was no way to turn back time.

The stakes were brutal and binary. You and the people you were charged with protecting either lived or died.

Over time, Lock had allowed the same belief to dictate his personal life. He had been lucky enough to meet the woman of his dreams. Carrie Delaney had opened up a whole new world for him. They had met in New York and fallen in love. Then she had died in front of his eyes while fleeing two kidnappers.

He had always figured that had been his one shot at true love. But now, much to his surprise, it looked like he'd been wrong. From nowhere a woman had entered his life who stirred some of the same feelings he had experienced before.

"Ryan?"

Carmen Lazaro's voice drifted across the perfectly set table, snatching him away from a storm-swept Topanga Canyon road where Carrie had died and his life had changed for the worse. He looked across the table at her. She was a tall caramel-colored beauty, with lush chestnut hair and mesmerizing brown eyes. Raised by a Mexican mother and Guatemalan-Irish father, she had grown up in East Los Angeles and studied law at UCLA, graduating in the top one percent of her class – three part-time jobs to pay her way through college had prevented her from coming out on top. She had turned down a fistful of big-money offers from white-shoe law firms to carve out a far less lucrative, but more rewarding, career as a criminal defense attorney in downtown Los Angeles.

"Ryan?" This time Carmen's voice was a little more insistent.

"Sorry?"

"Can you stop working? Just for one evening?"

He was puzzled. "Working?"

"You're miles away and when you're not miles away you're scanning the room like someone's about to pop up from under a table-cloth with a machine gun."

She was right. He had been checking out their fellow diners. It was a habit carried over from work. He was constantly scanning his surroundings, performing a second-by-second risk assessment. Looking for something in the environment that didn't quite chime.

Over the years, the presence of the abnormal, the absence of the normal, had come as close as he'd gotten to having a mantra. It had made him a first-class bodyguard, and a second-rate date. This wasn't the first time Carmen had pointed it out.

He threw her a placatory smile—not that he was known for smiling or placating people but Carmen was different. Big-league different. "I apologize. You have my full, undivided attention," he said, taking a sip of water.

"Yeah, right. Tell you what, I'd settle for half to three-quarters."

"Deal."

"What are you so on edge about anyway. You know what the cops call this part of town, right?"

He didn't, but he guessed it wasn't going to be complimentary. Cops were rarely complimentary about the world. They'd seen too much of it. "Go on."

"They call it West Latte Division."

A cursory glance around the main dining room of Mélisse confirmed Carmen's point. The area from Marina Del Rey to Malibu and all the way inland to the B-neighborhoods of Beverly Hills, Brentwood and Bel Air, was about as upscale and genteel as you got in the sprawling Greater Los Angeles area. Here, what most people would consider crime was rare, and serious violent crimes were rarer. When they did happen, they captured the front pages, and were dealt with swiftly. Drive ten miles and homicides were commonplace. But the closer to the Pacific you got, the richer the residents, and hence the safer the streets.

A movie-star-handsome waiter materialized at their table to take their order. He flashed an overly familiar smile at Carmen as his eyes fell a little lower than was professional. "Madam, are you ready to order?"

Lock didn't blame the guy. If you dated a woman as drop-dead gorgeous as Carmen Lazaro, you got used to the reactions of other men. Carmen had confessed to Lock early on that one of the reasons she liked him was that he was secure enough not to be bothered by it. He didn't get defensive or, worse, jealous. He was one of the few men, perhaps the only one, Carmen had dated who had enough self-confidence not to be irritated by the attention she attracted when they went out together.

For Lock's part it wasn't a strategy. It wasn't even conscious. He just figured that if they were together then they were together. Being jealous or possessive never made a relationship better. It could only achieve the opposite.

His attention shifted briefly from Carmen and the waiter. Outside the restaurant on Wilshire Boulevard, a black Ford Mustang with tinted windows had pulled up into a loading area directly opposite. It sat there, engine idling, no one getting out. No one getting in either.

"And for you, sir?"

Lock didn't get much of a smile. Then again, he didn't have the waiter trying to stare down his shirt either, so he figured it was a wash. He glanced back at the menu. "May I have the steak, cooked rare?"

"Cooked rare," the waiter said, like he didn't quite believe that was how he wanted it.

"As in, wipe its ass and throw it on the plate," Lock said, keen to ensure there wasn't any ambiguity in the kitchen about how he liked his steak.

"Yes, sir."

As the waiter collected their menus, Lock glanced back to the Mustang. It was still parked across the street, the faintest shimmer of heat coming from its tail pipe.

"Ryan?" Carmen said, clearing her throat. "You're doing it again."

Pushing back his chair, Lock got to his feet. "I have to use the bathroom, be right back," he said, heading, at speed, toward the restaurant's front door.

Carmen called after him, "The bathroom's that way."

He half turned to her. "The one next door's nicer."

"Ryan!"

4

He dodged round the hostess, who was busy greeting a party of six, and pushed through the door. As he made the sidewalk, the Mustang bolted, narrowly missing a white Prius as it took off at speed down Wilshire, running a red light on 11th Street. A few seconds later it was a distant memory.

Lock looked round for a Santa Monica Police Department cruiser. No luck. He turned back toward the restaurant. Carmen was waiting for him at the door, clearly less than pleased.

"What was that?" she said, her toe tapping the floor.

Lock shrugged, and did his best to look innocent. "What?"

"Don't play dumb."

He could feel an argument brewing. "There was a strange car parked across the street, like they were up to no good. I went out to take a closer look."

"And?" Carmen asked.

"And nothing. They took off."

Carmen rolled her eyes at him, but she was smiling.

"What can I tell you? Old habits die hard."

Carmen studied him. "What do I have to do to make you relax?"

Lock smiled. "I'm sure we can think of something."

She reached out, slipped her hand into his and led him back to their table. For once he was happy to let someone else take charge. "I'm sure we can."

~

As the waiter came with the check, Carmen's cell phone pinged with an incoming message. She had already laid her American Express card on the table, ready to pick up the tab.

Lock handed it back to her. "I got this."

"You got it last time," Carmen protested.

"Last time was Fat Burger. I don't think that counts as me buying you dinner."

Carmen didn't argue. It was unusual for her. She was big into making sure that she paid her fair share, even though the money he was pulling down must have been three times what her office could afford to pay her. Her brow furrowed slightly as she scanned the text message.

"Problem?"

"We just had a deposition rescheduled for tomorrow morning. I'm going to have to swing by the office on the way home and pick up some papers."

Carmen's office was downtown. A forty-minute drive from where they were.

"I can drive you."

"That means I'd have to come back here for my car. It's easier if I just go myself."

"You sure?"

"Ryan, you do know that I managed to navigate this city on my own for years before you came along?"

"I was thinking you might like the company, is all."

Carmen smiled. "Tell you what, you go back to my place. Open a bottle of wine for us, light some candles, and I'll be there as soon as I can."

He didn't answer straight off. His mind was still on the black

Mustang that had been parked outside and taken off when he'd walked outside.

"Or we can forget it and you can go back to your place on your own. Maybe call up Tyrone if you get lonely later on."

That got his attention. He'd spent enough time on his own with his business partner Ty Johnson to last two lifetimes. "Think I'll go with your first proposal, Counsellor."

"Wise choice, Mr. Lock," said Carmen.

OUTSIDE, the valet pulled forward Lock's car, a pearl gray Audi RS7. It had been kept up front, its position secured with a tip.

The Audi blended nicely with LA traffic. It wasn't too ostentatious, but could move like greased lightning when he needed it to. Deleted badges meant that most people assumed it was a regular Audi and had no idea what lay under the hood—a four-liter V8 engine that went from zero to sixty in under four seconds.

Lock thanked the valet for his cooperation, and pulled out onto Wilshire Boulevard. A half-block down he eased into a spot on the street, and watched in his rearview mirror as Carmen got into her Honda.

Everything seemed normal. He started to feel a little bad for keeping eyes on her. His guilt soon evaporated as her Honda pulled out of the restaurant driveway, and the black Ford Mustang he'd seen earlier fell in behind her.

He waited for them both to pass before he, too, pulled out into traffic. He doubted the guys in the Ford had seen him, but he hung back anyway.

It looked like his hunch had been correct after all. The question now was, who were the guys in the Mustang and why were they following his girlfriend?

5

C entral California Women's Facility
Chowchilla, California
Chance stared down from the top tier at Ginny Browell, who was sitting alone at a table in the far corner of the pod. All the other inmates were backed up into the opposite corner, as far away as they could get in such tight quarters. They shot nervous glances at Browell and whispered among themselves.

Before Ginny, there had been Gerard Browell, the serial rapist who had terrorized large swatches of southern California for almost ten years before he'd finally been caught. It was a long time to evade the law. Longer, Chance now thought, to evade justice.

Browell specialized, if that was the correct term, in leaving his victims barely alive. Never quite finishing them off, even when it would have been easier and, for his continued freedom, safer to do so. Many were so traumatized by their experience that it took the police months to extract any kind of useful witness statement.

The sheer terror that Browell left his victims as a legacy meant that descriptions of him varied wildly. After his arrest the police discovered he had deployed a variety of disguises from fake facial hair to dressing up, on a few occasions, as a woman. It was this that he would later use against the State of California to argue that he had the right to gender reassignment.

Once he had been granted the right to change gender, he immediately began petitioning to be moved to a correctional facility for women. Anyone familiar with Browell and what he had done had a strong hunch that he wanted access to fresh stock of fresh victims. Nonethelss his case attracted a pool of people with the best of intentions and equally bad judgment.

His attorneys managed to successfully petition the CDCR (California Department of Corrections and Rehabilitation) for his transfer. The CDCR didn't want to do it, but had judged it less costly than losing a multi-million-dollar lawsuit that would also set a legal precedent they could be held to in future.

They had sent him here because it was the highest security facility they had for female inmates. Which still meant it wasn't all that secure. At least, not compared to places like San Quentin or Pelican Bay.

Chance had followed Browell's case with interest. She'd been rooting for him. Where the others had seen a threat, she had seen an opportunity. Browell, Gerard or Ginny, didn't scare her. There was nothing he could do to her that she hadn't already suffered as a child growing up in foster care.

Chance strolled to the end of the walkway and started to make her way down the metal stairs. Ginny Browell looked up at her. There was a predatory flicker in Ginny's eyes that Chance recognized. Blonds had been Gerard's type. Chance doubted that had changed. All well and good, she thought. It would make this a lot easier.

At the bottom of the stairs, she ignored the rest of the ladies, and headed straight for Ginny. Chance had a broad smile on her face as she pointed at a seat. "You mind if I sit here?"

Ginny seemed taken aback. On guard. That was to be expected. "Go right ahead," she said, in an affected Southern accent that grated on Chance, like nails down a chalkboard.

Chance opened her clenched fist to reveal a roll of candy. "Here," she said, passing it to Ginny. "I thought you might not have been allowed to bring commissary with you."

Commissary was the stuff you could legally buy. Ramen noodles, candy, and toiletry items, like soap and shampoo, were the big sellers. There was lots of other stuff you could get that was illegal and would be confiscated by the guards if they found it. From Chance's experience, it was a plain fact that there were more drugs floating around jails than out on a regular city block. Drugs helped the time pass.

Ginny held the roll of candy in her open palm. "You put poison in it?" she asked, again with that sickly *Gone with the Wind* accent.

Chance reached over and snatched it back. She flipped the top piece of candy from the roll with her thumb and popped it into her mouth. Ginny's eyes were still narrow. "Take a piece from the middle."

Chance shrugged. Did just that. She opened her mouth, flicking her tongue, and curling it as she dropped in the second piece. Slowly, seductively, she licked her lips and made a show of how much she was enjoying it. It was a performance designed to test her theory that Ginny Browell was just as driven as Gerard had been. "Tastes so good," she said, dropping her voice to a whisper and locking eyes with Ginny.

Reassured, Ginny reached out her open palm toward Chance. Chance smiled and placed the candy roll on the table. Close enough that Ginny would have to reach for it from across the table.

"Go ahead, sweetie," said Chance, her left hand disappearing below the table top and pulling the shank from where it was tucked into her pants. It consisted of a rigid black plastic handle with a sharpened metal blade. Chance had made it by melting down Styrofoam cups (the Styrofoam reconstituting as a hard plastic resin) and removing a metal disk from a fire sprinkler head, which she then sharpened to a point. It was more for slashing than stabbing but that was all she needed to get started. Behind her, unseen by Ginny, a couple of the other ladies were reaching for their shanks.

Chance would get the party started. Then the others would join her on the dance floor. That was the plan.

Ginny Browell leaned over the table. Her head was forward, her back at an angle. As her right hand went to pluck the candy, Chance grabbed Ginny's wrist, pulling her off balance. Her free hand came up with the shank. She slashed directly across Ginny's neck.

Ginny roared and reared back. She was strong. Stronger than even Chance had anticipated. But Chance kept a tight hold of the wrist as Ginny swung a punch with her free arm.

The fist came in from the side in a long arc that gave Chance plenty of time to raise the shank blade. The blade sliced across Ginny's knuckles. Blood was spurting everywhere now.

The alarm had already sounded. There was a rush of movement from behind Chance as the others swarmed toward them, like the bench clearing at a baseball game to defend a fellow teammate. Only this was planned. Everyone had already been told what they had to do. Some were to go to the unit door to slow the guards. Others would help Chance with what came next.

6

G inny rose from the table, half stumbling, half falling back toward the entrance door. Clarissa, the meth-addict who had killed her children, was already there with her little posse, blocking any escape. She didn't look like much but she was strong. She shrieked and waved her arms wildly, her curly red hair falling over her eyes as she slashed her nails at Ginny's face.

Chance advanced toward the melee. She handed off her shank to someone. They took it and passed her a fresh weapon. This one was a Christmas-tree deal made from pieces of metal scrounged up over the last month. It was barbed, tapering toward the end. That made shoving it in easy, but pulling it back out a whole lot harder.

Ginny was still fighting. Hard. Kicking and punching. Catching people too. A bulldog-faced woman, doing life for killing her girl-friend's grandparents, was sent spinning backwards by a kick to her stomach.

That gave Chance an angle. She rushed into the squirming mass of bodies, the shank held down by her side. At the last second she brought it up and around, pushing off with her back foot and twisting her hips to get momentum. The tip pierced Ginny just below her ribs on her left side.

Chance kept pushing, using everything she had to force the metal deeper. Past flesh and into organs. Slicing blood vessels. She watched as Ginny's eyes began to roll in her head. "See how you like it," she said, her face close to Ginny's.

Blood foamed at the corner of Ginny's mouth. Another improvised knife slashed across Ginny's face, the blood splashing Chance as the blade sliced through Ginny's eye.

Kicking out one last time with her feet, Ginny wailed. The sound came to an abrupt stop. Her body slumped as life left her. She fell backwards.

Guards in full riot gear were pushing their way through the entrance and into the unit. Batons swung into the air. A Taser crackled as its barbs sank into Clarissa's back. She jerked back and forth as thousands of volts shot through her, like a puppet with its strings yanked.

Chance began to grab women and pull them back, away from the guards. She urged them into their cells. "Come on now. It's done," she shouted.

They scrambled past her as she stood, her arms folded across her chest, a blood-soaked avenger. A baton slammed into the side of her leg. Chance smiled. The pain was just that. A physical sensation. Nothing more.

Slowly she put her hands down, palms open, and allowed herself to be bundled to the floor and shackled.

"You've gone and done it this time," one of the guards shouted in her ear, so loud that it hurt worse than being hit.

"The hell you talking about? I didn't do nothing," she said.

"You gotta be shitting me. We saw you. It's on camera."

"I told you. I didn't do nothing. I was giving her candy."

Her denial drew more disbelieving grunts and declarations from the guards. They had all watched her murder Ginny Browell. She had started it, and she'd finished it too, with that Christmas-tree shank.

The other inmates in the unit had helped, but Chance had done the real damage.

Chance knew it too. Of course she had done it. But doing something and it being proved in a court of law, well, those were two
different things. And Chance was going to have her day in court. Her
attorneys would make sure of it.

ock hung back in traffic, making it unlikely anyone in the
Mustang would see him, but close enough that if the occupants tried anything while Carmen was driving, the Audi's
powerful engine ensured he could close the gap within a few
seconds.

He followed Carmen and her new buddies all the way down the
10 freeway to downtown. Traffic was light, which in Los Angeles
meant it was moving at close to the posted speed limit, albeit in fits
and starts.

Carmen exited via the 101 interchange. The Mustang followed.
Now that sunset had turned fully to evening and it was dark, Lock
tucked in a little closer. As far as they would see, if they noticed him
at all, he was just another set of headlights among the mass.

At the bottom of the ramp, Carmen hung a left onto Grand. He
held his breath, hoping she would park on the street. That would
make keeping eyes on her, without being seen, a lot easier. And he
didn't want to be seen—not yet anyway.

Four blocks down, she turned into the parking structure next to
her office building. Lock immediately pulled in behind a parked car,

keeping enough of a gap that he could maintain visual contact with the Mustang.

The Mustang hung back for about fifteen seconds, then followed Carmen's car down the ramp and into the parking lot. *Ten, nine, eight, seven . . .*

He counted slowly. At zero, he pulled out from the parking spot.

At the bottom of the ramp, he powered down his window and took a ticket. The barrier lifted and the Audi headed back up the concrete ramps to the fourth floor where Carmen usually parked.

Up on four, he glimpsed Carmen's back as she pushed through the doors that led from the parking area to a glass-sided walkway that connected to her office building. The Mustang was already in place, parked a few rows back. A quick look told him no one had exited.

He eased the Audi into a space where it was partially obscured from the Mustang's view by a concrete support. His hand slipped to the butt of his SIG Sauer P229. The handgun of choice for many professionally trained close-protection operators, it was loaded with a fresh clip and good to go.

While Carmen collected the papers from her office, he planned on asking the occupants of the Mustang a few questions. The answers they provided had better be adequate or their night was about to take a very unexpected, not to mention unwelcome and potentially fatal, turn.

Lock's attention stayed on the Mustang. It would have been dangerous to assume that whoever was inside it was acting alone. Another car carrying accomplices could swing up the ramp behind him at any moment.

He doubted it. But it was possible. And possible was enough to trigger caution.

A fragment of paranoia popped into his mind. Could one of the Mustang's occupants have gotten out already and gone after Carmen? Highly unlikely. But, again, possible.

He decided it was best to be on the safe side. He dug out his cell phone, pulled up Carmen's name and tapped to make the call. He wanted to make sure she was okay. If she didn't pick up, he'd change his approach, pull the guys from the Mustang and do a quick head count, at gun point if need be.

To his relief, she answered almost immediately.

"Hey, where are you?" she asked.

The question he'd hoped she wouldn't ask. Whatever he said now would be a lie—either a direct deceit or one of omission. Lying to the woman you loved wasn't good, regardless of the purity of your intentions and how good your reason.

To hell with it. He'd take it head on.

"In the parking structure next to your office."

He took a breath and waited for the inevitable explosion. Carmen might be a polished professional all-round classy lady and demon defense lawyer, but she also had a feisty Latin temper. It was one of the things that had attracted him to her. But, as with any attractive quality, it came with a downside.

"Excuse me?"

"Can I explain?"

"I think you'd better," she said, her voice full of the implied threat that it had better be good, and he'd better get to it fast. He could see now why she was widely regarded as the scourge of the Los Angeles District Attorney's Office, their prosecutors, the LAPD, any number of expert witnesses, and even one or two judges.

"When we were at the restaurant there was a Mustang parked outside. The same car followed you downtown. I'm looking at it now."

She didn't respond straight away. A good sign in this instance. "How did you know they were going to follow me?"

"A hunch, which in this case comes down to years of watching out for this kind of stuff."

There was another pause at her end.

"Where are you now? Precisely," he asked her.

"Just walking into my office."

That was good. Her office had a security guard stationed in the lobby twenty-four hours a day, seven days a week, 365 days a year. He was low-paid, likely poorly trained and incapable of stopping any real threat if it arose. But he had eyes on a bank of cameras, and he was, presumably, in good enough shape to raise the alarm if anything did go down.

"Were you aware of anyone following you inside?"

"No. Should I have been?" Carmen sounded spooked. Again, not a bad reaction. Better spooked and alert to her surroundings than the alternative.

"No. I'm ninety-nine percent certain they're both still in their vehicle. I just wanted to make sure."

"Listen, Ryan, I'm going to call LAPD, get them to send a unit down here to take a look."

It was his turn not to respond immediately. He was weighing that judgment. If they saw the cops, they might split before anyone could talk to them. It would also mean that they, and whoever had sent them (assuming there was another party), would know they'd been made. They could resume surveillance and Lock would have much less chance of spotting them. They'd be more careful not to be made by him a second time.

All of that would also mean that he might never get to know who they were or what they wanted with Carmen.

On the other hand, the LAPD might catch them, and even if they weren't arrested, he'd have some information to work with. He could do some digging, as could Carmen, and they'd know who they were dealing with.

"Ryan?"

He decided. "Call them. Tell them I'm here as well. I don't want them thinking I'm some kind of extra surprise and getting spooked when they roll up."

He gave Carmen a run-down on the Mustang's details, and exactly where it was parked. He also asked her to make sure that the dispatcher informed the responding patrol about the details of his vehicle, who he was, where he was and the fact that he was legally carrying a handgun.

Finally, he told her to stay put until he called her back and it was done. Assuming they hadn't left of their own accord before the cops arrived.

"Are you always this bossy?" she asked, once he'd finished giving her the instructions.

"Only when I'm working."

"I'm work now, am I?"

He smiled. "I thought all women were. The good ones anyway."

"Nice save."

The call ended. Lock dug in, his focus staying tight on the Mustang. Easing his SIG from its holster, he laid it gently on his lap, and took a closer look at his surroundings.

The parking structure was laid out so that the entry ramp, which took drivers up the levels, was on the eastern side. The exit, which took drivers back down in a series of similar loops, was to the south. Both the Mustang and Lock's Audi were facing west.

If they did see the LAPD cruiser as it crested the ramp and decided to get out of there, it would be easy enough for him to scoot ahead and block their exit to the south.

To avoid confusion, and no doubt for cost reasons, both the eastern and southern ramps were single lane. If he blocked the ramp there was no way the Mustang would be able to maneuver around him. If they tried, and scratched the Audi's paint, he'd give them something more to worry about than a field interrogation.

A few minutes later his cell chimed with an incoming call from Carmen.

"Okay, there's a unit on the way. Should I stay where I am?"

"Absolutely. I'll call you when they're done."

"This sucks. You know that, right? You're stuck in your car and I'm stuck in my office."

"It'll be over in no time," he said as, right on cue, the roll bar of the responding unit crested the top of the fourth-floor ramp. "In fact, here's the cavalry now."

He watched as the LAPD patrol car eased slowly toward the Mustang. He could see that it was a two-officer unit. The driver was a Latino sergeant with a barrel chest and the kind of close crop that guys went for when their hairline began inching back from their forehead.

Next to the sergeant sat a much younger female officer. She was African-American and still had the game face rookies wore when they were new to the job, eager to prove to the world, and maybe their training officer, just how in control of every situation they were. She shot him a less than friendly look as the patrol eased past the passenger side of the Audi.

So far neither the Mustang nor its occupant or occupants had made any kind of a move. They had obviously decided to sit tight and talk their way out of this.

"What do you mean we followed someone all the way here from Santa Monica, Officer? Must be a coincidence. Yeah, one in a million, right? Hey, what can we tell you? We often like to take a romantic drive downtown in the evening and just park where it's nice and quiet."

Somehow Lock doubted that answer, or any variation on it, would satisfy the two cops who had now pulled up directly behind the trunk of the Mustang, blocking any possibility of a last-minute escape.

He stayed put in the Audi. He assumed one or both of the two cops would head over to speak to him once they'd dealt with the Mustang. There was no point in his inserting himself into the middle of things. Cops tended to respond badly to citizens (that is, anyone who wasn't a cop) who did that, and he didn't blame them. It was best if he let them do their job.

A flash of movement inside the Mustang caught his eye. It took him a fraction of a second to realize what he was looking at. From his position he had a partial view of the Mustang's front passenger-side mirror.

He saw a hand come up fast, fingers closed around the stock of a gun. With the darkness and slight tint of the window he couldn't be a hundred percent certain, but it looked to him like a machine pistol.

9

The sergeant was already out of the cruiser and heading to the driver's side window. He had his service weapon drawn, but it was held down by his side. The rookie had the patrol car's passenger side door open, her weapon drawn and punched out toward the Mustang.

From where they were, neither cop had the view Lock did. They wouldn't see the pistol until it was too late.

Lock knew that anyone who draws a fully automatic weapon like that wasn't going to settle for a friendly chat and a ride to the local precinct. In California, with its relatively strict gun laws, weapons like machine pistols came with the kind of jail time no attorney could talk their client out of—mandatory time.

Grabbing his SIG from his lap, Lock pushed open the driver's door of the Audi and rolled out as fast as he could. The older cop, alerted by the noise, spun round.

"Threat!" Lock yelled. with a nod toward the Mustang, careful not to raise his own gun just yet. Threat was standard close-protection language that covered everything, apart from an explosive device, the idea being that an IED or bomb required a different response from a gun, knife or other weapon. Not knowing if a regular cop would recognize the terminology, he followed up quickly: "Front passenger just drew his gun."

His weapon punched out, the older cop took a hesitant step back, almost losing his footing in the process.

The female rookie tensed, grabbing inside for the patrol's microphone. "Driver, passenger, keep your hands where I can see them."

Her words echoed around the concrete parking lot. They were met with silence.

Lock noticed that in the time it had taken for him to shift his attention to the two police officers and look back to the side mirror, the passenger had disappeared from the front seat.

What the hell?

A Mustang wasn't a limo or a town car. Hell, it wasn't even a large sedan or an SUV. The internal capacity would have made moving into the back of the vehicle a struggle. He was sure that the door had remained closed. And his eye would have been drawn to someone wriggling their way into the back. Unless . . .

A fresh jolt of adrenalin surged through him as his eyes flicked to the Mustang's trunk. The stumpy barrel of a gun pushed through a hole that been drilled just next to the trunk release. The black of the barrel against the black paintwork made it all but seamless.

The car had been modified. Most likely the rear seats had been removed, along with the panels that separated the interior from the trunk.

"Get down!" Lock screamed at the two cops, as he threw himself to the floor.

10

Lock's elbow banged painfully into the concrete, sending a jolt of pain up his arm. He shook it off, and kept moving, rolling underneath his own vehicle. An engine block, even a modern one with all its plastic and computers, made for a fairly decent bullet absorber.

He knew that the angle of the hole in the Mustang's trunk would make firing low to take him out tricky—if the gunman even thought to aim. A machine pistol was the ultimate small spray-and-pray weapon. What it lacked in precision it made up for in sheer rounds fired per second.

He righted himself so that he was lying on his belly, facing the rear of the blocked-in Mustang. The first burst of gunfire pulsed from the Mustang's trunk about a half-second later. The noise was loud and intense. The muzzle flared red and yellow.

His view obscured, he inched forward, the SIG still in his hand, not that it was of any use. The guy firing the pistol might not have had an angle to him, but the same went from Lock's end. And he sure as hell wasn't going to start trying to shoot out tires and draw fire toward himself just yet.

What he was looking at, though he hadn't realized it until now, was the difference between a civilian stop-and-search and one conducted by the military in a higher-risk environment. LA was a tough place to police, with no shortage of knuckleheads, gang members and all-round bad guys, plenty of them packing heat, but it didn't compare to Baghdad or Kabul.

The first rule of the hard stop in a high-risk environment was to establish distance. For someone to blow you up, they had to get close enough. You could take a bullet from a distance, but the more distance, the harder it was to hit a target. So the trade-off was between contact close enough to give you the information you required, and staying alive.

What these cops had done was to focus on preventing escape or evasion. Jam their cruiser behind the Mustang and block it in. Make sure the Mustang wasn't able to go anywhere. That had only raised the stakes for the occupants. They'd been transformed into the proverbial cornered rat—a situation that rarely ended well if you didn't have greater firepower.

He needed to get a better idea of what was going on. There was only way for him to do that.

Crawling forward another few inches, he could make out the back of the female rookie's feet, planted in a shooting stance. Judging by where they were placed in relation to the patrol car's wheels, he guessed she was still tucked in behind the passenger door.

He heard a couple of single cracks as one or both of the officers returned fire. There was a brief, almost surreal, moment of silence. Then a fresh burst from the gun poking out of the Mustang's trunk. Shifting forward and looking up, Lock could see the barrel of the gun pan fractionally to the shooter's left, in the direction, he guessed, of the male cop.

Yup.

Another staccato burst of gunfire coincided with another single round.

A woman's scream cut through the ringing in Lock's ears. The rookie. It had to be. She wasn't hit, though. It wasn't that kind of a scream. It was a sound that signaled a horrified reaction. Her partner had been hit, at least once, maybe more. He was down, and in a bad way. Lock would have put every last cent he had on it.

Patrol cops in the LAPD wore body armor as standard. It might have saved the sergeant. Unless he'd taken a round to his head, his groin or one of his legs. A head shot was what people feared, but a round through your groin or into your leg could be as bad. Lose too much blood, too fast, and you'd be in a world of trouble before you even realized it.

The ringing in Lock's ears was intense—it grew in pitch, an incessant mosquito buzz. He shook his head, more to clear his mind than his ears. He needed to improvise an AOA (actions on attack) plan—and fast. He couldn't just sit tight and watch two cops get slaughtered in front of him while he lay under his car.

First, he told himself, he needed a better visual. Pushing off with his elbows, he scrambled forward another few inches.

Now he had some kind of a low-level view of the patrol car. It wasn't pretty. The vehicle had been peppered with rounds. Narrowing his eyes, he could make out the older male cop lying on the ground next to the still-open driver's door. He was on his side, one arm in spasm. Blood had already pooled around him.

He made out the feet, lower legs and butt of the female rookie. She was holding her position, but had hunkered down, making sure she presented less surface area to the shooter. That was good.

Suddenly, she took a step back. Somewhere, in a register beneath the high-pitched ringing in his ears, he was sure he heard a solid *thunk*, like a car door being slammed shut.

He pushed off with his feet, his elbows and knees scraping painfully over the hard concrete, trying to inch himself forward again to get a better view. A pair of perfectly polished boots stepped slowly along the edge of the driver's side of the Mustang. The driver was headed toward the older patrol cop as his buddy poured in a fresh series of staccato bursts of fire toward the helpless female, who had started to duck-walk backwards, away from the patrol car and her partner.

It was safe to say that his time assessing the situation had just been abruptly curtailed. He scrambled to his feet, and stood directly in front of his car. His right foot fell back, and he narrowed into something akin to an inline boxer's stance as he raised the SIG.

11

To draw fire away from the rookie, Lock squeezed off a shot over the top of the patrol car toward the driver of the Mustang. His features were obscured by a full-face mask, but he was tall and white, with lank brown hair that feathered out from the sides of the mask. From the way he was behaving, calm and full of easy purpose, he was either high on something or this wasn't his first rodeo. From the way he held the gun in his hand, Lock would have said the latter.

Lock's shot was on line, but high. He'd had to build in a safety margin to avoid hitting the rookie. Aim much lower and he risked catching her if she decided to stand up. Trying to explain why he'd shot a cop, even by accident, didn't figure on his must-do list for this year or any other.

There was no question in his mind what the driver planned on doing. He needed to move the patrol car. But he wasn't going to leave a bleeding cop on the ground holding a gun while he stepped over him and into the front. He'd kill them both, then back up the patrol car.

The rookie seemed to figure that too. She was inching away as she returned fire. The drive for self-preservation was powerful. The problem was that once she cleared the rear of the patrol car she'd be wide open to both shooters.

There was a series of heavy concrete pylons set about forty feet apart behind her. If she could make it to one of those, she'd be in good shape. What she needed, if she was going to stand a chance, was someone to distract the two shooters.

Doing his best to stay low, Lock half duck-walked, and half ran, in a wide sweeping loop behind his Audi. As he moved he squeezed off two more shots. One for each shooter.

Taking her cue, the rookie turned and sprinted for one of the pylons: a blur of ass and elbows. Fresh rounds from the shooter in the trunk peppered the ground behind her heels. One round must have ricocheted up from the concrete and caught her because she let out a grunt and fell forward. Her arms windmilled as she tried to stay upright and keep moving.

She finally lost balance and went over a few yards short of the nearest pylon.

Meanwhile, the masked driver had reached the patrol car. He stood where he'd seen the older cop laid out. Lock knew what was coming. So did the cop. But neither of them could do anything to stop it.

Desperate to stop an execution, Lock squeezed off another distraction round. But the driver had ducked so that his head was below the sill of the patrol car and he had no angle.

There was a single shot. Then, for the first time in a minute, there was silence. Apart from the persistent ringing in his ears that he still couldn't clear.

Lock watched as the barrel that had been poking from the trunk of the Mustang was pulled back inside. The driver was already scrambling through the open door of the patrol car. There was a rumble as he started the engine.

He hit the gas and the patrol car lurched backwards. He must have turned the wheel because Lock heard a soft crunch as the patrol car reversed over the dead officer, several thousand pounds of metal making sure that the job was truly done.

A short distance away, the rookie was still down. Somehow, she'd held onto her gun. Her other arm grasped her calf, blood oozing from her pant leg as she dragged herself toward the safety of the pylon.

The patrol car kept moving back. Picking up speed until it was flat out in reverse. The driver was headed toward where the injured rookie was crawling the last few feet toward the concrete pylon.

Lock broke cover. He ran into the open, fell back into a shooting stance, his feet a little wider this time, and pulled the trigger of the SIG twice in quick succession, sending two fast shots toward the front windshield of the patrol car.

As soon as he'd taken aim, the driver's mask had disappeared from sight as he'd ducked down. Lucky for him. Lock's first shot missed, but the second slammed through the windshield dead center to where the driver's head had been a moment before.

The spray of glass into the cabin was enough to fractionally loosen the driver's grip on the steering wheel. The patrol car spun off course, the tires squealing against the floor as it went into a slide and came to a stop, side on to where Lock was standing.

Lock threw himself to the ground again as the driver's head popped back up. The driver leveled his weapon through the open passenger door and fired at him. The round ricocheted behind him.

The rookie had made it to the thick concrete support, a slick trail of blood tracing the final few yards of her journey. If she stayed put, and they didn't go hunt her down, she'd be safe where she was.

Not that he could be certain, the ringing in his ears seemed to have switched up a notch in volume, but Lock thought he heard the whoop of sirens down below at street level. Bad news for the two men in the Mustang.

Parking structures like this one were, by definition, easy to seal off. Their purpose was to securely contain hundreds of thousands of dollars' worth of vehicles. That meant being able to control and monitor access, with heavy-duty barriers and elevated concrete lips to make sure you didn't drive round a barrier, and cameras to make sure everyone entering and leaving was recorded for posterity.

The gunman driving the patrol car must have heard them too and taken the vehicle out of reverse because it lurched violently forward. The Mustang roared and backed up, turned and headed forward.

Both vehicles came to a stop in the middle of the parking area. The drivers sat parallel to each other as they conferred. Lock could hear them shouting, but couldn't make out the words for the buzzing in his head.

For a second he thought about firing toward them again, then decided against it. Help was on the way and the last thing he needed was some gung-ho SWAT team member taking him out because they had him down as one of the bad guys.

Instead he sprinted for the area immediately behind the pylon where the wounded rookie was. As he ran, he caught a flash of movement as the guy in the patrol car bailed out and clambered into the passenger seat of the Mustang. Before he'd even closed the door, the Mustang was on the move. It spun round in a narrow turn, and made its way toward the exit ramp.

This time Lock got a better look at both driver and passenger, although their faces were hidden by masks. What struck him again was how in control they were. Even hardened criminals would appear jittery and hyped-up, having just murdered a cop and shot a second. But these two seemed perfectly in control.

The driver sat back in his seat, his movements precise as he drove toward the down ramp. Next to him the passenger had some kind of long gun tucked between his legs, the barrel pointed toward the roof. His right hand reached over to the left collar of his jacket as he keyed a mic and spoke into it. Lock glimpsed something clipped to the front of both their shirts.

As the Mustang's front windshield passed under a set of strip lights, two pieces of glass on the front of each man's chest twinkled. Tiny camera lenses. Both men were wearing body cams.

Lock tracked the path of the Mustang through the iron sights of his SIG. At any moment they could turn and come back, finish off the rookie and take her out.

They didn't. They kept moving for the exit, no doubt aware that their escape was now time-critical. The sirens grew louder.

Kneeling down, he turned his attention to the young rookie cop. She was breathing hard, fighting for air. From what he could see she hadn't taken a shot to the chest, so her breathing was likely a result of panic more than a punctured lung or something equally deadly.

At the same time, reaction to being shot was critical. You needed some kind of fear response to damp down the pain and keep you conscious. But if your body overreacted—or, rather, you allowed it to —you could quickly find yourself in the exact deep trouble you needed to avoid.

"They're leaving. It's going to be okay," he told her.

Her eyelids fluttered. Her pupils were wide, her skin flushed and clammy. None of those was a good sign.

"What's your name?" He needed to gauge her level of response, and if he could shift her mind away from the panic she was feeling. If he could do that then her body just might follow.

"Officer . . ." she began, before taking a big gulp of air. Tears had formed in the corners of her eyes.

"No, your first name. What's your first name?"

She swallowed hard. Blood was still pooling around her, but as far as he could tell it had slowed. That was about as good a sign as he could hope for right now.

"Monique," she said, struggling to get it out.

"Okay, Monique, you want some real good news?"

That almost drew a smile. "There's good news?" Every syllable was a struggle to get out. The pain was kicking in as her body's initial hormonal response subsided.

Lock nodded. "You've been shot, but the medics are going to be here any second, and in the meantime you have a military-grade trauma medic here who's going to make sure you keep stable until then. So, you're covered."

That seemed to get through. As he spoke, careful to keep his voice low and calm, her breathing had returned to some semblance of normality.

"Mike. How's Mike?"

He guessed that was her partner. The question wasn't one he wanted to give her a truthful answer to. He dodged it. Not lying, but not being wholly truthful either. "We're going to make sure he's taken care of too." He reached back to his belt loop and grabbed his Gerber. He flipped open the knife. "Okay, Monique, I'm going to cut away your pants leg where you were clipped. I need to see what we have, and put some pressure on to slow down the bleeding."

A flash of red lights near the exit ramp took his attention. The Mustang was reversing back up the ramp at speed. It wobbled and the rear passenger side bounced off the edge of the ramp. It kept moving, going flat out in reverse until it had cleared the narrow confines of the exit.

As the driver of the Mustang spun the wheel hard, the car flipped direction 180 degrees. It was a perfectly executed evasion move. As Lock watched it, he dropped his Gerber and unholstered his SIG again, just in case. The more he saw of these guys, the more he was being drawn to one conclusion. They weren't gangsters, they were professionals. Military professionals. Or at least military trained.

Down by his side, Monique was struggling to sit up, curiosity and fear getting the better of her. "Take it easy," he told her. "That's the medics getting here now," he lied. If anything he needed her leg elevated, not her upper body.

At the top of the exit ramp, the reason for the Mustang's reappearance became clear as the red roll bar of a newly arrived patrol car crested the rise.

The Mustang was still on the move, headed in Lock's direction. He stayed crouched and raised the SIG. His index finger moved from the side of the gun to the trigger. It was his turn to breathe slow as he got ready to fire.

At the last second, just as he had the Mustang in his sights, it spun around again. Sparks flew from under the vehicle as the handbrake squealed. Another change of direction—this time it was headed for the pedestrian exit. The exit that led toward Carmen's office building.

He placed his SIG on the floor, and dug out his cell phone as gunfire barked from the Mustang, two patrol cars roaring from both entrance and exit and coming to a stop, one next to Lock and the fallen rookie, the other following the Mustang.

Both of the Mustang's front doors popped open. Driver and passenger bailed, each man with a black duffel bag slung over his shoulder. In their hands they cradled a machine pistol and what looked like an AR15 respectively.

Knowing what was likely to come next from the arriving LAPD units, he tapped on Carmen's name to make the call, hit the speaker button so that he could talk hands-free, and placed the cell phone on the floor next to his gun.

The patrol car that had gone after the two gunmen had stopped face on toward the pedestrian walkway. The guy holding the machine pistol pivoted around and squeezed off a lightning-fast spray toward his pursuers. The two cops in the patrol car ducked down. The machine-pistol guy sprinted toward his buddy, who had already pushed through the doors leading to the walkway.

Meanwhile, the other patrol car had stopped side on to where Lock was still crouched next to Monique. Both cops drew down on him. He made sure to keep his hands up nice and high, fingers spread, palms turned toward them so they could see he wasn't holding anything.

His eyes drifted to the cell-phone screen as the call connected and he prayed that Carmen would pick up.

One of the cops moved out from the patrol car, his partner's gun pointed straight at him. Still no response from Carmen. He looked back in the direction of the walkway. The two pursuing patrol cops had slowed up, not wanting to push through the doors in case a fresh burst from the machine pistol lay on the other side. He didn't blame them.

Behind him, more LAPD and emergency vehicles were pouring up both ramps and onto the level.

Keeping his arms high, he risked a response. "I called these guys in," he told the cop, who was closing in on him.

Slowly, the cop lowered his weapon.

"She took a single shot to the leg," continued Lock, "you need to get an EMS over here right now."

12

Point, the taller of the two gunmen, sprinted down the walkway, staying ahead of his buddy, Rance. Everyone who met him thought Point was a nickname, given to him because he was always the man out in front—the man on point, the tip of the spear. But it was his actual name.

From the open walkway linking the parking garage to the offices, he could see that the LAPD had closed the block to traffic. The cops' ability to control traffic flow from a central command point by accessing downtown's stop lights had come up on the briefing. Not that Point had ever anticipated having to deal with it—after all, this had been slated as a standard surveillance operation, not the main event.

But what was that saying about a plan never surviving first contact with the enemy? Lock following them and calling the cops, then the cops blocking their escape hadn't been part of the plan either. But, thought Point, as he jogged toward the office building's glass-fronted reception area, it may just have proved to be a blessing in disguise. Their hand had been forced. They might as well take care of the real business now. Because, with Lock on the prowl, they weren't ever likely to get another bite at the cherry.

Point stopped and half turned as Rance squeezed off a fresh burst from the machine pistol. A couple of cops had assembled on the parking-structure end of the walkway they'd just come through. The cops hunkered down, and quickly drew back from the incoming rounds.

They weren't going to play hero, Point figured. Not after seeing one of their own laid out dead back there. They'd cordon off the area and wait for the SWAT team to deploy. Which was why he and Rance needed to move fast on this extraction. Get in, grab the package, and get the hell out of Dodge before things really went south.

Point came up on the reception area. Rance was three feet behind, laying down single shots of cover whenever he saw any blue. This part of the building's reception was glass-fronted.

Point could see all the way inside to a long reception desk and, off to one side, a bank of four elevators. In front of the reception desk there was a seating area, with several black leather couches and a coffee table with magazines laid out on the surface.

Usually there would be a security guard behind the desk, even this late on a Sunday. He could control entry by pressing a button on the desk. He'd either already taken off or he was hiding. No matter, thought Point, as he raised his modified AR15 and fired a sharp series of rounds into the door.

The glass shattered on impact. Point raised his boot, kicked out some of the loose shards, and stepped through what was left of the door. He walked straight to the desk, skirted round, and came upon the security guard hunkered behind it. The man had his arms wrapped around his head, and his eyes firmly closed.

Point jabbed the guard's shoulder with the barrel of his weapon. "Wakey, wakey. Playing possum with us is only gonna get you killed."

The guard opened his eyes.

"Up onto your feet," said Point, hooking the barrel under the guard's armpit and using it to lever him upright.

Rance was standing in front of the desk, facing the walkway, the machine pistol aimed outside.

The guard rose. Point pulled out his cell phone, tapped it three times. He held up the screen to the guard's face. "This woman here. You're going to find her for us. You don't and I kill you. You do, and I let you live."

The guard nodded. He was shaking so badly he was barely able to stand. "Seventh floor," he said, his voice breaking.

"Okay," Point told him. "You take us to her."

The guard shook his head. "I can't. She already left."

"Bullshit," said Point.

"Yes," the guard said. "She heard the firing," he added, with a nod toward the parking structure. "She got scared, and she left."

Point took a step back and studied the man's face. His eyes were cast down at the floor. He swallowed so hard that Point could see his Adam's apple bob up and down. Point had enough experience to know a liar, especially when he had them at the end of his gun.

"Well, ain't that bad news for you," said Point, pulling out his side arm, raising it, pressing the business end into the middle of the guard's forehead and pulling the trigger once.

The bullet went in clean, and out messy, spattering blood, shards of skull and pink lumps of brain over the floor and reception desk. The man's body slumped slowly at first. Then gravity took over and he fell with a thud, legs and arms twisted, like the edge of a jigsaw piece.

Point started toward the elevators. "You stay here. Catch her if she comes through. We get any visitors, just holler."

Rance strode behind the desk, and sat himself down in the guard's chair. Something must have caught his eye because he waved Point back to the desk. "Looky here."

An elevator door opened. Point stepped in, pulled out the alarm stop so that it would stay where it was, then jogged back behind the desk to join Rance.

Rance jabbed a gloved finger at one of eight small monitors lined up under the desk. His finger traced a shadowy figure moving slowly down a corridor.

The package. On the move. And, better yet, heading toward a stairwell that would take her straight into their arms.

"Good looking out," Point told his partner, jogging past the elevator and heading to the adjacent stairwell. He had barely pushed the door open when a shot from outside slammed through the glass frontage and took out a chunk of wall just above his head.

Rance dove behind the desk. Point pivoted fast on his heel and spread his back against the wall.

"What the hell was what?" Rance said.

"Not a what, a who," said Point, as he saw a figure flit across from one side of the walkway to the other.

"Okay, who was that?" said Rance, barely able to contain his rage. Of all the ways to die? They always said it was the one you never even saw coming that ended it.

"That was the man himself," said Point. "Ryan Lock."

13

As long as Lock stayed close to the left side of the walkway, they had no shot at him. Not without moving closer to the door. Which would give him a shot at them. A trade he was prepared to make at this range.

He kept moving, staying close to the wall, and low enough that he hoped he wouldn't be seen from the street. SWAT would be either deployed or deploying, and Lock didn't want to contend with them in addition to the two assholes he already had to deal with.

There was still no response from Carmen's cell phone. He didn't even know if she was still in the building. He hoped not, but he couldn't be sure. Not without going inside and taking a look for himself.

Moving along the walkway, he finally made it within twenty feet of the shot-out glass entrance. He couldn't see anyone inside the lobby. But he wasn't counting on it being empty. If the situation was reversed, he would have stayed out of sight behind the desk and used whatever camera feeds there were back there to maintain a visual. As soon as someone stepped inside, he would have popped up and taken them out before they had time to return fire. The desk provided cover, and cover, if it was good enough, provided an element of surprise.

He took a knee where he was, and looked around for another entrance. Large office buildings like this always had multiple points of entry. If for no other reason than no one wanted their high-paying tenants having to jostle with cleaners, maintenance and the rest of the great unwashed. For that very reason it also meant that these entry points tended to be more discreet than a fancy glass and marble lobby.

From his current position he was coming up with nothing. There was only one thing for it: he'd have to try another level.

The building started at the ground, which was given over to retail units that extended for three floors as something approaching a mini-mall. Access from where he was came via a set of escalators around the other side of this plaza level.

To get there he would have to cross directly in front of the open lobby. He'd be absorbing almost the same level of fire (and risk) going the roundabout way than he would going in the front.

Or he could sit tight, and hope they didn't locate Carmen in the time it took the SWAT team to show up and flush these guys out.

He got back onto his feet, and took a very deep breath. Waiting wasn't an option. If it came to it, today was as good a time to die as any other.

14

Here goes nothing, Lock said to himself, pushing toward the fractured front door, and drawing an immediate burst of fire from inside the reception vestibule. Pieces of concrete kicked up around him. He squeezed off two quick shots and kept moving. His vision was a blur, the ringing in his ears intense.

He saw one of the gunmen duck back down behind the desk and fired at them again. The round plowed into the wall directly behind them. That counted as a good miss in Lock's book. In other words, he'd missed, but still given his quarry something to think about.

As he shouldered his way past the door, a stray shard of glass slashed through the upper arm of his jacket, cutting through his shirt and slicing the skin. He kept on trucking for a few more steps, then fell into a crouch and waited for the machine-pistol man to reappear.

Using a standard grip, Lock focused on the desk, his SIG out, his finger on the trigger, waiting for the first sign of movement.

It didn't come. The gunman was staying where he was.

Or was he?

The ringing in his ears was so intense in the relative silence that he couldn't hear any movement. He stayed crouched where he was.

He was waiting. But so was the gunman.

Lock suddenly figured out why.

He didn't have to take a peek from behind the desk. There were monitors back there. He could sit tight and wait for him to force the situation. Then take him out when he moved. Or he could slowly adjust his position and get the drop on him. Say, by moving to the end of the desk and taking a shot from round the side while he was looking dead center.

He was good. He had to give him that much.

It was time to remove his current advantage. Looking around, Lock quickly scoped out the main lobby camera. It was mounted high on the facing wall, directly above the desk. He tilted up quickly, steadied his breathing and took the shot.

Bingo. The plastic dome protecting the camera blew apart. Now the gunman behind the desk was unsighted. It was a minor win, but a win all the same.

Lock tacked to his right, moving closer to the elevator bank and the stairwell. Ten steps and he stopped, dropping back into a crouch.

A head appeared from behind the desk. He squeezed off a single shot. Missed low, his round embedding itself in the front of the desk. The head disappeared.

Not waiting around for the guy to gather his thoughts, Lock sprinted for the elevators. They lay at a ninety-degree angle to the desk. If he reached the corner he'd finally have cover. Then it would be up to the gunman to come after him. He'd be on the move and Lock would be in a position to pick him off.

Another spray of bullets tore across the lobby as Lock made it to the elevators. The gunman had hesitated and made his move too late. Lock hit a call button. The door of the elevator car nearest to him opened. Lock stepped in, hit the button for the seventh floor, and stepped back out. If the other gunman was already up on seven, all he'd have to do was wait around for the doors to open and Lock would be easy pickings.

Lock turned and headed for the adjacent stairwell. A thin stream of blood ran from his shoulder, down his arm and onto the back of his hand. Pushing through the stairwell doors, he took a moment to catch his breath, keeping an eye out for the gunman coming after him.

He started up the first flight of stairs. Every second or so he would check back on the entrance to the stairwell he had just come through to see if he was being followed.

On the next floor, he stopped and made another call to Carmen. Still no response. Maybe she didn't have her cell with her. Or it was on silent so she couldn't easily be found. If you were hiding for your life, the last thing you wanted was your phone chiming with an incoming call.

He killed the call and tapped out a quick text. He gave her his location and told her to text him back with hers. Rather than wait for a reply that might not come, he pressed on, grabbing the banister, and hauling ass up the next flight of stairs.

15

Point picked up the cell phone from Carmen's desk and scanned the text message on the screen. "Oh, ain't that sweet? He's coming to get you." He held the phone up in front of Carmen's face so she could read the message.

"You want I should write him back?"

Her hands cuffed behind her, and silver tape wrapped around her mouth, Carmen's eyes blazed with fury. She shouted through the tape, her words muffled and indistinct.

"What was that?" Point asked. "'Fuck you'? Now, that's not very nice, is it? Think I'll just leave this here," Point continued, his gloved hands placing the cell phone back on her desk.

Carmen kicked out at him. He stepped back so that she missed. He raised the back of his hand and slapped her hard across the face. Her nose cracked and started to bleed. She continued to glare at him.

He picked up the cell phone again and quickly tapped out a reply. He didn't hit send, instead laying the phone back on the desk where the message would be visible to whoever found it.

He stepped behind Carmen, closed his fingers around her cuffed wrists and pulled her arms painfully up her back.

"Let's take the elevator, shall we?" he said, as he propelled her toward the office door and out into the corridor.

Her arms wedged painfully high, she stumbled barefoot into the outer reception area, past the coffee machine, the paper shredder, and the desks usually occupied by secretaries and interns. The normalcy of her surroundings and her familiarity with them gave what was happening an almost surreal quality. It was like being trapped in a nightmare, only with no hope of waking.

They kept moving, she and the man with the gun. They walked out into the corridor and headed for the elevators. A car was already there, the doors open. She was shoved inside, and held, facing the back.

"Hey," said Point. "You ever been up on the roof?"

Carmen shook her head.

"Real nice view up there," he said. "Perfect end to a romantic evening."

He reached over and hit the button to take them to the top floor. As he waited for the doors to close, he keyed the mic button on his lapel.

"We're good. Meet me up top."

"Copy that," came Rance's reply.

16

L ock picked up Carmen's cell phone from her desk. A draft
text message was on the front screen, incomplete and
unsent. He scanned it quickly before he saw the first drops
of blood on the carpet. He lifted his arm, trying to work out, and
hoping against hope, that it was his blood.

It wasn't. He was no longer leaking from the shoulder.

Running back out into the corridor he looked around. No one.
The place was deserted and Carmen was gone.

There was no doubt in his mind that she had left against her will.
The message he'd just read told him that much.

He looked down, searching the carpet for more blood droplets.
There were two, each one about three feet apart. He followed the
trail. It ended at the elevators. This time he hit the button, any
caution on his part discarded.

Stepping into the elevator car as soon as it arrived, he tapped the
button to take him to ground level. It seemed like an eternity before
the doors closed again and the elevator began its descent.

He ticked off the floors on the panel. As he neared the reception
area, he slid back against the side of the car. The elevator shuddered
to a halt. The doors slowly began to open.

Even with the ringing in his ears, he could hear voices and the crackle of radios.

"We got someone in an elevator."

"Yeah, we have it covered."

"Only shoot on my signal."

The doors opened. He kept both arms firmly down by his sides and dropped his SIG onto the floor of the car as the area immediately outside the elevator bristled with SWAT team members in full tactical gear, their faces obscured, their weapons trained on him. He counted at least four red dots dancing around his head and chest.

This was not a situation that called for anything beyond complete compliance as they barked their instructions to him. He closed his eyes for a moment, the drone in his ears dialing up another notch as his heart sank into his boots.

Opening his eyes, he was shoved round, his arms grabbed by at least two people. Cold metal closed around his wrists. Another hand settled on his injured shoulder. He winced from the jab of pain.

He was turned round and pushed out of the elevator. A boot at the back of his knee, folded him onto the marble floor. Twisting his head round, he found himself staring into the still-open eyes of the building's security guard, half his skull blown away.

17

"You have no idea why someone may have wished to abduct your girlfriend?"

Lock shrugged. It hurt. Any kind of movement that involved shifting the position of his shoulder hurt. And his ears were still ringing to the point that it was painful. He wanted to clean up, grab a shower and get into some fresh, preferably non-blood-stained clothes. He also really wanted to punch the detective standing in front of him. Most of all he wanted to get the hell out of there so that he could find Carmen and kill the men who had taken her.

"None."

"Had she mentioned any threats?"

He shook his head. It was marginally less painful than a shrug, but still not great. "I already told you, no, she had not. The first I knew of any problem was when that Mustang showed up outside the restaurant this evening. The rest you know because I just told you. At least twice."

The detective, a guy called Stanner, planted his knuckles on the table and leaned over him. It was a gesture intended to intimidate. It might have worked on someone else but trying it out on Lock was, at best, misjudged.

"We have an officer dead and one in critical condition at UCLA Medical Center. So maybe you'll indulge me?"

Lock was done. He wasn't going to argue. He understood what Stanner was saying. Under different circumstances he just might have indulged him. But he'd given him everything he knew.

He stood up. He wasn't under arrest. He could leave at any time.

Stanner stepped in front of him, blocking his path to the door. Now Lock really was done. The two men stood, eyeballing each other.

Lock stepped to the side and walked past him. Normally he might have shoulder-checked him for good measure. Just so the guy got the message.

"Don't go anywhere," Stanner said, as Lock opened the door and walked out into the corridor.

"Come on, Stanner, you don't really think I'm on the wrong side of this deal, do you?"

Stanner kept his poker face. They had history. He might not believe Lock was involved in any way, but he wasn't a fan. That was fine with Lock. He wasn't a fan of Stanner.

"I have no idea what side you're on, Lock."

Lock struggled to contain his anger. "Any word on the helicopter that took them off the roof?"

Now it was Stanner's turn to be reticent. "None."

18

The sun threatened the horizon as Lock walked out of the new LAPD headquarters building on Spring Street, less than ten blocks from Carmen's office. Outside, a couple of news crews had set up, ready to squeeze the last juice from the pulp of the night's events.

Lock kept his head firmly down and headed toward the purple 1966 Lincoln Continental illegally parked next to a fire hydrant. The last thing he needed was any more questions about Carmen's kidnapping. He'd have to face the media some time, but he needed at least a day to process what had happened—and to come up with some answers of his own.

His business partner, and best friend, former US marine Tyrone 'Ty' Johnson, stood leaning against the driver's door of the purple monstrosity, which came with a carbon footprint that would drive an environmentalist to experience heart palpitations.

With Lock's Audi impounded as part of the investigation, Ty was providing transport for as long as it took Lock to get to a car-rental garage. Which, if he had any say in the matter, wouldn't be very long. The Tymobile might have been an accurate mirror of his partner's persona, but it didn't exactly blend into the background.

He waved away Ty's open-armed offer of a hug with a tap on his shoulder. "I'm joining you in the messed-up shoulder club."

Ty had taken a bullet to his shoulder six months previously. He was still undergoing rehab and physiotherapy for the injury. "Mother-fuckers," he said, the true extent of his displeasure shielded from view behind mirrored sunglasses. "We'll find her, Ryan. Find those assholes too."

He looked back to the satellite trucks. The Tymobile was drawing some attention and it was only a matter of time before someone picked him out and came looking for a few words of comment.

"Let's get out of here," said Lock, walking round to the passenger side.

Ty got into the car, turned the engine over, and they took off down Spring Street at speed.

Neither spoke until they were clear of downtown and on the freeway headed back to Marina Del Rey and Lock's rented condo. Watching the shoals of commuters slipping past them, sipping coffee from their travel mugs, rocking out to music or arguing with kids safely secured in the back of their cars, Lock had the same feeling of dislocation he'd had when he'd returned home from Afghanistan and Iraq. How could people go about their lives like this? Didn't they know what was happening?

He knew, even as they occurred to him, how naive those questions were. To protect themselves, people had become expert at ignoring what was outside their immediate realm. Back when he was serving, he had come to envy those who had the ability to hermetically seal their lives. It wasn't an option that had been open to him.

As they exited the 10 freeway, Ty breached the silence. "How you holding up?" he asked, the flick of his eyes obscured behind his Oakleys.

"My ears are still ringing."

Ty and Lock didn't go in much for heart-to-heart conversations. They happened, but they were rare. It wasn't that they didn't worry about each other. They did. It was more that men like them weren't much for tear-stained shared confessionals.

"You probably got tinnitus. If it don't go away, gimme a holler and I'll hook you up with something to help."

"Thanks."

They lapsed back into silence. Lock used his phone to check for any breaking updates. In place of information there was only lots of fevered speculation, but nothing new that had any meat on the bone, regarding who had taken Carmen and why. Nor was there any word from the LAPD about suspects, beyond a couple of grainy black-and-white images of the two men with their masks on.

The only consolation he had was that kidnappers didn't snatch people they wanted to kill. It took too much in the way of resources and planning. Not to mention risk. A murder, or for that matter an assassination, was almost always far easier to execute than a kidnapping.

That didn't mean kidnap victims never ended up dead. They did. All the time. It was why negotiating a release from a kidnap-and-ransom situation called for specialist skills.

From years of experience, Lock knew that the outcome to a kidnapping rested on a number of factors. Part of it was a straight equation that was balanced, on either side, with the stability of the kidnappers and the guile of the negotiators. Kidnap for ransom demanded a level of trust from a situation that inherently promoted suspicion. After all, who would trust someone who had done something as egregious as abduct, often violently, a family member, colleague, friend, or other loved one?

Successfully extracting someone alive from a kidnap-for-ransom situation involved a whole set of skills and psychological insights that most people simply didn't possess. It was also regarded as a rookie mistake for someone very close to the victim to become directly involved in their release. But what was he going to do? Leave Carmen to the experts? He had seen how that could go. No, one way or another, this was on him.

Ty's car drew glances as they reached Marina Del Rey. One of the least diverse areas of Los Angeles, about the only brown people the locals saw were foreign flight crew who used the hotels there as their layover base before they flew back out of nearby LAX. And, like the rest of upscale Los Angeles, domestic staff: maintenance guys, maids, and security guards. Actual brown and black residents? Not so much.

They turned into the driveway of Lock's apartment building. Ty pulled up front, waving away the valet-parking attendant who sprang from behind his station. Lock had gotten to know the young man well since he'd moved in. He was a good kid, and bat-shit crazy about cars. One day Lock had even allowed him to take the Audi to pick up his girlfriend. That small piece of generosity had earned him platinum-level service from then on in.

"Morning, Mr. Lock," the valet said, holding the door open for him, and doing his best not to react to what a sight he must have looked.

If he knew that Lock had been in the middle of events downtown, he wasn't about to let that knowledge slip. Discretion was one of the first lessons learned working at a place like this. That included keeping your mouth shut.

"Morning, Luis."

Ty got out and joined Lock on the forecourt. A Lexus pulled up behind them and Luis went to attend to the elderly white couple who got out. They both kept throwing horrified sideways glances at the purple Tymobile.

Lock heard the woman whisper to her husband. "I'm telling you, he's one of those rappers."

Her husband mumbled back, "If he moves in then I'm going to speak to the building management."

They scuttled past as Luis climbed into their Lexus and deftly eased it round the Lincoln. He lowered the window. "Just let me know if you need anything, Mr. Lock."

"Thanks, Luis. I will."

"You going to be okay on your own?" Ty asked him.

Lock shot him a grim smile. "I'll cope."

"That's not what I meant," he replied. "They might come looking for you here."

Lock glanced around at the white marble entrance, the perfect azure sky, and the hundreds of millions of dollars' worth of boats bobbing gently in the marina. "Not here they won't."

"I wouldn't be so sure."

"I'm not going to let my guard down, if that's what you're worried about," he told his partner.

"Good."

"Listen, I'm going to get cleaned up and grab some food. Then I'm going to pick up a rental car and head on over to Carmen's place." She had given him a key only a few weeks before. It had marked a definite shift in their relationship. A tilt toward domesticity, signifying something longer-term between them. They were no longer just dating.

"Why you need a rental?" said Ty, mock-offended. "You can use my whip if you need a car."

"Thanks, but I'll get my own."

"Okay. You need me for anything drop me a message," said Ty, getting back into his car. "I'm going to shake some branches. See if I can't get us some fresh intel on this crew that snatched up Carmen."

That was good to hear. Ty's sources were a little different from those Lock or the LAPD could access: his world tended to run more to the fringes of society, and that was a good place to pick up whispers about something like this.

Ty reached a huge hand toward him through his open window. The two men bumped fists. "Be safe," he said.

"You too."

"Badass motherfuckers like me don't need to worry, but I'll watch my back. How about that?"

"Sounds good." Lock watched him drive away, then headed into the air-conditioned lobby of the building. The concierge greeted him with a jaunty "Good morning, Mr. Lock."

His world might just have come to a screeching halt, but here in Paradise, life went on as normal. One day the same as the next. A bath-warm seventy-five degrees and sunny.

As he rode up in the elevator, he did his best not to think of

Carmen. Where she might be. How she might be feeling. How scared she was. He did his best to blot out all of that. But, like the persistent ringing in his ears, those thoughts he couldn't will away.

19

K een to get a start, Lock was in and out of his apartment in under forty minutes. Shaved, showered and as patched up as he was going to get, he headed back down to the lobby and signed the paperwork for the rental car that was waiting for him out front. His credit card and insurance details noted, he took the key and headed out to his new ride. It wasn't his zero to sixty in 3.7 seconds Audi RS, but it would get him from A to B until he could prize his own car back from the LAPD.

Luis looked a little crestfallen as he saw Lock ease himself behind the wheel of the Saturn. "Don't worry, Luis, it's temporary."

"Okay, Mr. Lock."

"Do me a favor, Luis. If anyone comes round asking for me, or there's anyone just hanging about, let me know. If you can, grab a quick photograph or note down what they look like and what they're driving. Don't go getting in trouble, but keep an eye out."

"Sure thing, Mr. Lock."

He palmed Luis a twenty with his business card. "Text me if you see anything."

He got into the rental car and took a few moments to adjust the seat position and mirrors, then check the brakes before he pulled out onto Via Marina and headed for Carmen's apartment in Culver City.

On the drive he thought about her behavior in the previous few weeks. She'd been tired, a little readier to be irritated or to overreact, but he'd put that down to her crushing workload. The truth was, no matter how fast they'd fallen for each other, he hadn't known her that long. Not enough to have a true baseline he could use to judge whether she'd been upset by something or had had any inkling of what was going to happen.

As realizations went about the woman you loved, it didn't feel that great. Then again, among much else, he'd been attracted to her by her apparent self-containment. She could be fun and flirty, but had an inner strength that drew people toward her.

She'd told him on an early date that one of the reasons she was such a good attorney was that people opened up to her in a way they wouldn't with others. It was more than that, though. They trusted her because there was a genuine goodness in her. He could see it in her eyes when she spoke. Sincerity wasn't much prized in these cynical times, but for a man like himself there were no greater qualities in a woman than truth and goodness.

He parked the Saturn on Duquesne Avenue and walked around the corner to the front of Carmen's building on Lucerne Avenue. Her building didn't have valet parking or a concierge. Instead it had two dead plant pots in the lobby and a row of mailboxes. He used the keys she'd given him to open her mailbox and flicked through it quickly, feeling a little guilty for the intrusion. The mail was mostly flyers and menus. He imagined her bank and credit-card statements were all accessed online.

Junkmail in hand, and the SIG on his hip obscured by his jacket, he headed up to Carmen's apartment. He was greeted at the door by the mewing of her cat, a ginger she'd found abandoned on the street. It rubbed itself against his legs as he made his way into the kitchen via the living room.

The apartment didn't appear to have been broken into. There

were no jimmy or pick marks on the door and everything was how he imagined she had left it.

He opened the refrigerator, found a fresh pouch of cat food, and put it into a bowl. He didn't know if he'd be able to check back in again later today so he also found some dried food in a cupboard, put it into another bowl and refilled the cat's water bowl to the brim from a jug of filtered water on the counter. He was more of a dog guy than a cat person, but he knew Carmen doted on the ginger fur ball.

Moving into the bathroom, Lock held his breath and used the scoop to shovel out a couple of small brown presents in the litter tray, dropped them into the toilet, flushed and put fresh litter into the tray. Having tossed back its meal in record time, the cat appeared behind him and started with the leg-rubbing again.

He put the bag of litter on the floor, reached down and picked it up. "Let me tell you, if I'd been around to have a say, you'd still be out there."

The cat put its paws around his neck, claws digging into the tear in his shoulder. Gently, Lock reached up and pulled it away and set the animal on the floor. "See? That's the kind of behavior I'm talking about."

The cat followed him back into the living room. Carmen's laptop, a MacBook Pro, lay open on the coffee table. This really felt like an intrusion, but extraordinary times called for extraordinary measures.

A password screen came up. He took a shot and typed in the cat's name, Merlin.

Voilà.

No wonder hackers had such an easy time of it. He was in. He scanned the desktop screen, his finger drifting over the pad to open Carmen's mail program. It was linked to her work account and there were hundreds of emails that she had received over the past day, never mind the past week.

He clicked on the sent folder. There were way less of them, which made them easier to check. Plus, he figured that something she had sent herself was more likely to contain a flag for any concerns she'd had.

He worked backwards, skimming anything that jumped out. The cat settled next to him on the couch. Lock guessed he missed Carmen too. They had that much in common.

Twenty or so emails in, his eyes were glazing over. Apart from a couple to her sister, everything was work-related and there was no mention of any personal concerns.

Her sister.

Even though her sister lived with her husband and kids in Arizona, she and Carmen were close. He found a number online and made the call. Carmen's sister picked up almost immediately, her voice tense and concerned.

Lock explained who he was and that he didn't have any fresh news, but he assumed she'd heard. She had. She was beside herself. How was she going to tell the kids about their aunt?

"Don't tell them anything for now. There's no point worrying them until we know more."

She asked him what had happened. He told her as best he could, leaving out the more graphic details of what he'd seen and learned subsequently.

"Listen, I was wondering if maybe Carmen had mentioned something to you. Perhaps she was worried about something or someone. I have a feeling this wasn't the first time she'd been followed."

"I'm really sorry, Ryan. She seemed stressed, but she didn't say anything about being followed or anyone watching her. The only thing she seemed bothered about was this new client of hers and how much of an asshole he was."

"Wait. Hold on. Which client was this?"

"She never mentioned that she'd been asked to represent Servando Guilen?"

"We tried not to talk about work if we could."

"Okay, I get that. Well, maybe you should look him up. Although I can't see how he'd be involved in doing this to Carmen. She was pretty much his best hope of ever being a free man again."

As he wrapped up the call with Carmen's sister, Lock ran a quick

Google search on Servando Guilen. His blood chilled as the first results appeared on the screen in front of him.

Carmen's sister had been correct. He had no interest in harming Carmen, but his criminal history suggested plenty of people out there would have a score to settle. And if the only way they could hurt him was via his attorney, well, that was exactly what they'd do.

Guilen was a career criminal from across the border in Mexico. He styled himself as a businessman but he'd carved out his multi-million-dollar drug and racketeering empire through raw fear, terror and lots of dead bodies. Men, women, children, police officers, politicians, he didn't care whom he took out.

It was a thought that offered Lock small comfort, but at least he could see why someone might go after Carmen if they thought it would hurt a man like that. Or was it someone else? Maybe a disgruntled client—or a victim of someone she had helped acquit.

He knew a man who could help him with the former. Someone who, despite his good character, had multiple connections in the world of gangs, both out on the streets and within the penal system.

As Merlin snuggled in tighter, dozing, he made a call to Ty.

"What's up, Ryan?"

"She was defending a guy called Servando Guilen."

"Oh, yeah, Mexican cartel guy, only he ain't Mexican."

That titbit of information hadn't featured on his internet search results. "Really?"

"No, he's from Honduras or Guatemala, somewhere like that. Operates out of Mexico, though. You want me to take a look into whether he was satisfied with his legal representation or not?"

"No, I'll cover that angle. I want your net to go a little wider. I was thinking that maybe it could be a former client holding a grudge. Maybe they decided they didn't like the deal Carmen cut for them. Something along those lines."

"Okay, I'll look, but I doubt it's that," said Ty.

"How come?"

"Well, a dude she messed up is gonna be cooling his heels inside.

And if they're on the outside she must have done something right so they ain't a problem."

It was a valid point. But it had a hole in it. Prisoners, especially those affiliated to gangs and organized crime, had a reach outside prison. They could put out the word via an array of communication channels and have someone killed or kidnapped on the street without ever taking a single step outside their cell.

He put that to Ty.

"I hear ya," he said, after a moment's contemplation. "I'll make a few calls, see if there's any word out."

20

T he parking structure, primary scene of the previous evening's gun battle, was already back in business. Lock guessed that the LAPD had gathered whatever forensics they needed. He hoped they'd be as speedy with the work on his car, although he suspected not. He imagined the building management had made some phone calls to expedite matters and keep the money flowing.

He rolled on up to level four. He was hoping that seeing it again would jog some small detail from his fragmented memories of what had gone down. He parked as close as he could to where he had before.

The view was completely different than it had been. Where before the place had been close to empty, now almost every space was taken.

Had that factored into the two men's decision to react as they had done? Would they have been quite so brazen and aggressive if it had been a weekday and the parking structure had been busy with office workers? It would certainly have made life more difficult for the kidnappers. All those people and vehicles would have made high-speed maneuvers next to impossible.

Getting to Carmen, then extracting her would have been much harder. There would have been more LAPD units in the area. Response time would have been faster on a workday in downtown.

Maybe it hadn't been a simple surveillance operation after all. Maybe they had been lying in wait for Carmen to return to her car.

He suddenly remembered something. Carmen's late night, and unscheduled return to the office, had been prompted by a message she had received. He had assumed it had been a text that had gone to her phone, but perhaps it had been an email. He should have checked when he'd been looking at her inbox on the laptop. He made a note to look again at her emails when he headed back later to see Merlin.

The front of the office building was still boarded up where the glass had been shot out. Apart from that, there was no sign that anything had happened. Two cops prowled the area between the walkway and the entrance. They checked him out, but didn't say anything as he stepped into the lobby

Inside, more repair work was going on. A temporary reception area had been set up. He wondered about the security guard who'd been slain in cold blood. He hadn't stood a chance. There had been no hesitation from the gunmen when it had come time to kill him. The more Lock thought about it, the more he was convinced they were former military. Or at least that they'd had military training.

At the temporary reception desk, he gave them his details and the reason for his visit. No, he didn't have an appointment, but if they could let Mike Mazarovitch, the head of Carmen's law firm, know he was there he'd very much appreciate it.

A few minutes later, he was given a visitor's badge to pin to his jacket, and directed toward the elevators.

THE ATMOSPHERE in the suite of law offices was somber but businesslike. People seemed to speak in whispers. That didn't chime with the impression of the firm he'd gotten from Carmen.

Lock sat waiting until Mike appeared and ushered him into the main conference room. In his late fifties, he had carved out a reputation as a fierce advocate for his clients, with a bruising style. He often lost at trial, but won on appeal, riling the opposition so much that they tended to make mistakes he could exploit later on to his client's benefit.

Like most defense lawyers, Mike was of the everyone's-entitled-to-the-best- defense-possible school. He didn't concern himself too much with the morality of whether or not he'd saved the guilty. It was this approach that had attracted clients like Servando Guilen. Men with low morals, but deep pockets.

"Please, Ryan, take a seat."

He walked to the window. "I'm good."

"Okay," said Mike, perching one buttock on the edge of the conference table. "We're all very shocked by what's happened. I've been a lawyer for over thirty years and I've never encountered a situation like this. Threats, yes. But this? No."

Lock cut to the chase. He didn't have time for pleasantries, and he guessed that neither did Mike. "Have the people who took Carmen been in touch with you?" he asked.

He shook his head. "No. With you?"

Lock matched his gesture. "Not a word."

That was bad news. Although it didn't mean a worst-case scenario. If someone was seeking ransom they would often let the victim's family or friends stew for a little while. Silence was a weapon. It could be used to soften people up for when they finally made the demand.

"What can you tell me about Servando Guilen?"

Mike hopped off the conference table. "Nothing. We don't discuss clients with outside parties."

That was the answer he'd expected but he chose to ignore it. "You think he's connected to this?"

That got a reaction. Mike's face flushed. "No, I do not. I think the idea is ridiculous. We're on his side. He's relying upon us, and Carmen in particular, to make sure he's a free man."

He could have pointed out that a second ago Mike had said he didn't discuss clients. "I asked if you thought he was connected in some way. I didn't ask if he did it."

"You mean, is someone trying to undermine his trial?"

He nodded.

"Possible, but it seems like a naive strategy. There are other defense lawyers if he loses one. Listen, Ryan, we're all devastated by this. I'm sure you are too."

He had no idea but Lock's main emotion wasn't devastation. That wouldn't get Carmen back home safe. He was white-hot angry, but he knew he had to channel it.

He stared out of the window to the street below. People were snaking their way along the sidewalk, going about their day. He doubted more than a few hundred people had given the crime more than a passing thought. As the days passed that number would dwindle.

"We have one of our own investigators working this," Mike continued. "He's looking into every possibility we can think of."

"Which investigator?" He knew Carmen and the firm used a half-dozen investigators to unearth evidence for them. Most were former LAPD or came from other branches of law enforcement.

"Carl Galante. I'm sure he'd like to sit down with you. See if there's anything you might have noticed."

"That'd be fine." Carmen had mentioned Galante to him in passing. He'd gleaned two things about him: he was good at what he did, but a difficult man to work with. She'd also hinted that he'd left the police department in San Diego under a cloud of suspicion that he might have been on the take.

"Great. I'll have someone in the office set it up. Now, unless there's anything else . . ."

"Just the one thing," Lock said, stepping forward, closing the space between them.

"What is it?"

"I plan on finding whoever did this, and when I do, I just might need a good attorney myself. If the kidnappers contact you, or anyone else in your office, you can pass along a message from me. If they hurt Carmen, I'm going to find them, and when I do, I'm going to kill them. Slowly."

Mike stared at him. "I'm not sure that's a good message to be passing on."

"Just make sure you tell them." He walked toward the conference-room door.

"Can I ask you something?" Mike said.

Lock turned back toward him.

"Are you sure you don't know who might be behind this?"

21

A s a kidnap victim, Carmen Lazaro had one distinct advantage. She had spent a lot of time around criminals. They were her clients and, as such, she had grown to know, if not to fully understand, how they thought. She was hoping some of that knowledge might be enough to keep her alive.

Carmen had defended four kidnap cases. Three had been gang-related: gang members abducting other gang members or their family. Those could be considered more as abductions because the motive often extended out beyond payment of a ransom to revenge or payback for some slight, real or imagined.

The other case had been a more straightforward kidnap for ransom. Or, at least, that was how it had started before it descended into a raging torrent of violence that had culminated in the deaths of a Silicon Valley entrepreneur, his wife and their two young children. The man she had defended in that case had told her he knew it was going to end in murder when his accomplice had used both their real names in front of the victims.

So far Carmen didn't know the names of either of the men who had taken her. She was clinging to that as a sign they didn't plan on killing her. Not just yet anyway.

They were playing this, as far as she could tell, like people who didn't want her to identify them. Which suggested they expected her to finish this thing alive.

The flip side was that they didn't talk to her. Not beyond issuing instructions. Any time she tried to strike up a conversation, to establish rapport with them (something else she knew was key to her staying alive), they shut it down or simply ignored her. Today, when the taller of them came in to give her lunch, it seemed it wasn't going to be any different.

When they'd finally hunted her down, they had blindfolded her. They'd also been wearing masks so she couldn't see their faces. She knew from their hands and necks that they were white. One had the slight trace of a Southern accent. The other sounded like he was from somewhere out west, maybe Oregon or northern California.

She was being kept in a bedroom of a house somewhere remote. She never heard any outside noise. Nor were there any traffic sounds, apart from what she assumed was their vehicle, which she could hear arriving and leaving. The only window in the room was blacked out: heavy material had been tacked around the frame.

There was a metal bedstead, a mattress, a chair that was secured to the floor, and a bucket to use as a toilet. The room was carpeted. The walls were bare and painted a sickly yellow. Light came from a floor lamp in the corner.

When she was alone, she was cuffed and shackled to the bed. Sometimes they would move her to the chair and shackle her there. That morning she had been blindfolded, and led outside to walk around. One had guided her by the elbow so she wouldn't fall.

She had been told that trying to escape was pointless. Even if she did get away, there was nowhere to run to. No one for miles around. Nothing she had heard contradicted that. And the way they had said it was so matter-of-fact that she didn't doubt them.

All of this was miserable. But it gave her hope. It meant they were taking it seriously. In her experience, serious criminals were rare, but easier to deal with. They knew all about risk and reward. Most of all they knew that killing someone, unless you had no choice, was not a good move.

Now she heard footsteps outside. A key turned in a lock and the door opened. The footsteps grew louder. She felt hands at her ankles as the shackles were removed. The hands moved up, unlocking and removing the handcuffs.

"Get up slow," said the Southern man's voice.

She did as she was told. She rubbed at her wrists as she stood.

"I'm going to take off the blindfold now," he said.

She nodded to let him know that she understood. She closed her eyes as he did it. That way she could open them slowly and let her eyes adjust to the harsh light from the lamp.

When she opened them, the man was wearing the same mask. But, this time, he was standing back from her. He threw her a newspaper, a copy of that morning's Los Angeles Times. She tried to scan the headlines, to see if her kidnapping was on the front page, but it was hard to focus.

"Hold it up, front page facing me," he said.

He held up his cell phone, a red light blinking to show that it was recording.

"Okay, say your name, and let them know you haven't been harmed. Then tell them they will receive further instructions soon."

"Who's they?" she asked.

His free hand fell to a Taser gun, tucked into a pouch on his waist. The message was clear and didn't require any embellishing with words.

"This is Carmen. As you'll see from the newspaper I'm holding, I'm currently safe and unharmed. You will receive further instructions soon."

He stopped recording and put his cell phone away. "Good. That was good."

"How long do you plan on keeping me?"

His eyes stared at her from behind the mask. "Just do what we say, when we say it, and everything'll be fine. That's all you need to know."

"How much is the ransom you're asking for? Because my family, they're not rich."

His hand rested back on the Taser. He unclipped the top of the pouch and took a step toward her. She saw the ripple of his biceps under his black T-shirt. "Are you and me going to have a problem?"

"No," she said, her voice cracking despite herself. "Not at all."

"Glad to hear it, because if I need to hurt you, I will."

The way he said it, with no emotion, and no flare of anger, Carmen believed him.

22

re you sure you don't know who might be behind this?

The question turned over in Lock's mind. He had pressed Carmen's boss to explain what he meant. Why would he even ask him something like that? Did he know something that Lock didn't?

He hadn't gotten any kind of answer. And he wasn't going to. The man was a lawyer, practiced in the art of being evasive when he had to be. All he'd said was that someone in Lock's position must have made a lot of enemies. He didn't know of anyone who would want to hurt Carmen but perhaps there was someone who wanted to hurt him, and they could do that via her.

It sounded like bullshit. Like he'd made a slip. But he'd quickly backtracked and Lock knew he wouldn't get any more out of him. He left the office before things got really heated and promised he'd speak with their investigator, Carl, as soon as he was available.

He called Carl on his way out of the office. It went to voicemail. He left his number and asked him to call as soon as he got the message. His next call was to Ty. He answered immediately. Lock put him on speaker.

"You have any news?" Ty asked.

"Nothing worth knowing."

"Gimme what you got anyway."

Lock brought him up to speed with his visit to Carmen's firm. As he spoke, his phone pinged. An email.

The sender's address was a string of letters, symbols and numbers. The message line read: "Proof of Life."

"Ty, hang on."

"You want me to call you back?"

"No. Stay with me. I just got an email that might be from the kidnappers."

Ty lapsed into silence. Not something he was noted for.

Lock tapped open the email. There was no message in the body. Just a link.

It could be a virus. Or some kind of hoax. It had come to his private email rather than the company's general information or enquiry address, but his email wouldn't have been that tough to track down if someone was determined.

"There's no message. Just a link."

"You sure this is from the kidnappers, Ryan?"

"I don't know. But I guess there's only one way to find out." If it was a virus he could have someone he knew clean up the damage for him.

His index finger hovered over the link. He hesitated. The email's title said that Carmen was alive. Proof of life was a standard kidnap-for-ransom protocol. Kidnappers didn't usually offer it up first. It was a bargaining chip they held: a small, but powerful piece of psychological power.

There was something else in the mix. Proof of life had to be in the form of evidence. A phone call. A photograph. A video. Something that was material, tangible and, above all, credible.

And evidence, no matter how carefully it had been constructed, contained information: clues that could be used against the kidnappers. Proof-of-life material had been used in many cases to locate the victim or victims. It had also been used after the kidnapping was over to identify and capture those responsible.

The one thing he knew so far. These kidnappers were not only highly motivated, and prepared to absorb a high level of risk, they were also highly skilled.

He pulled his finger back from the screen, and closed the email inbox. "Ty?"

"What did it say?"

"I don't know yet. Meet me at the strip mall on Lincoln in an hour."

Ty immediately picked up on where Lock was about to go with this. That was the benefit of working with someone for so long. You created an understanding that saved time and words. "Li's place?"

"You got it."

23

A shotgun across his lap, Point pecked two fingers at his laptop keyboard. Rance was pacing back and forth, one eye on the live feeds from their cameras, the other on Point.

"Goddamn it," said Point.

"What?" Rance asked.

Point swiveled round on the chair, got up and propped the shotgun in the corner. "He opened the email, but he didn't click through to the link."

"You're shitting me," said Point.

"Wish I was."

"See, I told you we should have just embedded it in the email. That way he would have watched it by now."

Point's features darkened. They'd already had this discussion. More than once. "And I told you that if we did that it's harder for us to remotely delete it."

"Maybe he thought it was spam. Or someone trolling him."

"Or," said Point, "maybe he's smarter than we figured."

24

L i Zhang was a grey-hat hacker. That meant he didn't use his considerable hacking skills to commit crime, but neither did he stay entirely within the lines of what was legal. His family had fled Communist China years ago, and their experience had given him a healthy distrust of authority. That had made him the perfect asset for Lock and Ty.

Lock had thought about letting the LAPD know about the email but had decided to wait. For one thing he still didn't know if it was genuine. For another, kidnappers usually got tetchy if you shared information with the cops. As he had no idea whom he was dealing with, he had made the decision to err on the side of caution.

Grabbing his cell phone, Lock walked to the back of the strip mall and knocked at the door. Ty opened it and nodded him inside. He followed him down a stub of corridor and into a back room. It was dark, apart from the light thrown up by various monitors and screens. Racks of computers, motherboards, and hard drives took up almost every available inch of wall space.

Li was perched on a stool at his workbench. He spun round as they came in.

"I already brought Li up to speed," Ty told him.

Lock handed the cell phone to him. The young hacker took it, turned it over a few times in his hand and placed it on the bench. He nudged past them to one of his wall racks and grabbed a plastic storage box. He opened the lid and began rooting around among a mass of cables. He pulled three out, trying to locate one that was compatible with the data port of his cell phone.

"Unlock the phone for me, please," he said.

Lock stepped over to the bench and tapped in the four-digit code. Li frowned. "Four three two one. Really?"

Lock shrugged. He had a point. It wasn't the best code.

"When I get through with this you should let me run a review of the security on all the devices you use. They probably have more holes than a colander," said Li.

"What about this?" Lock said, pulling him back to the task in hand.

"It came into your email?" Li asked.

He tapped the screen where the icon for Lock's email was. It opened. A few new messages had already come in. They could wait.

"You opened it already?" said Li.

"Is that bad?" he said.

"They'll know you opened it, that's all."

"But I didn't click through on the link," he told Li. "I know they can set things up so they're zapped once they're opened. I thought you could make sure that doesn't happen."

"And maybe get us more information about who sent it and where they are." Ty added.

Li had the cell phone plugged into a black plastic tower. The screen of his main monitor lit up with lines of scrolling green text. Lock was getting dizzy just looking at it, never mind working out what, if anything, it all meant.

"I'll do my best. But it depends on how sophisticated these people are with this stuff. Assuming this is even them."

His fingers flying lightly over the keyboard, Li set to work. It seemed to take an age before he was ready to open the link. The room was warm and growing warmer by the moment. Lock could feel a line of sweat forming at the bottom of his neck and beginning to roll down his back.

The worst part of a kidnap was the paralysis. Both Ty and he were used to being active, and staying on the front foot. Now they were chasing ghosts. Hopefully Li could change that by giving them something, anything, to work with. Because right now they had jack.

"Okay," Li said finally. "We're good to go. I already started a trace on the email. And if anything's there when I click through on this, it'll be saved to the hard drive, along with whatever information there is." He glanced over his shoulder at Lock and Ty. "Ready?"

Lock nodded.

Li clicked on the link. It opened in a separate window in the corner of the large monitor that was still filling with incomprehensible text.

A video player popped up in the new window. For the first few seconds there was black screen then Carmen appeared. She was standing alone in a darkened room with a light directed at her. She looked tired, but otherwise in good health. There was no sign of any bruises, cuts or abrasions that he could see.

She stared straight down the lens. "This is Carmen. As you'll see from the newspaper I'm holding, I'm currently safe and unharmed. You will receive further instructions soon."

The video ended less than half a second after she had uttered the last syllable. It cut back to black, then finished.

Li was staring at the screen. He tapped at some keys. He turned round to face them. "Good call. They had it set to auto-delete from that website as soon as it was viewed. But, don't worry, I saved it."

That he'd made the right call didn't mean Lock was happy. They had the video, and it might contain clues that would lead him to Carmen. But it wasn't anything he could count on.

Li startled as the cell phone rang. It was still hooked up to his cable.

"You want to get that?" he asked Lock.

"Answering won't mess with what you're doing?" Lock asked him, wanting to be certain.

"No, it's all good."

He picked up the cell phone. The number had been withheld or it was unavailable. Not an uncommon occurrence.

He tapped the answer icon and raised the cell to his ear in case it was a client, or something private. "Yes?"

There was a rush of static that stung his still buzzing eardrum.

"Mr. Lock?"

The voice at the other end of the line was distorted. It sounded male, but beyond that he couldn't make out any details. He waved at Li to record it, if he could. Li shot him a thumbs-up.

"Speaking."

"That message was to be deleted for a reason. Mess us around again, or try to figure out who we are, and we'll kill her. Am I understood?"

Suddenly the hot, stuffy room was icy cold. "I understand," Lock said.

The line went dead. His mind was racing. Not just with how much smarter and more sophisticated they were than he'd given them credit for. But he was also wondering how, having taken this risk, he could turn it to his advantage.

He doubted the video Li had managed to download would yield anything useful. Certainly not a location that would be specific enough to help them find the room. But the LAPD weren't to know that.

25

C hance pushed her hands through the slot in the cell door. She really needed to do something with her nails, she thought. They'd gotten badly chipped in the fight with Ginny Browell, then the guards. Not that she could hope for nail polish any time soon. Not in the SHU (solitary housing unit), where all but the most basic essentials were denied.

She watched as the cuffs snapped tight around her wrists. The guards were mad at her. She knew they'd be getting their ears chewed off by the warden because he was getting his chewed off by his bosses. And they were getting their ears chewed by a bunch of politicians in Sacramento. All because she'd done the world a favor and taken out that scumbag rapist Browell.

The world was upside-down crazy, she told herself. Always had been for her. All she could do was ride the wave, stay true to the Fourteen Words, do her best by God, and see where that wave took her.

As instructed, Chance pulled her cuffed hands back through the slot and turned to the wall. The cell door opened and guards moved in. Six of them.

"Six of you for little old me?" she said.

"Stay facing the wall. Hands up on your head. Keep them there too. Legs spread."

Soon her feet were shackled, her cuffs and leg chains hooked to a belly chain. She shuffled out into the corridor. At the meshed observation windows of every other cell door she saw the faces of women from her unit. They screamed words of support as she was led down the corridor and into a small side room.

Inside there were two detectives from the local police department, a man and a woman. They introduced themselves. Chance was polite in return. There was no reason not to be—they were just doing their job.

"So," the woman said, "would you like to tell us in your own words what happened here earlier?"

Chance smiled sweetly. "Not without my lawyer present. I am entitled to a lawyer, right?"

"Of course," said the guy.

"Oh, and before y'all ask any more questions, I'll be pleading not guilty. So you can save yourselves a whole bunch of time and air asking me your questions because I ain't going to be telling you anything."

With that, Chance tuned out. If they said anything else, it didn't appear to register. After a few more minutes, the guards came back to return her to the SHU.

26

D etective Stanner hard-stared at Lock across his desk. From the way the vein on his forehead was pulsing, Lock made an educated guess that he was beyond annoyed.

Lock had just challenged whether the LAPD should retain control of a major headline-grabbing investigation. Stanner didn't like it. Lock didn't blame him, but he was doing what would help Carmen. Right now that was devoting more resources to finding her. More specifically, federal government resources in the shape of the Federal Bureau of Investigation.

"How can you be so sure she was in Colorado?"

Lock wasn't. In fact, there was no clue on the video as to where it had been shot. But out of state meant the Feds could be involved. So Lock had decided to stretch the truth.

"And this video they sent you, it deleted as soon as you watched it?" Stanner asked.

Lock tossed his cell phone across the desk to him. "Look for yourself, or have your tech guys check. You'll both find I'm not lying." *Well, not about that, anyway.*

Stanner grabbed the phone from the desk, and got up. "Oh, we will."

He stood, blocking Lock's exit. To get out, he'd have to go round him. "Kidnappings are time-sensitive," Lock told him. That wasn't entirely true either. Not beyond the initial abduction. Once kidnappers had fled with a victim, time could be a plus or a minus, most often a plus that brought them to the table to get their money. "I want the FBI contacted now."

He wasn't sure if he was overselling it or not. All he knew was that Stanner looked angry enough to take a swing at him.

"It's not your call as to whether we call in the Feds," Stanner told him.

Lock eyeballed him back. Refusing to blink. Meeting his gaze and holding it. "Correct. And it's not yours either."

"It's a matter of procedure. As soon as a person is believed to have been transported over state lines, it's incumbent upon the relevant authority to alert the FBI, if they haven't already been alerted."

Glancing down, Lock saw that Stanner's hands were bunched into fists. The gesture told him his ploy had worked. He had no choice. Procedure gave him the last word. He could try to play it down with the Feds. The more he did that, the more likely they were to take an interest.

When a five-hundred-pound law-enforcement gorilla wanted to keep hold of a case, that case became very interesting indeed to anyone else who caught wind of it. It was human nature.

27

A howling cat greeted Lock's arrival at Carmen's apartment. The food bowl was empty. Not a morsel left. "And what if I hadn't come back?" he asked Merlin.

His question was answered with· more high-pitched yowling. Yeah, Lock was definitely a dog guy. He dug some more dried food from the cupboard and topped off the bowl. The cat hunkered down and set to work eating. As he pigged out, Lock moved through into the living room, and powered up Carmen's laptop.

Logging into her email account, he quickly checked the inbox around the time of their dinner in Santa Monica. There were several emails. One was from her boss, Mike, at almost precisely the time he remembered her getting the message that prompted her to head back to the office.

He clicked the email. It was brief: *Carmen, really sorry about this, but I need you to pick up the Wilder affidavit from the office tonight and review. I need someone over it before tomorrow's meeting. Mike*

So, this was the email from Mike that had sent her hurrying back to the office. Funny he hadn't mentioned it when Lock had spoken with him. Then the crack about Lock knowing who might be behind the kidnapping. It was time that Lock had another little chat with him. This time, on his terms.

~

HEADLIGHTS OFF, Lock sat in the rental car and waited for Mike. He had already made a call to check he was in his office. He'd also made a call to find out what car he drove. Now he was parked directly behind it. All he needed was for the man himself to finish work.

While he waited, he called Li.

"Hey, Li, it's Ryan. You have any news for me?"

"On the video, no. It could be anywhere. There's no radio or television noise in the background. No sound of any cars or anything else, so it's somewhere quiet, but that's all I can tell you for sure."

Lock hadn't expected any different. "What about the visuals?" he asked, hopeful that a closer inspection of the video would maybe reveal something similar to the items he'd invented to get the LAPD to involve the FBI.

"A room and a camera. There isn't anything we can use to narrow things down. Sorry, Ryan."

"Don't be sorry. I appreciate your help on this." It was true. He did. He was paying Li handsomely for his work, but it was at the edge of Li's comfort zone, and it wasn't as if he was short of eager clients. Guys like him were becoming more and more valuable as crime moved online, and everyone, private security companies included, struggled to keep up with the bad guys.

"But I do have some good news for you. Well, maybe. It's kind of weird so I don't know if it's actually good news or just a dead end that these guys set up for someone like me."

"Go ahead. What did you find?"

"Well, the email was zipped all over the place before it came to you. No way to trace its true origin, really. But they kind of messed up with the video. That's why I'm not sure what I found is genuine."

If they had messed up, it would have been the first time. Or maybe not. They had been reckless during the kidnapping. They could have split and tried again at Carmen's place or somewhere else. Instead they had engaged in a gun battle that carried a lot of downside. "How'd they mess up?"

"Well, they put the video up on a hosting site. You know, some place you can upload stuff that you want to share. It was set to private so only you had access, but they still had to register an account, and they weren't quite as slick at covering their tracks when they did that," Li told him.

From his limited knowledge of such stuff, Lock knew that every computer that connected to the internet had a unique IP address logged somewhere. There were ways of concealing or misdirecting the address you were using if you wanted to hide. That was what most criminals did. But even then there were sometimes ways of electronically tracking it back to where the person really had been.

"Anyway," Li continued, "these guys tried to hide their original IP address when they uploaded the video to the file-sharing website, but I managed to track it."

Lock's heart jumped. This was potentially huge. He'd have to do some explaining to the LAPD and the FBI as to how he'd come by the information, having told Stanner that the video had auto-deleted, but he was sure he, or rather Li, would find some elaborate explanation and baffle them with jargon. In any case, if it helped them locate Carmen he doubted anyone would care too much how they did it. "Great work, Li."

"Yeah, but like I said, don't get too excited. First, it's a general IP address that could have been used by dozens, maybe hundreds of people. There would be a lot of sifting through to see who it might be."

"And the second?"

"Well, I was thinking it would have been uploaded at maybe a Starbucks or somewhere. But it wasn't. The file was uploaded at a US Army base."

"You're certain?" Lock asked him.

"Hundred percent. Weird, huh?"

Maybe not, thought Lock. Maybe it wasn't weird at all. Maybe it fitted with what he'd seen already. "Li, can I call you back?"

Mike was walking, briefcase in hand, toward his BMW 5-Series.

28

I f Mike was surprised to see Lock, he didn't show it. Lock guessed that was another characteristic of a good courtroom operator – a passable poker face when someone sprang a surprise on you.

"You'll have to make this quick, Mr. Lock. I told my wife I'd be home for dinner by eight."

This guy was a piece of work. Lock would give him that. Carmen had regarded him not just as her employer but as a mentor and friend, and he was worried about his wife burning a casserole.

Lock stepped out in front of him, blocking his path to the driver's door of his BMW. "It'll take as long as it takes."

Mike smirked and put down his briefcase. "I've spent my entire professional life dealing with criminals. Men, and women, who've done unspeakable things. I don't respond to the tough-guy act. It might have worked with Carmen, but it doesn't make any kind of an impression on me."

Lock matched his smirk. "There's no act. But I need the answers to a couple of questions and you're not going anywhere until I have them."

"This is known as false imprisonment," he said, trying to push past.

Lock didn't budge.

"If you persist with this, I'll have no other option but to call the cops," Mike said, reaching into his inside pocket for his cell phone. He started to tap in 911. "I know you're upset about Carmen, but this behavior is completely beyond the—" He tapped the final one.

Lock plucked the cell phone from his hand, deleted the 911 call with his thumb, powered the phone down and handed it back to him. "Here. I'd hate for you to add theft to my rap sheet. Try it again and I'll drop it. By accident, of course."

Mike's face flushed. Good. The dynamic had tilted. He could bluff and bluster and quote the law all he liked, but right now it was just him and Lock in an empty parking garage with no one else around. And even if someone did pass by there was nothing in his body language to suggest this was more than guys catching up before they headed home.

"This is absurd."

He made another move to push past Lock. This time he put a little more effort behind it, like he wasn't kidding around anymore. Unfortunately for him, neither was Lock.

Lock's right hand came up to his throat. His right boot stomped down hard on Mike's Italian-leather-encased left foot, holding him in place. Lock didn't want to leave any incriminating indents from his fingers around the man's throat so he settled for pushing his thumb hard into the trigeminal nerve at the point between the top of his jawbone and his ear. "Painful, huh?"

Mike blinked.

"It can get a lot more painful too. So you're going to answer my questions and then you can be on your way."

"I'll have you arrested."

"No, you won't," Lock told him. "Because you know more about this than you're letting on."

He let up on the pressure just enough for Mike to be able to concentrate a little more fully on his responses, which would determine how the next few minutes of his life went, and how late he'd be for dinner with his wife.

"How come you seem so relaxed about what's happened to Carmen, Mike?"

He reached up and Lock allowed him to push his hand away. "Two words. Servando Guilen."

"What about him?"

"Come on. Do I have to spell it out for you? Carmen is part of the key to him ducking life in Pelican Bay or Florence."

Both were ultra-high-security American prisons. So called Supermax facilities from which escape was pretty much impossible. The Bay was California State, and Florence was a federal facility, located in Colorado.

"Do you really think someone like Servando is going to allow his defense team to be compromised a few weeks out from his trial like this? Right now he'll be moving heaven and earth to work out who took Carmen and make sure they give her back."

"And if they don't?"

"They'll spend the rest of their lives looking over their shoulders."

"He's told you this?"

"He doesn't have to. And if he did, I'm not going to confirm or deny. You can try all the strong-arm tactics on him you like, but attorney-client privilege isn't something I'll compromise. Not with a client like this."

What he'd said made sense. No question.

"Someone took Carmen to fuck with Servando?"

"I didn't say that."

"No, you said it was connected to him somehow."

"That's my hunch. But it's nothing more than that. A hunch. If someone had wanted to compromise Servando they wouldn't kidnap Carmen. It's way too much effort, and it could wound him but it wouldn't make a conviction any more certain. Hell, if he wanted, he could hire any number of attorneys. It's not as if money is an object."

Lock wasn't sure if the last part was true. From what he'd read about the Guilen case, the Mexican and US governments had located and frozen a number of his bank accounts and other assets. Money was almost certainly an issue.

"Okay, last question. How come you didn't mention it was you who asked Carmen to come back into the office?"

"Oh, come on. They were following her. If they were looking to kidnap her they could have taken her from somewhere else just as easily."

"Not when I was with her, they couldn't."

"Listen, if you think I had anything to do with this you should go talk to the LAPD. They'll think you're as nutty as I do. I'm sorry this has happened, but it has nothing to do with me. If you really want to speak to someone outside law enforcement who might have an idea what's going on here, then go speak to Guilen. Assuming he'll see you, which I very much doubt."

29

Servando Guilen was being held at the Men's Central Jail in downtown Los Angeles. Also known as the Twin Towers, it is the world's largest jail facility and covers one and a half million square feet.

As befitted a criminal of his standing, Guilen had been placed in the secure housing unit. It wasn't that he needed protection. Any prisoner so much as looking at him the wrong way would face swift and decisive retaliation. His isolation came down more to a lifestyle choice on his part. He wasn't a man given to mixing with the commoners, and the Towers had more than their fair share of those, not to mention rapists, murderers and psychopaths.

The next morning, Lock left his cell phone and everything else, apart from his wallet, in his rental car and walked the few blocks to the central reception. His identification was checked, and he got in line with the other visitors. Apart from a handful of attorneys and clergy, they were overwhelmingly female. They were also predominantly African-American and Hispanic.

Once he was through the security check, Lock followed the line of people into the visiting room. Guilen was already seated at a table in the corner. Apart from a two-day stubble, he looked the same as he did in the photographs Lock had seen of him. He was a handsome guy in his late forties, with glossy black hair and an easy smile. If you had to guess his occupation without knowing who he was most people would plump for TV news anchor or thrusting young entrepreneur, which in a way he was. It was just that his business was narcotics trafficking.

"Mr. Lock," he said, putting out his hand. Such a move would usually have earned an immediate reprimand from a guard, who would read the gesture as a way to receive contraband. No guard so much as dared to glance his way. It was a minor miracle that he wasn't just allowed to walk out of the place, such was the fear he inspired.

"Thanks for taking the time to meet me," Lock said, shaking his hand.

"Please." Guilen motioned for him to sit down as casually as he would have if they were in his boardroom in Mexico City. The immediate impression he gave was of someone who was perfectly calm and composed. "Time is one commodity that I have an abundance of," he said. "And can I say how sorry I was to hear of Carmen's kidnapping? I understand that you and she are very close."

"Yes. I was hoping you might be able to shed some light on what happened to her."

Guilen steepled his fingers in a professorial gesture of studied contemplation. "Believe me, Mr. Lock, I have my people out there as we speak trying to answer just that question. And when they find those responsible for this . . . Well, from what I understand about your life, you're a man of the world when it comes to these matters."

It didn't take a man of the world or otherwise to know what Guilen meant. If and when he found the kidnappers, he'd have them executed. Assuming, of course, that there wasn't more to it. Just because Lock couldn't see an angle as to why he'd be involved didn't mean there wasn't one. Men like Guilen operated their business empires like a game of three-dimensional chess, their motives often obscured by layers of subterfuge and deceit.

"I appreciate your efforts, but if I find the people responsible before you do, you won't have to worry about what happens to them. I'll take care of it."

The drugs baron shot him an amused smile. "I don't doubt it for a moment. You know, my business could always use someone with your experience and abilities."

"I'm sure," said Lock, looking around the room, his eyes settling on the bars on the windows. "But I like to stay on the right side of the law."

Guilen's eyes crinkled. For a moment it was hard to imagine that this man had personally ordered the deaths of hundreds of people, men, women, even children. "But you like to walk close to the line as well?"

"Not as close as you. Did Carmen mention to you that she had received threats?" Lock asked.

"No. I only wish she had. I would have put measures in place to ensure that something like this didn't happen."

"If your people do discover anything . . ."

"I'll make sure they inform you. Carmen is my lawyer, but she's become more than that since I've known her. I regard her as family."

Lock wasn't sure Guilen's was a family that any sane person would want to be welcomed into. The narco-cartels, like most large criminal enterprises, consumed their own as much as they did strangers. He wondered if he should tell Guilen about the email sent from the army base. Maybe his people could do some digging. He decided against it. Guilen could help, that much was true, but Lock wasn't sure he could be trusted.

LOCK DUG out his cell phone from the center console next to the driver's seat. Six missed calls and as many voicemail messages. Three of the calls had been from Ty. "Sorry, Ty, I was in visiting Servando Guilen. Had to leave my cell in the car."

"Okay. Well, listen up, I got some news."

Ty sounded hyped. Lock could only hope he'd made a breakthrough because, so far, he had the same amount of information he'd started out with—zip.

"Go ahead, Tyrone."

"You not see the news?"

"Ty, would you just tell me what you're talking about, or do I have to guess?"

"The news about that crazy white supremacist, Chance, carving up some rapist in prison. You know, the one we ran down in San Francisco."

Lock remembered her all too well. His heart sank. "I thought you meant you had news about Carmen."

"No, sorry, dude. But I spoke to a buddy who works at the base and he's going to do some poking around for us. See if we can't find out who sent the video."

That was something, but a military base was a big place. Many were equivalent in size and sprawl to a small town. It was worth a shot, but it would take time, and time wasn't something they necessarily had on their side. They needed a solid lead, and fast.

"So what's the story with Chance?" Lock asked.

Chance was the daughter of a white supremacist and leader of the notorious Aryan Brotherhood prison gang, who had gone by the name Reaper. Freya had helped engineer her father's escape, then led the authorities on a merry dance. It had ended in San Francisco where she had been involved in an assassination attempt on the President of the United States. Lock and Tyrone had foiled it. Chance had been sentenced to life without possibility of parole, in the process becoming a martyr to the ever-growing white supremacist movement.

"You hear about this cat called Gerard Browell?" Ty asked. "Got gender re-assignment surgery, became Ginny, and transferred to the women's central prison at Chowchilla."

"I heard something about it."

"Okay, so Browell wasn't in there twenty-four hours before Chance carved him up like a Thanksgiving turkey."

"So what's that got to do with Carmen?"

Ty sounded irritated by the question. "I don't know. But it's kind of a coincidence, don't you think? Carmen goes missing and all of a sudden Chance is in the news."

"You said it. It's a coincidence. Chance is still in prison, right?"

"Yeah, but . . ."

Lock's cell pinged with another incoming call. "Ty, listen, I have another call. Keep speaking to as many people as you can. Maybe see if your buddy at that base can talk to some of the higher-ups. Find out if they have anyone on base currently under investigation."

People assumed that everyone in the military was on the up and up. That was the case for ninety-nine percent. But the military, like any organization, had its bad apples. The good thing, though, was that service personnel were usually pretty perceptive (their lives depended upon it), so even if they didn't always nail the odd rogue, they often had a good idea who they were.

"Will do."

"Thanks," he said, switching calls.

"Is that Ryan Lock?"

It was a man's voice, but he didn't recognize the number.

"Speaking. Who's this?"

"Carl Galante. I'm the investigator from Carmen's office. Sorry it took me so long to get back to you. Listen, I'm real sorry about what's happened, and I just wanted to let you know that if there's anything you need, anything at all, you have only to ask."

There was something. Lock had asked the cops for it and been almost laughed out of the office. "Carl, would you be able to get me a copy of the closed-circuit security cameras from the office building?"

Carl hesitated for a second. "I already looked at all the stuff. See if we'd had any visitors before the kidnapping. Or if there was anything from the abduction that the cops might have missed."

"Carl, I'd really appreciate it if you could get me that footage. I'm in the weeds here right now."

30

C arl Galante had a goatee, collar-length hair, and was wearing shorts and a Dogtown Venice surf T-shirt. From the checking he had done before their sit-down, Lock knew that the ex-cop came with a solid reputation. There was nothing in his past to suggest he might be involved in any way with what had happened to Carmen.

Carl slid into the booth across from him, thumped down a heavy envelope and slid it across the table to him. "I got you a copy of the threat assessments we've compiled over the past three years. Everything's there. Names, numbers, background information and whether the threat was credible or not."

"I appreciate it." Lock picked up the envelope and placed it next to him on the bench seat. Even allowing for the fact that it covered a three-year span, there was a lot of paper.

"I also included a couple of USB drives with all the relevant video footage from our cameras," Carl continued. "If anyone asks, you didn't get any of it from me."

Lock studied him for a second. "Why so helpful?"

Most people would have taken offense at such a question. But Carl had spent twenty-plus years in law enforcement. He understood

Lock's natural suspicion. Especially given the circumstances. "I like Carmen. She's a good person with a good heart."

"You're right. She is." Lock patted the envelope. "Thank you."

Carl shrugged and took a sip of water. "I've been through everything, but nothing jumped out at me. I figured it couldn't hurt to have you take a look, see if you spot anything that I or the cops have missed."

"There was nothing recent that gave you cause for concern? No one with a grudge, or maybe someone looking to upset Servando Guilen's defense?"

"Something connected to Guilen was the first thing I thought about when I got the news. You know, broad daylight, brazen, lots of shots fired. It's definitely cartel-style stuff."

"But?" Lock asked.

"If there is a connection, I haven't found it."

That didn't mean it wasn't there. "Guilen didn't think so either, and your boss thinks it's connected to me somehow."

That drew a smile from Carl. "He said that?"

"Not those words exactly, but yes."

"And what do you think?" Carl asked.

Lock had asked himself the same question. There were enough people out there who'd be more than happy to see him suffer. He'd always stayed on the right side of the law, or at least fought for the good guys, but he'd hardly been a choir boy. He believed that sometimes an eye-for-an-eye strategy was the right fit. And that some individuals couldn't be negotiated with.

But why wouldn't someone who wanted revenge just come for him directly? It wasn't as if he hid away. He would have been easy enough to find if someone was determined to do so. "I don't know," he said.

Carl seemed to weigh that answer and find it reasonable enough. "So, Mike gave you a hard time, huh?"

Lock felt Carl had more to say about his boss. But he'd have to proceed with caution. Mike was still the guy who cut Carl a check every month, and that meant something in this economy, even for a retired cop with a good pension. "I don't think he's a fan,' he said. 'Plus I gave him a little bit of a hard time back."

"Yeah, I heard about that."

Lock decided to offer Carl a concession, hoping it might persuade him to open up a little more. "I may have gone a tad overboard. But you have to understand, Carmen means everything to me." That last part was true. She did mean the world to him. He couldn't imagine his life without her. Not now.

"I get that. She spoke about you to me once or twice. You know, in passing. She loves you."

Lock decided to cut to the chase. Neither of them had come here to discuss how good his relationship with Carmen was. "So what's the deal with your boss?"

"You mean why doesn't he care too much for you?"

"Yeah."

Carl took a breath. "This stays between us, right?"

"Of course."

"I think he has a thing for her. Or, at least, had."

"You mean, Mike and Carmen . . .?"

"Oh, no," Carl said, quickly correcting himself. "Like an affair? No, this was pretty one-sided. I'm not even sure he told her how he felt, but anyone who was around the office could see it."

That would certainly explain his hostility, but Lock wondered if Carl was trying to suggest anything more sinister. It seemed a stretch, but people were capable of all kinds of strange behavior if they'd had a romantic advance spurned. "You're not suggesting he may have been involved in this?"

Carl laughed. "No. No way. But it does mean I can't have him knowing I gave you any of this stuff."

Lock reassured him it would stay between them, paid the check for the water and coffee, and grabbed the envelope. It felt heavy in his hand. He hoped that somewhere inside there would be a scrap of something he could use to find Carmen.

Out on the sidewalk, he shook Carl's hand. "Thanks. You didn't have to do this, but I'm glad you did."

"Just go find her and bring her home. If I get wind of anything from inside the firm, I'll be in touch. Although it looks like I'm going to be crazy busy after that shit-show up in Chowchilla."

Lock froze. "Chowchilla? The Central Women's Prison?"

Carl looked at him, puzzled. "Yeah. You know it?"

"Know the name. So how come you guys are involved with something up there? It's a long way from Los Angeles."

"Oh, we represent the women who killed that other inmate. You know, Browell, the rapist."

"Wait. The firm represents Freya Vaden?"

"Yeah. Have done for about the past five years. Why?"

31

His head still spinning, Lock drove back to the west side. He planned on watching the footage at Li Zhang's office on Lincoln Boulevard in Marina Del Rey. Not only did Li have large high-definition monitors, he also had software that could enhance any image or segment of video he needed to take a closer look at. From there he would head back to his apartment and work through the papers Carl had given him.

As he drove, he turned over what Carl had told him about their representation of Freya Vaden, a.k.a. Chance, in his mind. When Ty had mentioned her to him earlier he'd thought it nothing more than a macabre coincidence. And, anyway, she was in prison. For good.

But now he knew that Carmen's firm represented her? He wasn't going to lie: it was unsettling.

After Carl had dropped it into the conversation, Lock had pressed him for more details. For one, he wanted to know exactly what work the firm did for Vaden. She couldn't have had any reasonable expectation of getting out via an appeal. The evidence against her had been as clear cut as it got. Among other things, she had tried to kill the President of the United States, in full view of dozens of witnesses. Witnesses that included cops, Secret Service agents, himself and Ty.

If it hadn't been for them, she would likely have succeeded, and America would have been plunged into who knew what. Possibly a race war, which was what she and her allies had been hoping to spark.

No, Carl confirmed. She knew she was going to die in prison. She had retained the firm's services to fight a series of battles as to how her son, who had been born while she was awaiting trial, was raised. Due to her own father's incarceration, Freya had been raised in foster care. During that time she had been abused. That, and her separation from her father, had transformed her, somewhat understandably, into a very angry woman intent on taking revenge on the system. She was determined that she exert some control over her son's upbringing.

Suddenly he could see how Carmen's law firm would have offered their help on a *pro bono* basis (without taking payment). Carl had stopped him when he'd said that. They weren't working *pro bono*. They were being paid their full fee.

That piece of information had stopped him in his tracks. How the hell was a woman like Freya Vaden able to pay such huge attorney fees? They would run into tens, likely hundreds of thousands of dollars.

"She has lots of friends," Carl told him.

"The kind of friends who can cover those costs?" he'd asked him.

"I said lots, not wealthy."

He'd explained that Vaden had become the Joan of Arc to many sections of the white supremacist movement. In fact, she was one step up from the Maid of Orleans. She was a living martyr.

Even though she was in jail for a series of homicides, and terrorist-related crimes, she was seen as a victim of race mixing. A victim who had chosen to fight back.

In a world less twisted, and allied to a less hateful ideology, even he could glimpse the power of her life story. Cast into the darkness while her father was imprisoned, she had grown up not only to aid his escape but had come within seconds of achieving the dream of many on the lunatic fringe by murdering America's first African-American president. Now she herself was being forced to share her father's fate, while her son was made to suffer as she had, separated from his family.

"So what was she trying to achieve?" he'd asked Carl.

"She wanted the boy, Eich, to be raised by friends of hers in the white supremacist movement. You can imagine how that request went down."

Lock had stopped him. "The boy's name is Ike?" he said, making a note.

"E-I-C-H. After Adolf Eichmann."

Of course it was.

"Anyway," Carl had continued, "when she didn't get her way, she filed a series of motions, and also made sure that the foster family who were looking after the kid were harassed to the point where they handed him back."

"So the kid went back into the system?"

"Exactly. The law of unintended consequences."

"What's the current status of all of this?"

"Stalled. But the firm is still working on it."

"Was Carmen involved?"

"Not as far as I know. Why?"

At that point Lock told him about how his life had intersected with Freya Vaden's and her father's after a friend of his, Ken Prager, an undercover Federal law-enforcement officer, had been murdered by white supremacists. Carl had let out a low whistle.

"So, what do you think? Is there a connection?" Lock asked.

"There's no evidence of one. Nothing direct anyway. But I don't care much for coincidences like this."

LOCK PULLED the rental car into the parking area in front of the strip mall on Lincoln. For a moment, he sat there and didn't move.

Was it really possible that Freya Vaden was involved in Carmen's kidnapping? Apart from the Servando Guilen case, it was all he had to go on. He glanced at the thick envelope Carl had given him. Maybe Carmen's abduction was connected to neither. It was more likely that the identity of the kidnappers, or the person they were working for, was in that envelope. A disgruntled client, a victim (or victim's family member) of someone Carmen had helped to acquit. Attorneys were hardly the most popular people, and that went treble for attorneys involved in what passed for the criminal justice system.

Grabbing the envelope, he swung open the driver's door, got out, and headed for the side of the building. As he got close to the small rear entrance to Li Zhang's lair, he stopped. The door, which Li always kept closed and locked, wasn't just open, it was hanging from its hinges.

His right hand fell automatically to his SIG. He eased it from its holster, and moved toward the wall, the barrel covering the door. He had spoken with Li only a half-hour before.

That was both bad and good news. The bad was that Li was almost certainly inside when whoever it was had shown up. He'd told him that he was there, was going to get something to eat, but was going to wait for him first. But the half-hour window also closed down the possibility that whoever had done this had already left. There was every chance that they were still inside.

He decided to work on the assumption that they were. Instead of calling out, he sidestepped quickly across the door, the SIG punched out, the inner pad of his index finger across the trigger, ready to fire.

32

The stub of dark corridor lay in front of him. The lights had been switched off, and the contrast of the gloom to the sunshine outside made it hard to see. Gun in hand, he stepped through the door.

If someone was moving around inside, he couldn't hear them. He still hadn't shaken off the ringing in his ears from the gun battle. He needed to get it checked out as soon as he had some free time. But, right now, free time didn't seem likely. As soon as he felt like he was getting any kind of a foothold with Carmen's kidnapping, some other element spun off into chaos.

No matter. All he could do was focus on the task in hand. Half blind, and half deaf, he edged slowly down the corridor. The door at the end was open. On the other side lay Li's main work space.

He passed another door on his right that led into a small kitchen and toilet area. This door was closed. He decided to leave it for now and circle back round once he'd checked the workspace for Li. At the end of the corridor, he placed himself with his back to the corridor wall.

Moving fast, he dropped down, spun round and moved through the door. The room was empty. But it had been trashed. Stools were toppled over. One was upside down, the seat on the floor, the legs in the air. A couple of computer monitors also lay on the floor, their screens smashed in. Keyboards, hard drives, and other hardware were scattered around them, in pieces. Every surface had been swept clear.

The chaos was such that he couldn't tell if anything was missing. In any case, the only person who would have an answer to that would be Li Zhang, and he was nowhere to be seen.

Blood was spattered across the far wall. His heart sank. He was still clinging to the hope that Li had ducked out to get some water or juice from a nearby store while he waited for Lock to get there.

He crossed to the blood spatter. He was careful not to touch it, even though his and Ty's DNA was all over the room from previous visits. It was definitely fresh. There was some hair as well, and a dent in the plaster, like someone's head had been grabbed and shoved hard into the wall.

Backing up, he picked his way across the floor to the door. A chunk of green computer board scraped under his shoe as he headed back out into the corridor.

His heart sank with every step. This didn't look like a robbery. Behind him, thousands of dollars' worth of tech equipment that could have been fenced for at least five hundred bucks lay smashed to pieces, worthless. The bloodied dent in the wall wasn't good either. He couldn't imagine a lanky kid like Li offering much resistance, so smashing his head into the wall—if it had been his head that had made the dent—came off like overkill.

On the plus side, he hadn't found him yet. So maybe he'd been taken. It was strange to realize that he was actually hoping he had been. Or that he'd somehow fled to safety.

The door leading into the small kitchen was in front of him. He took a deep breath, flattened himself against the wall and reached for the handle. He pushed it down and went through the door all in one swift movement.

Tracking a quick 180-degree view of the kitchen through the iron sights of his SIG, he was confronted by more blood. A lot more. The tiled floor, walls, even the kitchen cabinets were splattered with it. If it was Li's, it was a lot to lose and still be breathing.

"Li!"

No response.

The door that led off the kitchen to the small toilet in back was ajar. A foot prodded out, the toes pointed up. Red Chuck Taylor low-tops and a once white, now red, sports sock. He squelched his way through the blood, and pushed the toilet door open.

Li Zhang's body lay on the floor. His head was jammed between the edge of the toilet bowl and the sink. His eyes stared lifelessly at the ceiling. There was no need to look for a pulse. He was gone. Lock had seen enough of the dead and dying to know when it was too late.

His chest was bare, with a brown-black mosaic of knife puncture wounds and slash marks. Someone had really gone to town. He swallowed hard. Li had likely crawled in here to try to escape the onslaught, or after his attacker or attackers had left, only to bleed out on the floor.

His left arm was stretched out, as if he'd been grabbing for the edge of the sink when he'd collapsed. It was then he caught sight of the mirror above it.

Someone had left a message in a series of smeared-blood letters. He narrowed his eyes to make out what it said.

Tracking goes two ways.

Then, beneath that, numbers: *14/88/18*

33

The first part of the message was self-evident. Li had helped them trace the email that had been sent. In turn, they had chased him down, then butchered him. If they were white nationalists, as the blood-graffiti suggested, they would have taken additional pleasure in murdering an Asian man.

The numbers below were more mysterious to the untrained eye. Unless you were familiar with the world of white supremacist and neo-Nazi groups. Each number signified something different: "88" signified the letter H, repeated twice, which stood for "Heil Hitler"; "18" stood for A and H, the initials of the German Führer and the man responsible for the Holocaust that had killed six million people, most of them European Jews.

The "14" was a little more circumspect, more of an insider thing. A number that most members of the public would have no idea about.

It stood not for an initial or initials, but for the so-called Fourteen Words, which had been coined by hero, and martyr, of the white nationalist movement, David Lane. Lane had led an organization called the Order, which had been behind the murder of Jewish-American radio talk-show host Alan Berg. The words were, "We must secure the existence of our people, and a future for white children."

In Lane's world there was a conspiracy against white Aryan people by a secretive Jewish group they referred to as ZOG or the Zionist Occupation Government.

All of a sudden, Freya Vaden's possible connection to what was happening with Carmen seemed a lot more likely. Lock backed out of the bathroom, then went along the corridor, through the broken door and out into the light. Looking down, he saw that he'd left a trail of bloody footprints in his wake. He pulled out his cell phone and made two calls. The first was to 911. The second was to Ty.

The 911 operator told him she would have a unit on scene in under five minutes. In this part of town, he didn't doubt it, and he guessed there would be a lot more than one in that time. Marina Del Rey was hardly noted for violent crime. A half-mile down the road in Venice Beach, it was a different story but the marina was quiet.

As he stayed on the line with her, he walked around to the front of the strip mall. Sometimes a perp or perps will hang out near the crime scene to take in the aftermath of the mayhem they have created. In this case, he doubted it, but there was always the possibility. Strange people did strange things.

Traffic was busy on Lincoln Boulevard. A homeless man pushing a shopping cart down the sidewalk stared at him. Looking down, he realized he was still tracking blood. He had some on his shirt, too, and, of course, he was carrying a handgun in his holster. Lock called over to the guy, "Hey, were you here ten minutes ago?"

"No, I wasn't nowhere ten minutes ago." He took off, pushing his shopping cart so fast it threatened to tip over.

Lights flashed in the distance. He saw them before he heard the scream of sirens. Ty finally picked up his call. "What's up?"

Lock told him about Li. His partner didn't say anything. "Ty? You still there?"

"I'm heading over."

He wasn't sure an irate six-foot-five-inch retired marine would be a useful addition to the crime scene. "No, hold off. Meet me at my place in an hour. We still need to look at the footage and the papers Carl gave me. Two of us will make it go a lot faster."

A patrol car breached the entrance to the mall at speed. It swept into a turn and stopped a few feet short of him.

"Ty, I gotta go."

Two cops got out of the patrol car, weapons drawn. Lock held up his hands.

34

"Stop! Right there!"

Sidestepping the papers scattered across his living-room floor, Lock grabbed for the remote control, and hit the freeze-frame button. Ty stood next to him, and they studied the CCTV footage from Carmen's abduction on the wall-mounted television screen.

"Okay, go back," said Ty.

Lock handed the remote to him. Ty stabbed at a button, putting the images into slow-speed rewind. They moved back a few frames at a time. He tapped another button to freeze the image.

On the screen the taller of the two men was walking across Carmen's office. He was still masked, and nothing about the footage struck Lock as any more significant than what they had already watched. "What am I looking at here, Tyrone?"

Ty took two long strides toward the screen and stopped so that he was side on. He jabbed a long finger at the man's arm. The sleeve of his jacket had ridden up. "The ink," he said.

"What about it?"

"Can we take a closer look?"

"I don't know. Maybe." Lock hurried back to his laptop, which was sending the video footage to his TV. He had some image manipulation software that was capable of sharpening and also of zooming in on a particular section. The only problem was that, since they had begun to rely on Li's expertise, his skill at using it had gotten a little rusty. He pulled down a few menus before he found what he was looking for.

Ty's finger jabbed again at the section of the image he wanted to examine more closely. Lock managed to highlight and find the correct command to blow it up.

Ty was right. The guy had a tattoo emblazoned just above his wrist. But he still couldn't tell why Ty was so excited by this discovery. Tattoos were hardly news. They'd become so commonplace as to be almost invisible to Lock. It looked to him like some kind of cross. He peered at the blown-up section of image. "Ty, we already know they're almost certainly white supremacists. A swastika doesn't get us any further forward."

Ty peered intently at the tattoo. He was clearly seeing something that Lock wasn't. Finally, he glanced back over his shoulder. "You're correct. A swastika don't. But," he said, tracing the outline of the battlefield cross down to some tiny letters and numbers, "the name of the dude's infantry company sure as shit does."

"You can't possibly read that," Lock told him.

"No, but when we get that ink blown up, that's what it's gonna be." Ty stuck a massive hand toward him. "I'll bet my life on it."

35

Rance rolled up his shirt sleeves and plunged his hands into the warm, soapy water in the sink. He rubbed them together, then took them out, rinsed them off under the tap with cold water, and dried them.

He pivoted round to the kitchen table, and picked up the wooden tray he'd already set with coffee, orange juice, toast, a bowl of cereal and milk. Their guest had barely eaten since her arrival, but he figured that had to change. It was important for their mission that she at least gave the appearance of being in good health.

Outside, he could hear Point's dog, Bito, barking its fool head off, unhappy that it had been left alone in the cab of the truck. He put the tray down, and pushed out through the screen door and over to the vehicle. The dog was sitting on the bench seat, its huge front paws resting on the top of the steering wheel. The inside of the windshield was covered with slobber and condensation.

Rance hauled open the driver's door, and the dog launched itself out of the cab. Holy fuck, he'd never got over the size of the beast. Even for a Rhodesian Ridgeback, it was a monster. Maybe a hundred twenty pounds, all of it muscle, and almost three foot tall at the shoulders.

Point had named it Benito after Mussolini, but over time that been shortened to Bito. Rance had never cared for the animal. It had a look in its eye he didn't trust. But it had come in plenty useful, not only as a guard but for other work. It had a good nose, was a relentless hunter, and unforgiving when it came to a kill.

Maybe that was why it set him on edge. He had seen, up close and personal, on more than occasion, the damage it was capable of inflicting.

Rance walked back into the kitchen, careful not to let the dog follow him in. He grabbed a couple of frozen chicken feet from the refrigerator and tossed them outside. That would keep Bito occupied while he gave Carmen breakfast.

He picked up the tray again, and checked himself. His mask. He had forgotten it, not for the first time. He walked through into the living room, retrieved it from the couch, put it on and went back to the kitchen to fetch the tray.

~

CARMEN STARTLED as the door opened. She had been asleep. Last night one of the men had offered her an Ambien sleeping pill and, exhausted, she had accepted it. It wasn't as if they couldn't do what they wanted to her without drugging her. She was completely and utterly at her captors' mercy.

The shorter of the two men walked in with a tray. The sight of food made her stomach turn over. But she knew she needed to eat. Especially as the nausea she was experiencing was more likely the result of this trauma than anything else.

During the night, her period had arrived, bloodying the sheets and leaving her even more depressed than she already felt. Something she hadn't imagined was possible.

Her mouth was as dry as cotton as she struggled to lift her head. "I need to use the bathroom," she told her captor. "And I need some tampons."

From behind the mask, she saw the man's eyes dart down to the bloody patch on the sheet. He quickly looked away.

That was the reaction she had been hoping for. As she had drifted in and out of sleep, she had realized that the arrival of her period could be turned to her advantage. Many men were squeamish about such matters, which she could use to gather a few moments of privacy. Privacy could be used as a window to escape.

"Okay," her captor said. "I have some in the other room. I'll go get them."

Her heart sank a little. She'd hoped he would have to go out to get them, leaving her alone. No such luck.

"Can you at least release me so I can get cleaned up? I don't mind changing the sheets. I wouldn't expect you to . . ."

If she could be free and have him out of the room, even for a few seconds, she would have an opportunity to make a run for it.

"It's okay," he said. "Blood doesn't bother me none."

The way he said it, his eyes lingering between her legs, his initial embarrassment gone, set her teeth on edge.

He walked out of the room, leaving her prone and vulnerable. She was starting to regret taking the sleeping pill. It had left her mind fuzzy when she needed it to be sharp.

But she'd been so tired.

He reappeared a minute later, clutching a white plastic bag. He dug out a fresh box of tampons and another of sanitary pads and put them next to the tray.

He came over to the bed, and began to free her. "I'm going to take you through to the bathroom. Get cleaned up and do what you need to do. Don't even think about trying anything. If you do, I'll hurt you."

She believed him. But he had said "hurt", not "kill". That choice of words gave her some small hope. If they'd wanted her dead, they could have done it easily by now. "I promise," she said.

His eyes flickered behind the mask, meeting hers. Without being able to see his face, she couldn't read his intentions.

"Is it okay if I take a shower?" she asked, praying he would say yes. She could use the noise of the running water as cover. Assuming, of course, that he didn't stand sentry outside the door, or that if he did, there was a window she'd be able to climb out of. She was fairly sure that the house was all on one level, so that was something.

"Sure. But don't take long about it. Get yourself cleaned up, and out again. Any longer than five minutes and I'll be coming in, whether you're decent or not."

36

Carmen closed the bathroom door behind her. She was light-headed and her legs felt alien, like ghostly appendages that might, at any time, stop supporting her weight.

She caught sight of herself in the mirror. Her long hair was greasy, dank and tangled, her face was puffy, her eyes dull. She splashed some water over her face, trying to shake off the sensation that her brain had been wrapped in cotton wool.

Crossing to the tub, she pulled back the plastic curtain, and turned on the shower, which ran directly into the bath. She got in and set to work quickly scrubbing the worst of the grime from her body, and the blood that had dried between her thighs.

A minute was all she would allow. She counted down from sixty as she cleaned up. At one, she left the shower running, and quietly stepped out, dried off, and broke open the box of tampons.

She removed a tampon, ripped open the packaging, and inserted it. She dried off, grabbed the shorts, bra and T-shirt she'd been given. Her hair was even more tangled. That couldn't be helped. She had maybe three minutes left of the time she'd been allotted. She hoped it would be enough.

She walked the three feet to the door, and slowly turned the handle. She would pop her head out and, if he was there, she'd ask for toothpaste and a toothbrush.

And if he wasn't, if the corridor was empty, she'd make her move. If she was caught after that, she would take whatever was coming.

~

THAT GODDAMN DOG.

It was out there in the yard, barking its fool head off about something. A few days before it had cornered a cat under the house. Rance had practically had to Taser the damn thing before it would give up digging. That was all they needed, some little old lady coming round looking for her missing kitty and seeing a woman tied to the bed.

He could hear the shower running. She'd be good for a few more minutes yet, and it wasn't as if the bathroom window was big enough for her to climb out of.

He walked outside and called to the dog. "Hey, Bito. Here, boy."

The dog loped across to him and stuck its muzzle into his groin. He pushed its head away and it growled. It looked up, saw the mask and started barking, the ridges on its back quivering. Not a good sign.

Rance peeled off the mask. The dog seemed to calm a little, but kept barking. Rance pulled another frozen chicken foot from the bag he was holding, opened the truck door, and tossed the foot in. The dog took off after it. Rance slammed the door. It would have to stay there for now.

He walked back to the house. It was time to tell the woman that shower time was over. She should get her ass dried and back in the bedroom. In the kitchen, without thinking, he put his mask on the table.

Outside the bathroom door, he stopped and knocked. He could still hear the hiss of the shower. What was it with women and long-ass showers? Growing up, Rance had had three sisters and getting into the bathroom had proved a near impossibility. And when he did get in, there was never any warm, never mind hot, water left.

He knocked on the door again, this time a little more insistently. "Hey, time to wrap it up in there."

The shower stayed on. He didn't want to barge in on her, like some pervert, but she was testing the limits of his patience.

He knocked a third time. "Okay, I'm going to count to ten, and if that shower ain't stopped, I'm coming in, whether you're decent or not. Y'hear me?"

As CARMEN FLITTED past the truck, a huge caramel-brown dog lunged against the window, barking frantically, its teeth bared. Not that she needed any encouragement to speed up, but she did, sprinting for a copse a hundred yards away. The trees were about the only cover she'd seen anywhere near the house. Otherwise the only feature was the rough dirt track running up to the house.

With no idea how long it would take to reach a road, and other people, from the track, she'd decided to make for the trees, where at least she'd be concealed from immediate view of the house.

As she ran, small rocks and the hard scrabble ground cut into the soles of her feet. She picked her steps with more care, but that only slowed her down. She tried to block out the pain and discomfort and kept running.

Slowly, she found sensation returning to her body. The fog in her brain began to clear. It was as if her body was on auto-pilot.

One foot in front of the other, she told herself. That was all she needed to do.

She'd had frightening experiences before. Things she'd thought she would never get through. Her first time in court had been one. As stupid as it might have seemed, that had been almost as scary as being kidnapped. Maybe worse, because here she had only herself to worry about. In front of a judge, she had shouldered the responsibility for another human being.

Her right ankle folded under her. She stopped, brought up short by the fresh jolt of pain. For the first time, she dared to glance behind her. She couldn't see anything, apart from the dog locked inside the cab of the truck, its vast square head pistoning up and down as it barked at her. Its chest heaved and the ridges along its back rippled so hard that Carmen shivered with terror. If it was between a kidnapper with a gun and this monster of a dog, she would take her chance with an itchy trigger finger every time.

Come on, Carmen. It's a twisted ankle.

She pushed on toward the copse. Soon she had breached the tree line, and was hidden from the house. She sank down, her back to a tree trunk, and massaged her ankle.

Gingerly, she stood up again, placing more weight on the ankle. It was painful, but she was sure she had only twisted it. At worst, it was a sprain. Something she could power through. She moved forward through the trees.

Twenty feet later she had reached the tree line on the other side. She blinked, not sure whether she could believe what she was staring at. A road. A big, beautiful two-lane blacktop road.

In the distance she could see a car on the horizon. It was heading straight toward her.

Tears of sheer relief welled in her eyes. She was safe. Or at least within touching distance. She stepped out onto the blacktop and held her arms up above her head, ready to flag down the car that was heading straight toward her.

37

R ance kicked open the door. The bathroom was empty. She must have snuck out of the house when he was dealing with the dog. Point was going to be P-I-S-S-E-D. But only if he found out. If Rance could get her back before that, there was no need for Point to know.

Outside, the dog was still barking. Man, that was all he needed.

He caught himself.

The dog. Of course.

Why go hunting for this stupid beaner bitch when he could let the dog do the job for him? Hell, Bito lived for shit like this. He'd think he'd died and gone to doggy heaven.

Rance walked back into the bathroom. He looked around for something that would have her scent. It didn't take long.

Perfect.

He reached down to the floor and came back up with a pair of blood-stained panties. Pinching the edge between his thumb and forefinger, he ran back out.

At the truck, Bito was practically foaming at the mouth. Rance pulled his Taser from its holster, just in case the dog turned on him.

They had a shock collar for it, but Point got all sensitive about using it on Bito.

Rance pulled out the key fob and lowered the window. He shoved the bloodied panties through the gap. The dog pushed its muzzle into the cloth. Its tail whipped back and forth with excitement as it inhaled the scent.

"Okay, Bito. You ready?"

Rance stepped to the side of the truck, the Taser in his hand, and ripped open the door. The Ridgeback bounded out. It swung round to look up at Rance. His hand tightened around the trigger of the Taser. "Go on, Bito. Seek!"

That was the command he'd heard Point use with the dog. It worked. The dog's head slumped forward. It nosed the ground. It moved forward, sniffing. It began to head toward the trees.

That made sense, Rance thought. Make for cover.

The dog padded forward, its nose still glued to the ground. Rance fell in behind it, the Taser still gripped in his hand. He might not have to use it on the dog. But he had a feeling he'd be using it real soon.

THE CAR SLOWED as Carmen flagged it down. She could see a woman behind the wheel. No other passengers. The woman had long blond hair, and was wearing a T-shirt. She stopped the car next to Carmen, doubt entering her eyes as she saw her bedraggled state. For a second Carmen thought she might drive on.

Carmen motioned at the woman to lower the window. To her immense relief, she did, the window gliding down and the woman leaning out.

"Please, I need a ride."

The woman looked at her. "Where?"

"Anywhere. Wherever the nearest police precinct house is. Or if we see a patrol car we could flag it down."

The woman was still staring at her.

She was freaking her out with all this talk of cops. And she was probably speaking too fast. She must look like some crazy lady, probably high on meth, who had just crawled out of the woods behind them.

Carmen took a deep breath. "I know I look . . ."

The woman's expression was slowly shifting from one of puzzlement to something approaching nerves, all the way on through to fear. It took Carmen a second to register that she wasn't looking at her. She was looking at the woods behind her.

Carmen glanced round. The dog that been in the truck, the huge brown one, was running through the trees. It was headed straight for them. A ways behind it, she could see a figure following, struggling to keep up.

The woman was fumbling to open the rear door. Carmen grabbed the handle. It was locked.

"Please, open it," she screamed at the driver.

"I'm trying," the woman yelled back, panic-stricken.

The dog was getting close. A few seconds and it would be right on top of her.

The more panicked they became, the more the woman fumbled. Finally there was a click. Now Carmen could hear the dog, as it raced, panting, toward the car. She could hear the man too. "Go on, Bito. Go on!" he shouted.

Carmen grabbed the door handle. This time it opened. She launched herself into the back seat.

"Close it!" the driver screamed. "Close the door!"

Carmen twisted round, and made a grab for the door. She slammed it just as the dog reached the blacktop a few yards in front of the car.

There was a reassuring clunk as the woman hit a button to lock all the doors. Meanwhile, the dog had skidded to a halt, its back legs shooting out behind it as it struggled to keep its balance and gain traction on the road surface.

It was Carmen's turn to scream. "Drive!"

The dog was facing the car. It wasn't barking, just staring intently at them.

The driver had frozen, her hands gripping the steering wheel tight. She was staring at the huge dog as it began to move to the side of the car. She reached down and placed the car in Drive. The color had completely drained from her face.

Carmen wanted to reach into the front and slap her. "Hit the gas, lady."

The woman seemed to finally snap out of her terror-induced daze. "Right," she said, her foot moving to the gas pedal.

Suddenly the dog launched itself at the driver's window. There was the sound of shattering glass, quickly followed by a series of growls, and the sound of tearing flesh. Instinctively, Carmen pushed herself into a corner of the back seat as the dog set about the blond woman.

With its back legs still outside the car, its teeth clamped around her neck. Its front paws came up, raking their way down her chest, tearing first her shirt and then into her flesh.

Blood spattered across the inside of the windshield. The woman's screams only seemed to drive the huge animal into more of a frenzy. It let go of her neck, and Carmen's could see its muzzle was covered with blood.

More blood arced across the seats and the windshield as the attack continued. The dog's back legs raked frantically against the side of the driver's door as it forced its way further inside the cabin. Its weight pressed down on the woman's chest, pinning her into her seat as it clamped its jaws around the top of her head, and slowly began to peel her scalp away from her skull.

Carmen was in the very corner of the back seat now. She reached her hand back, feeling for the handle. Even though her captor had to be outside, she had to get out of the car. If she stayed it would be a matter of time before the dog turned on her. If she had to die, she didn't want to die like that.

The tips of her fingers found the groove of the handle and she pulled it back. The door opened and she tumbled out backwards. The driver's screams had fallen away to silence.

Lying on her back, Carmen pushed herself to the other side of the road. She could still see the dog's torso pressing the driver back into her seat, but the blood spatters thankfully spared her any more detail.

There was the sound of a Taser crackling. The dog gave a whimpering cry. Another shot. The dog twitched, the arc of its spine arching, then slumped forward, its head flopping onto the dashboard.

Carmen looked up to see a man holding a Taser standing above her, looking down. The mask was gone. She was surprised by how young, almost boyish, he looked. He had blue eyes and sandy-brown hair. Only his stare, hard and unflinching, told the story of who he was. He pocketed the Taser, coming back up with a handgun.

"Look what you done," he said, waving the gun toward the blood-soaked interior of the car. He reached down and grabbed Carmen by the hair. He hauled her up and onto her feet. The gun prodding painfully into her spine, he drove her round to the driver's side of the car.

"You stand there," he told her. "Move and, so help me God, I'll kill you right here."

She did as she was told. She had no other choice.

She watched as he opened the driver's door and hauled the the dog out of the car, grabbed its collar, opened the rear door and manhandled it into the back seat.

When that was done, he cut the woman's seatbelt with a knife and shoved her across into the passenger seat. He got out and waved the gun once more at Carmen.

"Get in."

Shaking uncontrollably, she clambered into the back seat with the dog. It panted and drooled thick gobs of bloody saliva but otherwise it was quiet. The gunman climbed into the driver's seat, spun the wheel and drove the car off the road and into the woods. Threading his way carefully through the copse, he brought them back to the house.

When they got there, he ordered Carmen out. They were both covered with blood, their clothes saturated. He moved the dog back into the kennel area before coming back to get her. Ordering her out of the car, he marched her straight into the bedroom, made her lie down, then tied and cuffed her to the bed.

He walked out of the bedroom, slamming the door and cursing under his breath. A few minutes later she smelled gasoline. Then she saw the orange glow through the bedroom window as he torched the car.

Finally, there came the sickly sweet smell of burning flesh.

38

About an hour after the stench had been carried off on the wind, the bedroom door opened. Carmen had been staring at the ceiling, scared to close her eyes because each time she did she relived what had happened in the car.

She twisted her head round. The man stood in the doorway. No mask.

"You can get a shower in a little while. If you want to," he told her. He sounded sad more than angry.

She knew his dispensing with the mask was bad news. Kidnap victims who had seen their captors were less likely to be released alive. Especially in cases where the kidnappers had gone to great pains to conceal their identity.

"Thank you," she said.

He didn't warn her about trying to escape. He didn't have to. Not after how her first attempt had ended.

39

It was dark by the time Ty and Lock pulled into the parking lot of Casey's Irish pub in Lancaster, forty-five miles north-east of Los Angeles. Lancaster was less than twenty miles from the army base at which the email had been sent. The proximity of the meeting to the base wasn't a coincidence.

Ty sat next to him, his cell phone in his left hand, his right resting on the butt of his gun. They were waiting for a phone call from someone who might be able to tell them more about what they'd discovered.

Those few frames of security-camera footage had finally given them the break they needed to find Carmen. At least, that was Lock's hope. More detailed examination of the images had not only confirmed Ty's hunch about the tattoo, it had narrowed the field from 'These guys look and act like people with military training' to something much more specific. They needed a guide to this uncharted territory. Ty had hit his contact list hard and, after a lot of false hope and dead-ends, had found someone.

They were there to meet with an infantry staff sergeant by the name of Kyle Miller, a multi-tour combat veteran, still serving out what was likely his last few years. His value to them was two-fold.

First, he had inside knowledge of the precise unit they were looking at. Second, and perhaps most crucially, he was prepared to talk, albeit off the record.

Ty's cell buzzed. He tapped the answer icon. "Yeah?"

He listened for a second and gave Lock a nod. It was Miller. "Got it," said Ty, ending the brief call. "He's inside. Back booth. Said we can't miss him."

∼

MILLER WAS CORRECT. He was hard to miss. Even sitting down, he was a mountain of a man. He sat, as promised, staring into his beer, at a booth in the very back of Casey's. The bar was crowded enough that they had to muscle their way through the crowd to get to him.

Lock pushed his way through the crush at the bar as Ty went to sit down with Miller. With a twenty held out in front of him, he managed to wave down one of three bartenders. He ordered three beers.

Someone nudged his elbow. He looked round. A guy with a John Deere ball cap scowled at him. "Hey, buddy, I was next."

Lock made eye contact and held it, not blinking. He wasn't in the mood. His lack of a response seemed to throw the guy. He wasn't following standard-issue bar-fight procedure. He says something, Lock says something, and on it goes until someone throws the first punch.

The bartender placed three mugs of beer on the bar in front of him. Lock handed him the twenty and told him to keep the change. Gathering up the mugs, he shouldered his way back through the throng as Mr. I Was Next shot him daggers.

At the booth, he put the beers on the table and slid in next to Ty, who introduced him to Miller. Miller sank what remained of his beer, and moved on to the fresh one.

"Ty's brought you up to speed?" Lock asked.

Miller nodded. Up close he was even more imposing. His biceps were thicker than some guys' necks. He either spent a lot of time in the gym or he was on the juice. Lock guessed the latter.

"I've been expecting a call like this for a while now," Miller said.

"You know the guys on the tape?" he asked him.

After Ty had spoken to Miller earlier that day, he had sent him some screengrabs of the security-camera footage from the office building.

"I couldn't say for sure which one it was. But it was at least one of them."

"You're sure?" he asked.

Miller took a gulp of his beer, draining almost half of it, and stared down at the mug. "How come the third beer is never quite as good as the first?"

Lock took the question to be rhetorical.

Miller hunched forward a little across the table toward them. "I'm as sure as I can be. I only ever saw that ink on guys from that team. It wouldn't have any meaning to anyone else."

So they were military. Lock decided to leave the obvious questions, such as 'What team?' to one side, and give him the space to tell them the story in his own way. "The floor's yours."

"Okay," he said. "Before I get into the nuts and bolts, the first thing you guys have to understand is that the army I joined back before those fuckheads plowed those planes into us isn't the army we have now."

Ty gave a sage nod of agreement. Declining standards in the military was one of the few topics beyond sports, women and raising hell that he got truly passionate about. It was a recurring theme that stretched back over the generations. The guys who fought now weren't as good as the guys who had gone into Iraq and Afghanistan. And, of course, according to the Vietnam vets, those guys weren't made out of the same stuff as them. In turn the men who had ground it out in Vietnam weren't fit to wipe the asses of those who had served their country in World War Two. And so on and so forth.

But Lock knew from his own experience that Miller was about to make a slightly different point. One that rested more on verifiable facts than a rose-tinted view of how great the good old days had been when everyone next to you in the army was a stand-up guy and an all-American hero.

"Don't get me wrong," said Miller. "I've served with some great individuals, the best of the best."

Lock sensed the "but" just around the corner.

"After we went into Iraq and realized we just didn't have the bodies we needed to do the job, well, let's just say that there were guys allowed to join who would have never got past the recruiting office back in the day."

Lock had a feeling he wasn't talking about their physical shape. That was something the military was good at: taking your average couch potato in their late teens or early twenties and turning them into something approaching a ready-for-action soldier.

"Guys who were banging, or who already had jackets, and then there were guys like the ones I'm talking about who were straight-up Nazis or skinheads."

That translated as active street-gang members, people with criminal records, and the white supremacist crowd, some of whom had found their way into the Big Green because it was better than their current life or offered them a way out. And others who joined up for more nefarious reasons. In the case of white supremacists and their ilk, either because they wanted to legally kill brown people or because they figured that the skills the army could provide would come in handy in civilian life Stateside.

"I'm guessing these guys weren't gangbangers," Lock said, trying to steer Miller back to the men who likely had Carmen.

"How'd you run into them and how many of them are we talking about here?" Ty asked him.

Miller drained the last of his beer. "There was six."

Ty and Lock exchanged a look. *Six?*

They were going to need another round of beers.

40

"As far as I can tell," said Miller, settling back into the booth with a fresh beer "it started with Point and Rance. They hooked up in basic. Point was a Hammerskin and Rance was with some other white power group, but they somehow managed to stay together all the way to deployment. They were the start of it all."

The Hammerskins were the most prominent of numerous white supremacist skinhead groups. They were noted for their love of white power music (driving punk rock with racist lyrics) and their willingness to engage in acts of violence, most often directed against minorities or gay, lesbian and transgender people.

Formed in Dallas, Texas, in the late eighties they had a presence in cities across the country and a number of affiliated international groups in countries as far apart as Germany and Australia. Structured similarly to outlaw motorcycle gangs, such as the Hells Angels and the Mongols, the Hammerskins made members earn membership, often by committing acts of violence.

Membership entitled them to wear a Hammerskins 'patch', a fabric badge sewn onto a jacket or, for more devoted members, the

Hammerskins logo (two hammers crossed to resemble a pair of goose-stepping legs) tattooed onto their body.

"No one did any checks when they joined up?" Lock asked Miller.

A wry smile spread across his face. "Don't ask, don't tell covered a lot more shit than anyone really knows. Recruiters had targets to hit. Hell, Point even had a bunch of ink on his arms. Lightning bolts. Crossed hammers. I found out later that when the recruiter asked him what it was, he told him it was stuff he saw in the ink shop that he thought looked really cool. End of discussion. Recruiter had his target to hit."

"What about later on?" said Ty.

"Did people ask questions? Sure they did. But here's the thing. Point and Rance from an army point of view? They were like gold dust." Miller took another sip of beer. "It wasn't just that they were good soldiers. They were hardcore. You needed to go outside the wire on some suicide mission? Them and their buddies were the go-to guys. They loved action. Loved it. They were like our answer to the Taliban or the insurgents. Didn't care too much whether they came back safe or not as long as they got a chance to go out there and light up some bad guys." He spread his arms. "If you're a commander, what's not to love about that?"

"Tell me about their buddies in the unit," Lock said. "There were six of them, right? I'm assuming they didn't come in as Hammerskins too."

"No, they got drawn in after they were placed in that particular unit. You both served?" Miller asked, looking from Ty to him. They nodded. "So you know how it goes," Miller continued. "You take a small group of guys, most of them still wet behind the ears, and they go along with whoever has the biggest set of balls. Or whoever the alpha male of the group is."

"And who was the alpha?" he asked

"Point, by a mile. Dude had charisma. Even I'd give him that much. And he took care of business for everyone in that unit."

"But he was just a grunt?" Lock prompted.

"At the start. But about three missions in their squad leader took a bullet during a patrol. Point stepped in to fill the vacuum."

"So do you have any idea who our guy is?" Lock said, pulling out a fresh copy of the screengrab of the masked kidnapper with the tattoo.

"Not for definite, but I'd bet good money it's one of them. They all had that tattoo when I ran into them."

"And they're still serving?" Ty asked.

"That I don't know for sure. But it should be easy enough to find out. I can email you all their names."

"We'd appreciate that."

His mug was close to empty again. Lock had one remaining question. He reached into his jacket pocket and pulled out another picture. He placed it on the table in front of him, and shifted it around so Freya Vaden's face was staring up at Miller.

Before he'd even asked, Miller took a look and a fresh smile lit up his face. "The White Queen," he said, jabbing a finger at the photograph. "That's what they called her."

41

They headed out of Lancaster, Miller's last words of caution ringing in their ears. *These are dangerous men. They're well trained, battle-hardened, and they're plenty used to killing.*

As Lock drove, Ty pulled up searches on his phone of the four names that Miller had provided. One was dead, killed in action five years before. Another had been convicted of a racially motivated attempted murder and was doing a dime in Leavenworth. That left them with the two men Miller had told them about.

Before they'd left Miller had told them more about Point and Rance's fascination with Freya Vaden. Since Ty and Lock had caught up with her in San Francisco, Freya a.k.a. Chance, had, unsurprisingly, become an icon of the white power movement. A living martyr. After the first attempt on the life of the president and his family, she had tried to finish the job. Not only that, but her birth father had been a leading member of the Aryan Brotherhood, a prison gang close to white supremacist royalty. On top of all of that, with her blond hair and blue eyes, she was the epitome of what white supremacists saw as the physically ideal woman. To men like Point and Rance, she must have appeared to be like some fairytale princess, sealed off in a high tower by the evil forces of the federal government.

Not only, Miller told them, did they carry a picture of her with them, they had taken their adoration one step further. Several of the men in the unit, Point included, had written to her. And, with plenty of time on her hands, she had written back.

"So, what do you think, Ryan?" Ty asked him, glancing up from his phone. "Handle this ourselves or turn it over?"

In Lock's mind there was only one possible answer. He wasn't going to let anything, his ego or thirst for revenge, get in the way of Carmen's safe return.

"Let the LAPD, the Feds, and the USMP deal. We can keep trucking, but we're going to have to let them know what our moves are so we don't step on their toes."

"Agreed," said Ty.

Under the circumstances, it was the only call. Lock planned to stay on the trail as long as he could, but he and Ty couldn't possibly compete with the resources those three agencies could bring to bear. The only thing they had to worry about was letting this crew know they were on to them. If they realized that, they might not want to leave Carmen alive as a witness. Hence it was important he shared whatever move he made next with the authorities.

Ty's cell buzzed with an incoming call. He flashed the screen in his direction as he glanced over. It was Staff Sergeant Miller. Before they'd left him he'd promised to make some calls on their behalf and see if he could raise some current information on where Point and Rance were, these days.

"Here, I'll put him on speaker." Ty tapped the screen, taking the call.

"Hey, Sarge," said Ty. "Just to let you know, Ryan's with me, and I have you on speaker."

Miller didn't respond.

"Sergeant Miller, are you there?"

The voice that responded didn't belong to Miller, but Lock was sure he'd heard it before.

"Miller's gone. And if you say one word to the cops your lawyer bitch girlfriend will be going the same way."

Before the person at the other end finished, Lock spun the wheel, cutting across a lane of traffic, the rental car thumping over the median as he headed back toward Ventura and Casey's pub. "I didn't plan on speaking to the cops," he lied.

"That's good."

"But if you don't hurry up and tell me what you want and when you plan on releasing Carmen, I won't have any choice."

"Understood, we appreciate your patience," the man said. "But don't worry, it won't be much longer."

42

It didn't take them long to find Miller. As they hit the outskirts of Lancaster, an ambulance and two Ventura County Sheriff's Department patrol cars blew past them, sirens and lights working overtime. Lock tucked the rental car in behind them, and followed.

Their route took them straight back to where they had met Miller: Casey's. Lock parked a block south. They got out and walked back toward what was now an active crime scene.

Patrol cops were busy securing the area. Casey's had been sealed off, its patrons corralled inside for questioning. He could imagine that more than a few of them wouldn't be entirely resistant to the idea of being locked inside a bar.

A small crowd had already gathered on the sidewalk. He scanned the faces for Point or Rance. He didn't recognize anyone. Neither did Ty.

A patrol cop wandered down toward the crowd of looky-loos. "Anybody see anything?"

Even though he'd likely been the last person to speak with Miller, Lock wasn't about to start talking to any cops. Not in public view, and certainly not after the warning he'd just received from Miller's cell phone.

His cell. It was a long shot, but occasionally long shots came in.

He stepped back from the crowd, dug his own cell phone out of his pocket and called Stanner.

Without revealing the detail of the information Miller had given them, he quickly brought him up to speed on the meeting and how they'd just discovered that the man they'd been speaking with had been attacked. He told him that the assailants might still have Miller's phone and Stanner might want to try to locate it. As he finished the call, Ty looped back to find him.

"What's the story?" Lock asked.

Ty shrugged. "Came out of the bar, and took four bullets from a guy in a car. Two in the chest, two in the head. Was probably dead before he hit the deck. Guess they snatched his cell, split, and called to give us the good news."

"Okay. In that case there's no point hanging around here."

They started back toward the car. Lock threw a couple of glances over his shoulder to see if any of the cops, or anyone else for that matter, was watching them. No one was. No one that he could see anyway.

43

"So what now?" Ty asked, vocalizing the question that Lock had been turning over in his mind for the past half-hour.

"I don't know. The Feds and the cops have a better shot at running them down than we do."

"But if they find out we gave the cops the info then Carmen's in even deeper than she is at the moment," Ty said, finishing up for him.

Lock loosened his grip on the wheel a touch. "Maybe we're both asking ourselves the wrong question."

"So what's the right one, Ryan?"

"Why are they doing this?"

"Isn't that kind of obvious now?" said Ty.

"Is it?"

Ty reached down to push the seat all the way back. Like most cars, the rental wasn't constructed for a man of his size. "Miller pretty much told us," said Ty. "These boys have a thing for Chance. We're responsible for chasing her down and making sure she was put behind bars. All she needed to do was drop your name into the conversation and that would be enough."

"So why not just kill me? Going by what they just did to Miller, they could have popped up any time and taken me out. I probably wouldn't even have seen it coming. They would have had the element of surprise going for them."

Ty took a moment to chew that over. "They could have, but maybe killing you wasn't enough. Maybe they wanted to fuck with you first. Then kill you."

He had a point. It didn't entirely answer Lock's question. But it went a long ways toward doing that. Death wasn't always enough. He could see that Chance, rotting away in a maximum-security prison, just like her father before her, would want him to suffer. And the best way of making someone suffer was to target those they loved.

But Ty's theory also had its drawbacks. Lock was suffering, but he was also on guard. The element of surprise was gone. They had to know that hurting Carmen would make the hunters the hunted.

He put that to Ty. His response was a heave of his wide shoulders. "There's five of them, plus who else? And there's one of you, two if they include me. You going to tell me that guys like that don't feel safe with those odds? From what Miller told us, these guys are tough. Real tough. Killed-motherfuckers-in-cold-blood tough."

He was right. People like that weren't going to be intimidated by his reputation. They'd likely see someone like him as a worthy opponent. Someone who offered them a real challenge.

"I still don't get it," he muttered, switching lanes, moving over so that they could transition onto the 405 freeway.

"Because maybe there's nothing to get. These assholes are twisted as all hell. You're trying to apply logic to a bunch of brainwashed dudes who probably never graduated high school. They talk about recreating the master race, but you've seen them. They're the shallow end of the gene pool after the swamp's been drained."

Lock's cell phone sounded an incoming call. The number had been withheld.

"Lock."

"I told you it wouldn't be long."

It was his old friend the anonymous caller. He wondered if it was Point, Rance or one of the others. "What do you want?" He was growing tired of games. He hadn't been bluffing when he'd said that if they didn't tell him what they wanted, or when they planned on releasing Carmen, he would hand the whole thing over to law enforcement.

"To meet."

"Where?"

"You headed back to Los Angeles?"

"Yeah, I just got onto the 405."

"You alone or with the nigger?"

The N-bomb startled him almost as much as Miller's murder. Then he remembered who he was talking to. "Ty's with me." There was no upside to lying. If they'd been watching the meeting with Miller, which was a nailed-on certainty, they would know he was with Tyrone.

"Sorry, I meant to say 'African-American'," the voice cut in.

"I'm sure you did."

"Slip of the tongue."

"So? I take it you didn't just call to say hi."

The voice at the other end of the line chuckled. It was a distinctive laugh with a phlegmy rasp at the end. Almost certainly a smoker's. He noted that small detail in case he needed it later.

"Nope. You ready for the good news, Lock?"

"Go ahead."

"We're at the beginning of the end. We're ready to deal."

Across from him Ty's eyebrows shifted up a fraction. He wasn't about to get excited. Not yet.

"So what do you want from me?" Lock asked.

"I said the beginning of the end, not the end. We'll get to that. First, the ground rules. Any of them are breached and she dies. Understood?"

"Understood."

"Excellent. So, first off, I'm going to send you a set of GPS coordinates. Plug them into whatever system you use, in-car navigation, Google Maps, whatever, and head there now. When you're there, we'll give you the next instructions. You have twenty-five minutes. A second over the time we've given you, and she's gone."

The voice disappeared back into the electronic ether. A second later a text pinged. He handed the cell phone to Ty, who opened the text: *37.0900N-120.1498W*

The rental didn't come with a navigation system. That was an additional option he had declined. He did his best not to use satellite navigation systems while travelling. His reasoning was double-pronged. First, they were essentially surveillance systems that you operated to keep tabs on your own movements, and could be compromised. Second, and more fundamentally, they made you lazy.

He'd always figured that at some point, sooner or later, he'd need to go back to good old-fashioned map and compass. It was no bad thing to keep those old-school skills sharp for when he needed them. However, with a time limit, this wasn't one of those occasions.

He motioned for Ty to pull up Google Maps.

Ty plugged the coordinates into the app. He held the phone up for him to see, a wry grin on his face. "Either they have a sense of humor or we're going to need a ladder and a lot of luck."

Lock took the phone and immediately hoped it was the former. They had to be messing with him. If they weren't, Carmen was as good as dead.

The coordinates were in the middle of the California State Prison for Women at Chowchilla. Most famous occupant since one of Charlie Manson's girls had died a few years back? Freya Vaden a.k.a. Chance a.k.a. (according to Miller) the White Queen.

He checked the time-to-destination that the Google Maps route planner provided. Its estimate, allowing for traffic, was thirty-two minutes.

A minute had almost ticked since the phone call. They had twenty-four minutes and twenty-two seconds remaining.

44

Bito's heavy paws thudding down the corridor roused Carmen from what had been a fractured sleep. She would doze off only for her mind to flash images of her attempted escape into her mind's eye. The splatter of blood on the inside of the windshield. The odor of meat from the dog's mouth. The desperate screams of the woman driver.

One or all of these would snap her awake. Her eyes would open. She would look up to the ceiling, remember the restraints cinched tight around her ankles and wrists as she went to move. Then, the worst part. Her realization that this was a nightmare she'd lived through. A nightmare for which she had been responsible.

If she hadn't tried to escape, that woman would be alive. Her mind was racing, asking questions to which she didn't want to know the answers. Had the dog attacked like that before? Had it killed someone previously? Did it have a taste for human flesh?

She'd heard somewhere that that was what happened with man-eating sharks. They had no natural inclination to attack humans. But if they did, they got a taste for them. After that people were prey. Was it the same with other animals?

In the corridor outside, she heard Bito being called away. A door slammed.

A few seconds later, more steps. A person. She didn't know which sound scared her more.

The door opened. She closed her eyes, pretending to be asleep. Someone came in. She could feel their presence above her.

"Wakey, wakey, Princess!"

A callused hand raked against her cheek. She opened her eyes.

Her captor. No mask. Any pretense of concealing his identity dispensed with.

"We're moving," he told her. "Oh, and if you try to run again, if I even think you're going to run, it's chow time for the hound. Nod if you understand."

Trembling, Carmen moved her head as she'd been asked to.

45

Lock leaned on the horn as they inched up to the bumper of a slow-moving station wagon that had decided to camp out in the fast lane. Finally, it scooted over, and he could hit the gas. In the passenger seat, Ty was hunched over the cell phone, checking for any live updates about traffic delays that might require them to reroute.

"It's going to be close, but we're good," Ty assured him.

He scanned the road ahead. Highways like this one, long and straight, were beloved of Highway Patrol cops looking to raise some revenue. The last thing they needed was to be pulled over. Even if he refused to do so, a pursuit would likely prove equally catastrophic – especially given their current destination.

"So what do you think the game is?" he asked Ty, as he tried to push every ounce of speed out of the rental while bitterly regretting not pressing the cops to release his Audi. Unlike the rental, it was engineered for the German *Autobahn* and, as such, was perfectly suited to devouring highway miles.

"The hell if I know. They can't expect us to roll on up there and ask the warden if he would mind releasing his number-one prisoner into our custody so she can have a white power reunion with her fan club."

He wasn't so sure. While the men who had taken Carmen had skills to match their readiness to deploy extreme levels of violence, they also seemed chaotic. What had gone down at the office when all this had begun had told him that much. They could have retreated and circled back round for Carmen. Instead they had chosen a much higher-risk strategy that had exposed them to greater risk of death or capture. As a group they were a weird mix of tactical and reckless.

Maybe it all connected back to what Miller had told them. Command had turned a blind eye to their affiliations because of their willingness, maybe even eagerness, to take on missions that verged on the suicidal. You went on enough high-risk missions and survived, it was easy to succumb to your ego, to believe that you were somehow different. That you were impervious to failure.

But if that was the case, and they wanted them to go spring Chance from jail, did they think he was in the same category? Or was their presence at the Chowchilla intended as either a distraction or just a plain suicide mission, with Ty and Lock as the guys going over the top?

They could second-guess all they wanted. But the answer lay five miles up ahead.

"Okay, next exit. Two miles," Ty informed him.

The rental was already flat out. He had his foot so hard to the floor that he was worried about the pedal snagging on the carpet and getting stuck. "Time?" he asked.

"Enough. Just keep rolling."

"That wasn't what I asked you, Ty."

"Seven minutes," he said, after a moment's hesitation.

"Damn." He slammed a palm into the top of the steering wheel. They were five miles away, but in two of those they'd be leaving the highway and hitting surface streets where the pace would be slower.

"Look, Ryan, we do what we can. For all we know Carmen's already—"

He pulled himself up without finishing. Lock could guess how the sentence ended. His jaw tightened. He flashed on Carmen's face, then Carrie's. That was what made this different. The echo of old grief.

Was that why they'd done what they had? Because they knew it would push him into a world of torment that went way beyond simply putting a bullet in his back?

If he was Freya Vaden and wanted revenge, what better way was there?

Shaking his head, he tried to refocus. This wasn't a time to get lost in those thoughts. Dead or alive, he'd have plenty of time to muse about revenge and its motivations later on. Right now he had to assume Carmen was still breathing until they knew different.

He looked at Ty as they bore down on the exit ramp. "Let's just go with what you said before."

Ty seemed puzzled. "What was that?"

"Keep rolling."

46

They pulled into the main public parking lot outside the prison with a minute to spare. They were still some distance from the precise coordinates they'd been given. Those lay on the other side of the razor-wire-topped outer and inner electrified perimeter fences, which were also peppered with guard towers.

With no opportunity to prepare, even if Ty and he had been willing to fight their way inside to get to Freya, a minute wouldn't have been close to enough time. He switched off the engine and exchanged a "Now what?" look with Ty.

On cue, the cell phone lit up with an incoming call. Ty was still holding it and passed it to him.

"We're here," he said.

"Where?"

"Outside in the jail's parking lot. The coordinates you sent are on the other side of the wire."

He braced himself for the reaction. When it came, it wasn't what he had expected.

"Yeah, that was his little joke," said the voice.

"What now?"

"Locate the main entrance and exit points. He'll text you the next destination in ten minutes. There's a gate about a half-mile down on the south-west corner. Right next to the SHU. You might want to pay special attention to that one."

"Wait, why do you want us to—?"

The call terminated before he could finish. The cogs in his brain were busy turning. Things were dropping into place. There was only reason they'd be looking at entrance and exit points.

"You thinking what I'm thinking?" he asked Ty.

"Yep."

"What do you reckon?"

"We should go check out that gate."

LOCK COULD HAVE GUESSED the next location before the coordinates finally pinged up on his phone. He waited for Ty to tap them into Google Maps and confirm his suspicions. He held up the screen for him to take a look.

This was one time that being right gave him no real comfort. He threw the rental car back into gear, and they peeled away from the prison, heading back toward the freeway.

47

They drove south-west on CA-99 until they hit the city of Madera, although the word "city" was a rather grand designation for a place with seventy thousand inhabitants. The coordinates took them directly to the newly built Madera Courthouse. They parked three blocks away and got out. He tugged a ball cap down low over his eyes and Ty pulled up the hood of his sweatshirt as they walked back to the building, which fronted onto a carefully landscaped open plaza.

Skirting the plaza, they began looking for the entrance to the holding area. It didn't take long to find it on the north-eastern side. A ramp led down into an underground parking area. From there a bank of elevators would take people back up into the court building. There was also a stairwell.

"They won't bring her down here," he said, as they started back up the ramp for the street.

"How come?"

"Look at the clearance. Way too low for anything much taller than a standard size SUV."

"I wouldn't be so sure," Ty said. "She's a special case. They won't be shipping her in on a bus with a bunch of other inmates."

He had a point.

~

THEY COMPLETED their tour of the courthouse exterior and made their way back to the car. There was no way to access the inside at this time of night, and it wasn't worth making an attempt. If they were going to be called upon to do what he thought they were, static interior locations were not the way to go, given the likely security presence around Freya Vaden.

There were a number of good reasons why inmate escapes that relied upon outside assistance most commonly took place while the object of the escape attempt was in transit. Static locations such as prisons and courts had layers of security in place. You had to get in and then get out – with the inmate. That took time, and time, the ticking clock, was your greatest enemy.

The passage of time allowed a counter-reaction, and for existing procedures to be put in place: roadblocks; search parties; alerts to law enforcement and the general public. Even if you did manage the escape, by the time you hit the road, you would already have triggered a pursuit. Helicopters were a prized form of transport for that very reason, but every prison had wires in place to stop them landing on their yards.

Inmate-mounted escapes were different. Properly designed, they could build in a period between the escape and its discovery that offered a window for flight.

The nature of an escape impacted heavily on the next component: evasion, or getting far enough away to avoid recapture, was the real determining factor. Getting away from custody was the part people focused on, the part that often required cunning, guile and imagination. But it was only the first half of the story. Ultimately what counted wasn't getting free. It was *staying* free.

With all that pinballing around his head, Lock and Ty sat in the rental car and waited for the next call. Five minutes went by. Then ten. Then a half-hour.

Was the silence planned? Another device designed to throw them off balance after the frantic pace of the last few hours? Or was there a problem at their end?

Here lay the inherent power of a kidnapper. The control of information and contact. They could call him, but he had no way of reaching them. Communication was a one-way street.

"You think he's gonna call back or was that it for tonight?" Ty said.

"Either way, let's start making tracks back to LA."

Ty didn't respond. Something was clearly weighing on his mind.

"Problem?" Lock asked him.

He grimaced. There was, but he didn't want to say it for whatever reason.

"Ty, my mind-reading skills aren't what they used to be. What is it?"

He was waiting for something insightful or profound. Maybe Ty had spotted a crucial weak link in the court security or come up with a way they could work round what they both guessed the kidnappers had in mind.

"Ty?" he prompted.

"Dude, I really need to eat something. Can we stop off someplace on the way back?"

48

A half-hour later, with Ty's stomach rumbling so loudly that Lock was afraid he wouldn't hear the next call from the kidnappers, they pulled in at the Black Bear Diner near Tulare. He wasn't sure, when it came to Ty, that the diner would live up to its promise to "Come hungry, and leave satisfied." Ty definitely had the hungry part covered, but it would take a lot of food for his partner to leave even close to satisfied. But the place was clean, the staff friendly, and the menu no-nonsense.

"I'm going to hit the head," he told Ty. "Order me some coffee and . . ." he did a quick scan of the menu ". . . the turkey plate."

Ty's head was already buried in the menu. "You got it."

He made for the restroom, as Ty flagged down a waitress and began to reel off items from the menu. Before Lock hit the door, he heard the waitress ask, confused, if other people would be joining them.

"Can't a man be hungry?" responded Ty.

In the restroom, Lock pushed open the door of the nearest stall, closed it behind him and threw up. His stomach lurched a few more times and then he was done. He flushed, walked out and cleaned himself up. Behind him a stall door opened and an elderly man walked out. He stood beside Lock as he washed his hands. His eyes kept darting in Lock's direction. He was building up to saying something. "Rough day?" he asked eventually.

Lock walked past him to the hand-dryer. "Something like that." As he hit the door on the way back out, his cell phone rang. He walked to the end of the corridor to get some privacy before he answered. "Lock."

"What did you think?"

It was the kidnapper.

"About?"

"The courthouse. More workable than the prison, right?"

"Neither," he told him.

He chuckled. "Good answer. I knew you'd be the right man for the job."

"Anything else?"

"You have coordinates coming in. When you receive them you'll have twenty minutes to get there. Previous rules apply so don't be late."

"I'd like to speak with Carmen."

Silence.

He heard the man's phone being set down. A few moments later a woman said, "Ryan?"

His throat tightened at the sound of her voice. Part of him now regretted asking to speak to her. He wanted to know she was alive, but hearing her voice made it all very real. It summoned emotions he couldn't afford. Not if he was to do what was needed to make sure she kept breathing. Right now he needed to be calm, and detached.

"Carmen, listen, everything's going to be okay. Just do what they ask, and I'm going to take care of the rest."

"I will."

"How are you holding up? Have you been hurt?"

The kidnapper came back on the line. "She's fine. Don't be late to the next location. Do everything we ask, don't talk to anyone else, and she'll stay that way. Break any of those rules and she's dead."

He clicked off. A second later an incoming text pinged on the screen with a fresh set of coordinates. He walked back into the dining area and headed over to Ty. Their coffee was on the table, but the food had still to arrive.

"We gotta go."

Ty looked at him like a kid who'd just been told that Santa would bring them coal and switches instead of a new bicycle. "Now?"

"Now."

Ty got to his feet as he laid down enough bills on the table to cover the food they'd ordered but wouldn't get to eat. He shook his head as he stared balefully in the direction of the kitchen. "Man, when we finally get to these motherfuckers, I'm really going to lay down some pain."

He followed Lock toward the door and out into the cold of the parking lot.

49

Eighteen minutes later, they rolled up a dirt track not too far from the freeway. On one side was a stand of trees, on the other a barren stretch of open ground. Up ahead was a single-story house. To one side, a chain-link dog run ended in a concrete kennel. On the other side of the house he could just about make out the rear end of a burned-out car.

Slowing to a crawl, Lock parked next to the kennel. That way anyone who was watching them from inside the house wouldn't have a clear line of fire toward the car.

This run-down ranch house in the middle of nowhere posed a different question than either the prison or the courthouse. Why the hell were they here?

His cell phone rang. The by now familiar voice at the other end of the line started speaking before he had the chance to say anything.

"The front door is unlocked. Go inside. Alone."

The call terminated. Lock relayed to Ty what he'd just been instructed to do.

"I don't like it. Why they want you to go in there alone?"

He didn't know. But there was only way to find out. "If they wanted me dead I'm sure they could have killed me by now."

"I don't know, Ryan." He stared at the house. "This place creeps me out. Let me come in with you."

He didn't disagree with him. It had a serial-killer vibe.

"It'll be fine," he said. "And if it's not . . ." He grabbed his Maglite from the glove compartment, handed Ty the car keys and got out.

Rather than walk to the front of the house, he skirted round to the back of the property, passing the empty dog run. He'd been asked to go inside, but no one had said anything about using the front door.

Behind him, Ty had already gotten out of the car and taken up position, his gun drawn, ensuring that the car remained between him and the front of the house. If he had to come out in a hurry, Ty could provide cover as well as alert him to anyone else trundling down the dirt track toward them.

Pushing on, he made it to the rear of the house. Like the front, the blinds had been drawn to cover every window. No lights were on. A few feet away he saw a 48-gallon wheeled plastic trash can. He lifted the lid, and shone the Maglite inside.

His cell-phone screen lit up. He took the call.

"Stop fucking around and go inside, like I asked you to."

He shifted the beam of the torch from the trash can to the rear of the house. A camera was mounted above the back door.

"Okay, enough of the cloak-and-dagger bullshit, what's inside?"

"You're starting to try my patience."

"The feeling's mutual. What's inside?"

"You'll know it when you see it."

Switching the Maglite to his left hand, he kept the beam trained on the camera. He pulled his SIG from its holster and fired a single shot at the camera. It shattered into tiny pieces.

"I'm done playing games," he said.

There was silence for a few seconds. "There's a folder on the kitchen table. Everything you'll need is inside."

"Thank you." He terminated the call.

A few seconds later Ty appeared from the other side of the house. "You okay?"

"Fine. Just trimming back some of their remote surveillance," he explained, flashing the torch beam back across the distended wires of what had been the security camera.

"You checked out the car?" Ty asked him.

He shook his head. "Not yet."

"There's a body in back. Looks like a woman, but who knows? It's pretty badly torched."

His stomach lurched again before he remembered that he'd only just spoken to Carmen, so whoever was in the car, it couldn't be her. He walked up to the back door, ran the beam of the Maglite around the frame, checking if it was booby-trapped. With Ty a step behind him, he pushed the door with the toe of his boot.

It swung open. He walked in, through a utility room with an old washing machine, and into the kitchen. There on the table, as promised, was a folder. He picked it up, and quickly flipped through the contents before handing it to Ty.

Ty thumbed through the pages from front to back. His face didn't betray much of anything, apart from some lingering resentment at having been torn away from a meal. He passed the folder back to Lock.

"So? What do you think?" Lock asked.

Ty took a deep breath and exhaled loudly as his partner flicked through the pages. "It's gonna be tough, but it's achievable. What's your take?"

"They could have given us some more time to plan but, yeah, it's doable."

～

Two minutes later, they were back in the car, the folder on Ty's lap as they bumped back down the rutted track. Lock looked over to his partner. "And what do you really think?"

For safety's sake, they had both assumed that the discussion they'd just had in the kitchen was being relayed back to the kidnappers.

This time Ty didn't hesitate before giving his answer. "I think we're royally screwed."

50

When it comes to revenge, most people lack one key quality: imagination. Have someone cut you off while driving, and you might, if you're having a really bad day, fantasize about running them off the road, or pulling them out of their car to punch them in the face. Usually revenge fantasies are fairly basic. They extend no further than causing discomfort, inconvenience, pain or suffering to the object of their wrath. What Freya Vaden and her fan club of white supremacists had cooked up was altogether more sophisticated.

In twenty-four hours she was to be transported from the Central California Women's Prison in Chowchilla to the Merced Courthouse to attend a preliminary hearing for the murder of Ginny Browell. In return for Carmen's safe release they wanted him to facilitate Vaden's escape from custody.

Kidnapping Carmen was more than revenge. It was revenge with a greater purpose: revenge that gave them leverage over Lock. Who better to aid Vaden's escape from custody than someone highly skilled in close-protection security? Better yet, by having him do it, he would be committing a series of criminal acts. The fact that the woman he loved was being held by these maniacs would cut little ice if he ended up shooting a US marshal in the line of duty.

If he was lucky, he could free the woman without blood being spilled. But that was unlikely. There was no way a team of US marshals charged with escorting Freya Vaden from Chowchilla to court were going to stand idly by while he took her. They would respond with lethal force. To achieve the mission, he would almost certainly have to respond in kind.

The absolute best outcome he could hope for, if he wanted to save Carmen's life their way, involved committing a laundry list of crimes that would see him behind bars for life, or spending it on the run, condemned to an ever-present fear of a knock on the door.

Unless . . .

51

Detective Stanner threw the folder onto the conference table. Outside, dawn was breaking over downtown Los Angeles as the city's commercial center slowly ground back to life. Ty sat next to Lock at the opposite end of the conference table from the assembly of law-enforcement officers. They waited for Stanner's response to what Lock had just told them, which was close to everything.

"You're a very lucky man, Mr. Lock," Stanner said finally.

There were many words that could have been applied to his situation. He wasn't sure "lucky" was one of them. Right now, he certainly didn't feel lucky.

He leaned back in his chair, trying to find some relief from the knots of pain that had formed in his shoulders and lower back. "How do you figure that, Detective?"

The woman sitting to Stanner's left, Special Agent Mirales from the Los Angeles Office of the Federal Bureau of Investigation, stepped in to answer the question for him. Mirales was only about five feet three inches tall, but she came with a fearsome reputation and a string of high-profile convictions that ran all the way from human trafficking to white-collar fraud.

Stan Petrovsky, from the US Marshals Service for the Central District of California, was next to her. He was in charge of prison services for the marshals. It would be his guys and gals who were charged with escorting Freya Vaden to court and back to Chowchilla. Usually the marshals' prisoner transport service extended only to inmates in the federal system, but the CDCR (California Department of Corrections and Rehabilitation) had balked at such a high-risk prisoner movement. The Feds, no doubt still bristling from Vaden not being their prisoner had graciously offered to step in.

"We've been following you. The prison. The courthouse. We've had eyes on you and Mr. Johnson the whole time," Mirales said.

His face must have betrayed his surprise. He usually knew when he was being watched. It was something he looked out for, even when he wasn't actively worried. Spotting a recurring vehicle or a face that popped up a little often for it to be mere coincidence was second nature to him.

"Drones," Mirales continued, by way of explanation. "They're way more effective than boots on the ground, and the government doesn't have to pay them overtime."

He felt himself bristle. He tried to dampen it down, but it was a struggle. "I'm flattered, all this technology to follow me around, but you haven't found Carmen."

"It hasn't been for lack of trying," said Mirales, doing her best to sound placatory.

Stanner sounded way less apologetic. "Count yourself lucky that you jumped the way you have. If you'd tried to go through with this without letting us know you'd be looking at a world of pain. We saw you outside the prison, and at the courthouse. It didn't exactly take a genius to figure out what was going down."

Lock stared at Stanner. "That's just as well."

He shrugged off the jibe with a smirk. "Smart guy."

Ty's hand thundered down on the conference table. The vibrations went all the way to the floor. The retired US marine levered himself up from his chair and stalked toward the other end of the table. Stanner visibly sank back in his padded conference chair.

"The only question that need concern us right now is how we're going to handle business in a way that no one gets hurt." Ty stood directly over Stanner. "And no one *includes* Carmen, motherfucker. You feel me, Detective?"

Cops aren't easy to intimidate. That goes double for homicide detectives, like Stanner. But they don't usually have a six-feet-five, 240-pound marine, who grew up in Long Beach, standing over them, glowering, with his hands bunched into fists. Stanner's face paled.

Mirales stepped in to play peacemaker. "I think we're all agreed on that."

Ty wasn't going to be easily defused. He kept glowering down at Stanner. "Are we?"

Stanner cleared his throat. Probably nerves. "Yes. Carmen's safety is a priority."

"Perhaps there's a way we can have our cake and eat it too," Lock said.

"Meaning?" Stanner asked.

"Freya Vaden stands trial for the Browell murder, and we ensure Carmen's release." He took a moment, then revealed what he hoped would be the clincher. "And we round up these guys before they do any more damage. I mean, how many bodies are they responsible for now, that we know of?"

There had been the rookie cop in the parking structure, the building security guard, Sergeant Miller, and the lady whose body had been found in the burned-out car. She had turned out to be a mother with four children, all of whose lives had been irrevocably altered by those assholes. There would be more deaths to come if they weren't stopped. He was in no doubt about that. The longer this had gone on, the less they'd had to lose, and the more reckless they had become.

Vaden's fan club gave the distinct impression that they were all out of fucks. Right now it was the one thing he had in common with them.

"So, what are you suggesting, Mr. Lock?" That question came from US Marshal Petrovsky.

Lock took a deep breath. What he was about to suggest would be a hard sell. Law-enforcement organizations were all about control, and he was about to ask them to surrender what control they had to him.

"Allow me to do what they've asked. I free Freya Vaden from custody."

The reaction from the other end of the table was a mixture of disbelief and bewilderment. Stanner laughed. Mirales and Petrovsky were satisfied with merely looking horrified.

"You said you've been using drones to have eyes on him. You can use that same technology to follow Vaden straight to these guys. Carmen's released and you can go in and scoop them up."

"Just like that?" Stanner smirked.

"No, not just like that. We'll have to sell the ambush and her rescue properly. Make it look convincing. That'll be the key to this."

"Do you really think they're going to release Carmen?" The question came from Mirales.

"I don't know. But I do know that if I don't play along they'll likely kill her. Carmen's a means to an end for them. It's me they want to drag into the middle of all this."

Petrovsky put down the pen he'd been doodling with. "So, assuming I were to agree to this, how would you play it? I mean, I don't doubt your abilities. You're highly trained, but so are my guys. They're not about to let go a high-value inmate like Freya Vaden just because you and Johnson here roll up on them."

Lock wasn't about to argue. He already knew that this was going to be the most difficult part of what he had in mind. They had to make the escape look convincing without anyone actually getting hurt. Even if the kidnappers weren't able to watch it go down, Vaden would be right there. If she smelled a rat, the exchange of her for Carmen could go south rapidly.

The exchange itself was another area fraught with difficulties. But for now he still needed to sell his plan to the three law-enforcement officials.

"I agree," he told Petrovsky. "And if this is going to work we have to make sure it looks like the real deal. It's not going to be easy, but it's doable."

Stanner waved a hand in his direction. "Okay. So, for the sake of argument, how are you going to do this?"

"Here's what I have in mind." He got up, walked across to the whiteboard on the opposite wall and picked up an erasable marker pen. "But before I get into the details, there's something else we all need to start thinking about."

"What's that?" asked Mirales.

He took a breath. "Why now?"

"What do you mean?" said Stanner.

"Well, she could have attempted an escape before. She has friends on the outside. Go on any white supremacist forum or messageboard on the internet. She's a rock star. So why try to get out now?"

Petrovsky leaned back in his chair. "Why *not* now? The motive's been there since day one. Why would anyone choose to spend their life in prison if they had a chance to escape? Maybe it's just taken this long for her to see an opportunity. Browell was the opportunity."

Lock's eyes narrowed. He wasn't buying it. "There's something else going on here. She needs to be out for some reason."

That drew a smirk from Stanner. "What? Like killing the president?"

Lock let the sarcasm wash over him. Glancing toward the window, he gave a slight shake of his head. "There's something else."

52

In her single-inmate cell in the secure housing unit at Chowchilla, Freya Vaden woke a little after three in the morning. She lay there in the darkness, unable to get back to sleep. She felt as excited as a little kid on Christmas morning. Or how she had always imagined that must feel. Her own Christmases, like the rest of her childhood, had been bleak, filled with abuse of every description.

But she had decided not to let it define who she was, or what she could become. That was why she had created Chance – a kick-ass, white race warrior, who would lead her people to salvation. So if Freya was excited to the point of feeling sick, Chance was cold inside: focused; calm; ready for war.

And the best part of all of this? Her rescuer was the man responsible for putting her here in the first place. The man who had denied Chance her destiny those years ago in San Francisco when he'd foiled not one but two attempts to kill the president.

What could be more perfect, more poetic, than being freed by Ryan Lock? Not that she expected him to go along with their proposal. He would try to double-cross her, she was sure. But she wasn't worried about that. Lock's betrayal was already built into their plan.

Someone tapped three times on the pipe that ran the length of the six cells in this part of the unit. It was Clarissa. She'd also been moved to the isolation cells after they'd killed Browell. Not that she'd been charged with anything for her part. And not that Chance cared too much either way. What were they going to do? Sentence her to another life-without-possibility-of-parole? Bring it on.

Chance hunkered down next to the air vent.

"You there, Chance?" whispered Clarissa.

Damn, thought Chance. Clarissa was as dumb as a bunch of rocks. Where else would she be? On a beach with George Clooney? "What's up, Clarissa?"

"Just wanted to wish you good luck for today."

Chance smiled. "Thanks."

"Catch up this evening, right?"

"Sure," said Chance, still smiling.

A HALF-HOUR later the cell-door slot slid open. A male guard's voice said, "Something for your purse, baby."

"Thanks, sweetie," said Chance, reaching for the foldable knife.

The slot slid shut. Chance weighed the knife in the open palm of her right hand. She popped it open to check the sharpness of the blade. The edge was razor keen. She folded it closed, slipped it inside its plastic sheath, pulled down her panties, squatted and slowly inched it up inside her body.

Now she was ready for the next stage of her journey to begin.

53

A green and silver California Department of Corrections and Rehabilitation truck stood outside the warehouse, which was located in the middle of a small semi-derelict industrial complex on the north-eastern outskirts of Fresno. Inside, members of a hand-picked prisoner-transport team made up of US marshals and CDCR correctional officers drank from Styrofoam coffee cups, and checked their equipment for the final time, impatient to get moving.

Lock and Ty had already been on site for twelve hours, running through how this would go down. Every single person on the transport team had been walked through the precise sequence of events. Around three a.m., they had taken an hour-long nap break in the truck. Both Ty and he were past masters at snatching sleep where they could.

Originally they had thought about staging the escape on the second day of Chance being in court. In a real-world extraction that was the time frame Lock would have selected. It would have given the escort team time to relax. Their levels of vigilance would be less than optimal.

Waiting for the second day had been ruled out for two reasons.

First, a legal issue might arise that could blow them off course. Second, they didn't want the kidnappers getting any antsier than they already were. So, day one, they had decided, was moving day.

The challenge now was to stage an escape that looked credible, without anyone getting hurt or killed. With the second part in mind, and after a protracted negotiation, the transport team had agreed to give up their live ammunition. The two who would be carrying firearms would use blanks. In return, Ty and Lock had agreed they would do the same. That way they could stage an escape that looked credible without the risk of anyone taking a bullet. In case things went south, the two armed marshals had live rounds secreted on the truck. Both Ty and he had several clips with live rounds attached to their front webbing. But anything already loaded in a weapon was a blank.

Lock checked his watch. It was almost time for the transport convoy to leave for Chowchilla. Ty and he would wait here until they left to take up their position along the route.

He jogged over to FBI Special Agent Mirales, who had volunteered to play the role of Chance during their practice run. She was climbing out of her CDCR jumpsuit as she chatted to Stan Petrovsky. It was an indication of the seriousness of the operation that they had both chosen to be there. They would be riding together in the rear escort vehicle, their presence in the convoy hidden by dark-tinted privacy glass.

He reached out to shake her hand, then Petrovsky's. "I just wanted to thank you both. This wasn't an easy approach to agree to."

"I don't know, it's been kind of fun playing the bad gal for once." Mirales smiled.

Petrovsky was a lot less light-hearted. "Just make sure you don't fuck up on your end."

"I won't."

"You'd better not, because if Vaden goes missing while she's with you there's going to be the shit storm to end all shit storms, and I plan on retiring with a clean record on a full pension."

The second part of the plan involved swapping Carmen for

Chance. At that point a second, larger, team of law-enforcement officers would swoop in to scoop up Chance and return her to custody.
They also hoped to grab a kidnapper or two. Despite having names
from Sergeant Miller, the two men most likely involved had, unsurprisingly, gone to ground. They had the evidence on them, they just
didn't have the bodies.

The FBI had provided them with a vehicle. It was a barely used
double-cab Ford pickup that had been confiscated in a drugs bust
and fitted with a tracking device. A drone was also being deployed in
case the tracker failed or they lost the signal.

"I want Chance back in prison just as much as anyone else here,"
Lock reminded Petrovsky.

"You'd better, because it's your ass if this goes south."

One of the transport team marshals signaled that they were about
to move.

"Good luck," said Mirales.

Lock gave a curt nod. He was hoping that luck, good or bad,
wasn't going to be a factor.

54

Handcuffed, and manacled, with a belly chain linking the other two, Chance glanced down at the baggy orange jumpsuit. "This is bullcrap," she said, coming to a sudden halt.

The female US marshal flanking her right-hand side gave her a sideways glance. "Problem?"

"Making me wear this," she said. "It makes me look guilty. I should be allowed to wear my own clothes to court. Or at least give me a belt or something so half my ass isn't showing."

The female marshal prodded Chance with the end of her baton. "Keep moving."

Chance's eyes narrowed. "Or what?"

"Or we'll pick you up and toss you on this truck."

"I'd like to see you try," said Chance, as she began walking.

They had reached the sallyport. The guard Chance had hoped to see was waiting for them. She had worried his shift would be switched at the last second, or that he'd be reassigned to another unit. He had been her lifeline this past year, bringing her whatever she wanted and taking messages out. And all it had cost her were a few stolen sticky moments alone with him. A small price to pay for her freedom, she figured.

"Okay, let's do this," the guard said, walking toward the transport team.

Stepping back, he opened a door that led into a side room where a female correctional officer was waiting to search Chance for a final time before she was walked out. The officer had already been paid to make sure that any search was negative, regardless of what her torch beam illuminated when Chance bent over.

Chance walked toward the open door, shooting the woman a death-stare look as she went. They fell in step.

"Where's she going?" Chance asked the male guard.

"Peace of mind," said the woman. "I'm going to be sitting next to you in the van, remember."

Chance stopped suddenly in the doorway. Behind her, the transport team piled into each other.

Turning back, Chance stared at the female guard. "You sure that's it? You got a dykey vibe about you, girl. I think maybe you just want an excuse to sneak a peek at my coochy."

One of the other guards stifled a snicker.

The male guard, Chance's lover, puffed out his chest. "I hope you're not suggesting that any of my staff aren't up to performing a basic body cavity search."

A male marshal put up his hand toward his female colleague. "We'll let them do their job here, and we'll do ours."

The woman let it go with the briefest nod. Her face was still flushed from Chance's comments a few seconds before. "Fine," she said, conceding the point.

~

CHANCE STEPPED INTO THE ROOM. The door closed on her and the female guard, who wouldn't meet her eye. That wasn't uncommon here. It was an open secret among the officers that anyone messing with Chance would face consequences on the outside. And if Chance's friends in the white supremacist movement couldn't get to the guard, they would get to their family. No one wanted to deal with that.

The message that Chance sent out was simple. Make her life hard on the inside and her brothers and sisters would make your life hell on the outside.

"Okay, Vaden," the female guard barked, loud enough that everyone outside would hear. "Assume the position."

Chance rested her head against the wall, her legs splayed out at an angle, as the guard unclipped her torch from her belt.

A few seconds later, she announced, "Clear!"

Chance was led back to the door and handed back to the transport team. They fell in around her and walked her though the sallyport, down a corridor and out into the yard. The van was waiting, a rumble of smoke spurting from the tail pipe. They led her onto it and sat her in an aisle seat about halfway back.

One of the guards took the wheel, and the vehicle pulled through two sets of gates and out into the world beyond.

55

Ty tugged a ball cap low to shield his eyes from the sun. He sank down in the truck's passenger seat as a California Highway Patrol motorcycle cop sped past. The last thing anyone needed was a cop, who had no idea what was going down, being taken with a bout of curiosity and stopping to ask questions.

In the driver's seat of the Ford Super Duty F-450 truck, Lock tapped out a beat on the top of the steering wheel and looked down at his cell phone, checking the time.

Any moment now the van carrying Chance, with the two escort vehicles accompanying it, would be rolling down this stretch of highway toward them.

His cell vibrated, signaling an incoming call. He tapped the screen. "Yeah?"

It was the voice he'd come to recognize and loathe, the voice of the kidnapper. "You boys all ready for the big show?"

Lock took a long, slow breath. He'd been expecting this call. He knew the kidnappers would get antsy as soon as something they wanted was on the line. But he needed to remind them that this was a two-way street. He got them Chance, but they had to be able to deliver Carmen to him.

"We're in place, but I have to speak with Carmen first or the deal's off," he told them.

"And if she ain't here or I don't agree?"

"Then I make a call, the authorities turn back to Chowchilla and your heroine Freya Vaden rots away the rest of her miserable life in prison. Plus they come looking for you, real hard."

"You do any of that shit and your lady dies." He sounded pissy. Lock figured that was good. It showed he recognized that he needed Lock as much as Lock needed him.

Ty shot Lock an anxious glance from the passenger seat. Not that his anxiety prevented him reaching into a brown-paper bag on the dash and pulling out a protein bar, which he started to wolf down.

Lock took another breath. "Which means neither of us gets what we want. You want me to free Chance, then I need to know you've held up your end of the bargain and that Carmen's alive. If I can't speak with her now, I have to assume you've already welshed on your part of the deal."

"Okay, I'll put her on."

Lock felt a rush of relief spread through him as he heard Carmen say, "Ryan?"

"Hey, this is going to all be over soon. You okay?"

"Yes." She sounded close to tears. It was understandable. Lock could feel a lump forming in his throat. One thing was for sure, even if he got Carmen back safely, this wasn't going to be over. Not by a long way. He was coming after these assholes for what they'd put her through. They could get a shuttle to the moon and they still wouldn't be safe from his wrath.

Ty shoved the last of the protein bar into his mouth, and nudged Lock with his elbow. Lock looked up to see the lead vehicle of the prison convoy appear at the brow of the hill.

"Listen, Carmen, I have to go, but you hang in there. I'm going to be with you real soon and this'll be over. You hear me?"

Before she could answer, there was a rustling sound as the phone was taken from her. The call died.

Lock put the phone into his pocket, and started the engine as the prison van with Chance on board picked up speed down the hill toward them. Ty grabbed his duffel bag, opened the passenger door of the F-450 and jumped out.

"Ty, hang on."

Lock reached down and grabbed a spare set of ear protectors from the side compartment. He tossed them to his partner, who caught them one-handed and slipped them around his neck. He gave Lock a thumbs-up, slammed the passenger door, and moved fast toward a dried-out culvert that ran alongside the road. Two seconds later he had disappeared from view.

Spinning the steering wheel, Lock began to edge out onto the road, the nose of the truck pointing at an angle up the hill. He reached down to his webbing, making sure that he had his Gerber tactical knife to hand. Very soon, if the plan went as intended, he would need it.

~

CHANCE SAT on the bench seat, sandwiched between two US marshals clad in black tactical gear, and rolled her neck. "Suspension on this thing's shit. I'm going to need a massage when I get out of here."

She cast a suggestive glance toward the marshal who was sitting to her left.

"Full body," she added, just in case he had missed her meaning.

He turned toward her a fraction. "Shut up."

Chance's smile never broke. "The dominant type. I like it." She smirked, then switched her attention to the woman on her other side. "What about you, Princess? You want to break out the hot oil and have us some alone time? Prison's really opened up my sexual spectrum, if you know what I mean."

~

NEXT TO CHANCE, FBI Special Agent Mirales bit her tongue. It was best not to get drawn into any conversation with Freya Vaden. From reading her jacket, she knew that Vaden was a master manipulator of people. That, coupled with her unflinching ideological beliefs, was what made her so dangerous. At the same time, Mirales wasn't entirely lacking in empathy for what Freya Vaden the child had gone through to turn her into the monster beside her.

After Freya's father, a leading member of the Aryan Brotherhood, had gone to prison, her mother had passed. Freya had ended up in the care of the State of California and was sent to live with a foster family where she was subjected to years of physical, emotional and sexual abuse. Several members of the family had been involved in the sexual abuse, and by the time anyone was alerted to what was going on, Freya was already an adult and the damage was done.

Mirales shifted on the hard bench seat. Her body was already drenched in sweat from the heavy-duty US marshal's tactical gear she had borrowed for the journey. Marshal Petrovsky had been less than happy about her being part of the security detail inside the van but she had been insistent. It was important that Chance's initial escape went smoothly, if Carmen's life was to be preserved.

"What do you say, Princess?" Chance prompted.

Mirales put on her game day face. "Think I'll pass."

Chance smiled and sank back into the seat, rattling the chain of her ankle restraints. If they'd been on their A game they would have knotted the chain to shorten it. But they hadn't. "Your loss," she said.

Ty climbed into the cab of the escape vehicle, a van that closely matched, in color and markings, the one that was being used in the convoy. He fired up the engine, and watched as the very top of the transport van carrying Chance rolled past him down the hill.

Ty began to count down slowly from ten. At six he eased off the parking brake and tapped the gas pedal, easing the van out of from its hiding place and onto the edge of the freeway.

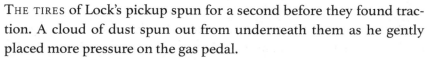

THE TIRES of Lock's pickup spun for a second before they found traction. A cloud of dust spun out from underneath them as he gently placed more pressure on the gas pedal.

With a side-on view to the convoy, he watched as the lead Suburban moved past him, a ten-foot gap between its rear and the front grille of the transport van. There had been no dry run for this part of the procedure, yet it was easily the most crucial. A fraction too much speed and he'd kill everyone inside, Chance included. A fraction too slow, and he could miss his shot.

His mind calmed as his eyes stayed level on the side of the van. A fraction of a second later, the front of his vehicle made contact with the rear side of the transport van. It fishtailed violently, the rear spinning out.

The airbag tucked inside the steering wheel deployed with a whoosh of compressed air, pushing Lock forcefully back into his seat. As the final breath of air filled it, Lock's hand was already around the handle of his Gerber.

He pulled the knife from his webbing, slashed at the airbag with one hand, and allowed it to deflate. He grabbed for the seatbelt and cut through that too. Then he shouldered the driver's door open and, drawing his SIG, stepped out of the truck.

WITH HER FEET braced hard to the floor, Chance watched as the two marshals flanking her jerked forward like puppets with their strings cut. She used the natural momentum of the collision impact to fold herself over at the waist. Spreading her legs as far as the ankle chain would allow, she lowered her front-cuffed hands to her crotch.

Her hand slid down below her waistband. With her index and middle finger, she reached up into her vagina, feeling for the handle. Finding it, she eased it down and out. With her other hand, she removed the protective plastic sheath from around the blade. She looked left and right. The two marshals either side of her had their eyes fixed firmly on the side panel door. They both seemed a little dazed, but not as surprised as Chance would have expected.

No matter. Right now that all worked in her favor. Holding the unsheathed knife in a hammer grip using her left hand, Chance let out a moan, and allowed her head to slump a little further forward. "Help me," she said.

"You okay?" the female marshal asked her.

"I can't breathe."

The female marshal unclipped her seatbelt as the last vibrations of the impact stilled. She got up and knelt next to Chance, whose face and lower body were masked by her long blond hair, which had cascaded forward.

Chance tightened her grip on the knife and waited for the gap between the top of the marshal's ballistic vest and the bottom of her helmet, a gap that exposed her neck, to come within slashing distance.

∾

THE MUZZLE of Lock's gun flared as he fired off three quick blank rounds toward the driver of the van, who ducked his head to take cover. Lock moved swiftly to the side of the van. He grabbed for the handle, stepped off to one side, and yanked it hard.

As rehearsed, the door opening prompted two, equally harmless, gunshots. Lock reached into a pocket of his webbing, pulled the flash-bang grenade out, checked that his ear protectors were snugly in place, and tossed it in around the side of the open door.

The deafening bang prompted a piercing scream. Lock's heart jumped as he feared he'd misplaced the throw. The intention was to roll it on the floor. A flash-bang was non-lethal. Unless it exploded directly in someone's face.

Pivoting on his heel, Lock punched out his SIG and swept around the edge of the open door. It took him almost a full second to process the scene that greeted him.

There was blood.

A lot of blood.

Both marshals lay on the van's floor, blood spurting from neck wounds. Kneeling between them, ochre red blood staining her hair, like a bad dye job, and covering her face was Chance. Clutched in her still-cuffed hands was a knife.

She looked up from her handiwork, and smiled broadly at Lock. "Well, if it isn't my knight in shining armor, come to rescue me."

Lock stared at her, still trying to get his head around what he was seeing. The inside of the van had been transformed in less than thirty seconds into a human abattoir.

A voice near the front of the van. Lock glanced over to see the driver, frantically keying his radio microphone.

"Officers down! Officers down! For real!"

With some difficulty, Chance scrambled to her feet. Keeping her head down, she duck-walked to the lip of the van, and hopped out. She straightened up.

Lock took a step back. She dropped the knife onto the blacktop and opened her palms to show him they were empty.

Lock could hear shots behind him. That would be Ty, playing his part by pinning down the rear vehicle, which contained the marshal's counter-attack team.

Only this wasn't exactly as rehearsed. Not anymore. The driver of the transport van had clearly gotten his message through.

Chance threw herself to the ground as a live round slammed into the van behind them, blowing a half-inch-sized hole in the bodywork.

They were taking fire, and it wasn't blank.

Lock followed Chance to the ground, and used his body to shield hers. Whatever lay ahead, he needed her breathing to save Carmen. Explanations would have to wait.

Glancing up he found himself staring into Mirales' lifeless eyes through the blood-splashed shield of her tactical helmet. Reaching down, he frisked Chance for any other weapons. She squirmed beneath him and let out a low moan.

"Oh, keep doing that. It feels good."

Someone who didn't know what Chance was capable of might have gotten embarrassed and given up on the search. Lock wasn't that guy. He ran his hands over every inch he could get to. Finally, satisfied that she didn't have another weapon, he stopped, grabbed the back of Chance's shirt and began to haul her underneath the van as a volley of fresh gunfire peppered it.

~

THE FIRST TY knew of the change in operation protocol was a bullet smashing through the windshield of his van. He had, as rehearsed, been bearing down on the marshal's counter-attack team from the rear, ready to make a show of engaging them before he rode to Lock's rescue further down the line.

Now, for reasons that weren't entirely clear to him, he was taking live fire from the same guys he'd been joking around with a few hours before. Thankfully, previous combat situations as a US marine had taught him that friendly fire was a more common occurrence than civilians might suspect and there was little point in bitching about it. Or, in the words of one marine buddy in Iraq, "Sometimes shit just happens, and you have to deal."

Dealing meant adjusting tactics, and fast. So, rather than sit there and engage with the Counter Attack Team, which, in any case, had been pretty much for show, Ty pulled down hard on the wheel of the van and buried the gas pedal to the floor.

He drove around the black Suburban holding the CA Team, taking fire as he did, and bolted toward the transport van. He slowed, spun the wheel one more time and came to a halt in front of it, the vehicle providing him cover.

Leaving the engine running, he ejected the clip in his SIG, jammed in a fresh one, holding live rounds, and bailed out.

Lock's head popped out from beneath the van. "What took you so long?" He shuffled forward on his hands and knees, and Ty saw he had a hand on the back of Chance's neck. She was covered with blood. So was Lock.

Looking past them, Ty got a glimpse of the inside of the van. Two dead marshals or, rather, one dead marshal and a dead FBI special agent. The live fire suddenly made sense.

Chance tried to wriggle out from under Lock, who tightened his grip on her. Ty reached out and pulled Lock to his feet, bringing Chance with him.

Chance struggled back round so she was side on to Lock. "Nice to see you kept your pet all these years," she said to him.

A fresh staccato burst of fire peppered the ground a few feet from them. Ty figured they could save all the catching up about old times for later.

"Here," Lock said, pushing Chance toward him. "Put her in the van. If I'm not there in thirty seconds, split and don't look back."

He tossed Ty his cell phone. Ty caught it with his left hand, pocketed it, and grabbed Chance, while he kept his SIG in his right hand. Pushing her ahead of him, Ty turned back toward his van. As he reached it he saw the lead Suburban spin to a side-on stop, blocking the road ahead. Ty threw Chance inside the van, and squeezed off a shot toward the driver's side front wheel of the Suburban. He hit it clean, his bullet ripping off a strip of rubber, as one of the marshals inside returned fire, the second of his shots coming so close that Ty felt the air part just over his head.

Turning, he saw Chance clambering behind the wheel. She reached down to throw the van into Drive. Ty jumped in and shouldered her into the passenger seat, her slender frame no match for his sheer size. "Hope you weren't thinking of taking off without me."

She shot him the trademark smile that had drawn so many people to their death. "Just trying to be a team player," she said, all sweetness and light.

He gave her a "Sure, you were" look, throwing his elbow out a little wider than usual as he flung the van into Drive, catching her rib in the process. "We ain't on the same team, lady."

He eased the van forward. Lock had maybe five seconds left of his allotted thirty. Ty felt torn. He didn't want to leave him. But he knew that, above all else, Lock wanted Carmen safe. In his pocket, Ty had the key to making that happen: Lock's cell phone and lifeline to the kidnappers. If Chance wasn't delivered, Carmen's fate would be sealed.

Ty kept easing forward, all the while counting down. He had the nose of the van facing the entrance to the old fire road that intersected this section of highway. The fire road was part of the reason they had selected this location for the ambush. It snaked for a half-mile over open ground before it was swallowed by a thick forest of Red Fir and Jeffery Pine that led, several miles later, to a lake. The route would give the illusion of providing cover from aerial surveillance. It was part of the sales pitch Lock had designed to make the escape seem credible to the kidnappers. This van was fitted with a tracker so that the authorities could locate them when the exchange was taking place.

Goddamn.

Ty had forgotten about the tracker. A good idea that would now ensure they didn't make it to the RV point.

One second more.

Ty's massive hands gripped the wheel. It was time to go.

A tap at the window. Lock stood there, a black box in his hand – the tracker.

With a swell of relief Ty threw open the door. Lock clambered over him and squeezed between the seats into the rear of the van. He dropped the black box on the seat. "Wouldn't get very far with this on board," he said.

"What about the eye in the sky?" Ty asked.

"I have an idea for that too. Just get as far down this track as you can in as little time as possible."

Lock unholstered his SIG and pushed the barrel into the side of Chance's head, just behind her ear. "Let's hope we don't hit any bumps," he said.

Chance was not a woman who scared easy. She turned her face

toward him, side-glancing him with razor blue eyes. "We hit any bumps and your girlfriend is dead," she said coolly.

Ty gunned the engine. The van's tires spun in the dirt, then found grip. They took off at speed, leaving two dead bodies and two Suburbans with shot-out tires in their wake.

56

The van lurched into the air, all four wheels briefly leaving the ground, as Ty hunched his long frame over the steering wheel. Lock reached through and clamped a hand on Chance's shoulder to prevent her head smashing into the van's roof and breaking her neck.

"You want me to ease off the gas here, Ryan?" Ty asked, as they continued to barrel down the fire road.

"Don't think we have that luxury right now."

"I hear you." Ty pressed down a little harder on the accelerator. The van's suspension groaned in protest as they hit a fresh series of ruts.

"You sure you want the Negro driving?" Chance asked Lock. "I mean didn't he kill your last girlfriend when he was behind the wheel?"

Ty glared across at her from the driver's seat. Lock chose not take the bait. Instead, he slipped his hand from Chance's shoulder.

"Hold on tight," said Ty, adjusting course a fraction toward a pothole near the edge of the road. As the van's passenger side sank into it and back out again, Chance rose in her seat, the top of her head slamming hard into the roof. She yelped with pain.

Lock put his hand back on her shoulder. "You want to play nice?"

"I was just saying. Jeez. No need to get so pissy."

"That's what I thought," said Lock.

They hit a rise in the road. A few seconds later, they cleared it. Spread out beneath them was a carpet of mature Red Fir and Jeffery Pine trees.

The van eased down the slope toward the forest.

"I think we done reached the Promised Land," said Ty, as the road took a turn and they closed in on the forest.

Lock didn't share his optimism. Not yet anyway. He could only imagine the shit storm that Chance's knife trick had caused back at the ambush site. The only chink of light was that, with so many law-enforcement agencies involved, and two individuals from two different agencies having been murdered, the frenzy would be such that it would slow the reaction. There would almost certainly be a huge pissing contest taking place right now as to chain of command and who was the lead agency. That might buy them some time.

A flicker of light that hadn't been there a second before. In the back, Lock shifted position so that he could better see the side mirror just beyond Chance. Red roll-bar lights. In the distance, but closing fast.

"Don't think we should count our chickens just yet," he said.

Ty stomped back down on the gas. The van lurched forward, heading off the fire road, and over the open ground, cutting toward the forest at an angle.

Even moving into the trees, Lock knew there was no way they could outrun whoever was behind them. He had to come up with an alternative. Fast.

57

P etrovsky swung a wild boot at the Suburban's front passenger-side tire. More rim than rubber, he had taken the vehicle as far as he could down the fire road before it had given up on him.

"Son of a bitch!" he shouted, as a couple of his subordinates eyed him warily.

It was no secret that Petrovsky had been the one person most opposed to Lock's plan of staging the escape. Right now it looked like he had been correct. It had blown up in their faces, and in spectacular fashion. Maybe now, he reflected, the other agencies might listen and he could run things his way.

An LAPD cruiser came screeching to a stop a few feet from Petrovsky. Stanner emerged and headed straight for him.

"What the hell happened?" Stanner asked.

"You see the bodies yet?" said Petrovsky.

Stanner's gaunt features darkened. He gave a curt nod. "Butcher shop."

He had likely seen hundreds of dead bodies and dozens of murder victims. So had Petrovsky. But somehow dead law-enforcement officials hit closer to home.

They were a more vivid reminder of each man's own mortality. Not just because there was familiarity but also because it was an affront to a hard-won established order. Cops and federal agents weren't supposed to die by someone else's hand. It was a challenge to the very basis of society. The first step to anarchy.

"Look," said Stanner. "We'll find them. It's just a matter of closing the net."

"And what about Lock and his buddy?" Petrovsky said.

"What about them?"

"Soon as they took off with her, they became part of this."

Stanner kicked the toe of his shoe into the ground. "Lock wants to get Carmen back. Vaden was part of that deal."

Petrovsky's face turned beet red. He struggled to keep his rage in check. "Not anymore she's not. If we can bring her home safe that's one thing. Far as I'm concerned, Lock and Johnson are fugitives now."

"If you recall, we agreed to do it this way," Stanner cautioned.

"No, you agreed, and I got railroaded. Either way, any deal terminated as soon as Vaden did what she did. I'd imagine the Bureau will see it that way too now."

"So we take Lock and Johnson into custody when we get them? Their attorney can argue their case. In court and in the media. That'll be like pouring gasoline onto a flaming pile of shit."

Petrovsky's expression told Stanner he wasn't done. "If they make it into custody . . ."

"What are you saying here, Marshal?"

"I'm saying that anyone who's actively involved will have to face the consequences of their actions. Up to, and including, the use of deadly force."

"You're going to kill them?"

"If that's what it takes."

58

Point finished a call and threw the cell phone back on the couch. Rance paced the floor behind him. Through the doorway, he could glimpse Carmen, cuffed and chained to a chair in the living room.

"That's another one down," Point announced.

"Where?" Rance asked.

"The place in Encino."

"Ah, shit, man."

"Chill. This was bound to happen when the heat came on. We still have more than enough places in the tank."

"Maybe if Chance hadn't killed that Fed . . ."

Point placed an open hand on Rance's chest. "You want to run that one by me again?"

"I was only saying that maybe we don't need any extra problems."

Point slowly shook his head from side to side. "Oh, and you don't think that Chance escaping was going to be a problem for us?" He took a step toward Rance, closing in, his eyes unblinking as he jabbed a finger into his partner's chest. "Let me explain something to you. This here is a war. As real as any of the other ones we've seen. Only the stakes are higher. A lot higher. We're fighting to take our country back. So you'd better buckle in because this is going to get a lot tougher before it gets easier."

Rance lifted a hand and pushed Point's hand away from him. "I get all that. But why go and kill a Fed when you don't need to?"

"Tell you what, you can ask Chance when you see her. How about that?"

The color faded from Rance's face at the mention of Chance. "Maybe I'll do that," he said.

"And maybe you won't."

A car horn sounded outside. Point moved to the window and pulled back the blinds a fraction. "They're here."

Rance joined him at the window. They watched as one black and one red Ford SUV pulled up outside the house. The doors of the two SUVs opened and men spilled out. They varied by age and size, but they had three characteristics in common: they were dressed in camouflage gear, they were heavily armed, and they were all, without exception, white.

"What did I just tell you?" Point said, turning back to face Rance. "This is war. The time for mercy is over."

The man who climbed from the front passenger seat of the red SUV appeared, from the body language of the others, to be the leader of this new, larger, group. He was huge, a veritable man mountain. Not tall, maybe only five ten, but muscular and broad. The sleeves of his black T-shirt strained to cover biceps larger than most men's thighs. He had long black hair and a thick black beard.

He walked up the front steps of the house and onto the porch. Point opened the door. He went to embrace the man. Padre blew him off, shoving a hand into his chest.

"You ready to do this?" Padre asked him.

"Yeah. Y'know they've hit another of our places?"

Padre stared at him. "Not our places. Your place. Let's be clear on that."

"Sure, of course," said Point, wrong-footed.

"Good," said Padre, pushing past him into the house. "Now where's the Mamacita?"

59

Ty's hands clamped around the steering wheel, the muscles in his arms taut. Thick black smoke belched from the tail pipe. Once distant, the sirens grew louder with every passing moment.

"Here's good," said Lock.

"You sure?"

"Nowhere's good, but a quarter-mile more and they'll be on top of us."

"Okay, brother. Guess it's time to de-bus."

Ty eased his foot off the gas and guided the van into the trees.

A dense canopy of branches enfolded the van as it rolled to a halt, brake lights flashing red. The door opened.

Lock clambered out, pulling Chance with him. She stumbled over a root as she stepped away from the van. Lock grabbed her arm and steadied her.

"Can't you take the cuffs off me?" she pleaded. "Before I break my neck."

"Sure," said Lock. "I'll get right on that."

Ty leaned out of the driver's window. "You'd better get gone," he said to Lock.

From the far distance came the sound of sirens. Louder still. Their pursuers getting closer with every second that passed.

"You too," said Lock.

Ty threw the van back into Drive, the wheels spinning as he circled around a tree, and headed back toward the fire road. Lock didn't wait to watch him leave. It was a situation that left no time for goodbyes.

Lock drew his SIG and turned toward where Chance was standing a few feet away. He pointed the muzzle at her. His finger fell to the trigger. The color drained from her face. She closed her eyes and murmured what sounded to Lock like a prayer.

"What the . . .?"

Lock lowered his aim and fired a single shot. The sound echoed through the trees, then fell away.

The chain securing the ankle restraints broke. She could move her legs freely.

She opened her eyes, fear turned to relief. She let out a throaty giggle. "Damn. You almost made me pee my pants."

Lock didn't respond. He holstered his gun, grabbed her arm at the elbow and guided her further away from the track. Pushing her ahead of him, he plunged deeper into the thick forest.

~

LOCK'S HAND fell on to Chance's shoulder. Without warning, he pushed her down into a crouch. Through the trees, they watched as flashing lights swept past.

The vehicles whipped along the tree line, in hot pursuit of the van. Lock stood. He stared at her for a second, his eyes meeting hers.

"Three rules. Do what I say. When I say it. Keep your mouth shut."

She rolled her eyes. "Yes, boss." She smirked. "Sorry, did I just break rule three?"

He chose to ignore her. Getting her to obey the last ground rule was always going to be a reach. He turned back toward the dense

woodland and started forward, Chance loping at his side, like a reluc-
tant puppy being leash-trained.

~

THE FRONT of the pursuing patrol vehicle slammed into the rear
bumper of the van. Ty lurched forward, only the seatbelt preventing
his chest going into the steering wheel and cracking his ribs.

Reaching over, he thrust his arm out of the window. He signaled
that he was about to stop. The patrol vehicle immediately behind
him halted. The parking brake off, the van was still rolling.

Two hundred yards ahead, the fire road curved around to the
right. Or, at least, Ty hoped it did. Either it was a curve or a dead end.
The narrowness of the track and the denseness of the trees on either
side made it difficult to tell which.

"I'm coming out. Don't shoot!" he shouted. He checked the mirror.
The driver of the lead pursuit vehicle pushed open his door, his gun
drawn. Using his door as cover, he took aim at the driver's door of
the van.

"Promise you're not gonna shoot me?" Ty hollered.

"As long as you do what you're told when you're told to do it," said
the cop.

"A lot of black folks have heard that line before," said Ty, moving
his other arm out of the window. "See? I don't have anything in my
hands. No reason to shoot me."

"Just make sure to keep it like that," said the cop.

Ty watched in the side mirror, as the cop began to move out
from behind the protection of his door. His gun punched out
ahead, he began to approach the van. Ty's eyes flicked across to the
side mirror on the other side of the van. A US marshal was making
a move, working his way down Ty's blind side. Eyes flicking from
one side to the other, Ty counted the men's steps as they
approached.

Seconds later both men were equidistant between the pursuit
vehicle and his van. Ty's foot moved across to the gas pedal.

Simultaneously, he pushed it down, at the same time moving his hands back inside the van and taking control of the steering wheel.

He watched as, behind him, the cop and the US marshal fell into a shooting stance and squeezed off a shot aimed at the van's rear.

Hunched over the steering wheel, Ty kept his foot on the gas. He struggled out from under his seatbelt and opened the driver's door, as the van barreled full tilt toward the turn in the road.

Ten yards short of the turn, he made his move. Pushing hard against the door to ensure it was fully open, he pulled his feet up from the pedals, pushed his hands against the steering wheel and dove out of the van. His shoulder slammed hard into the ground. His hip seared with pain as it also made contact. He kept rolling, allowing his own momentum to carry him through the gap between two pine trees. Catching a mouthful of dirt, he tumbled a couple more times, landing painfully with his back against a tree.

Meanwhile, the van sped on. With no one at the wheel, it missed the turn, and slammed, head on, into the trees.

TY WATCHED the cop and the marshal as they ran toward the van. He reached up and rubbed at his forehead. His hand came away wet with blood. He swiped off the worst with the back of his sleeve. He felt like he'd gone ten rounds with Tyson, but he didn't think anything was broken. Nothing major, anyway.

He levered himself up into a crouch. The cop and the marshal were almost at the van. It wouldn't take them long to figure out that he wasn't inside.

More men were coming up behind them. The narrowness of the track meant no one could move their vehicle beyond the ones that had already been abandoned by the lead pursuers. That, along with the terrain, leveled the playing field.

Ty moved in a half-crouch quickly behind a broad tree. As soon as he was certain he couldn't be seen from the track he started to move. A searing pain shot all the way from his right foot up to his hip and into his spine. He reached down, and, with long fingers, rubbed his leg.

He set out on a diagonal path that would give him the most distance in the shortest space of time. He could already hear voices behind him.

"He ain't here."

"None of them are."

"I told you, I saw him bail."

"What about the other two?"

"All I saw was Johnson."

"Great. Then where are the other two?"

Ty kept moving, his pace increasing as he shook off his body's shock. Soon, he was covering the forest floor with his trademark long strides. As he moved, the voices faded. But not before he heard one last voice that chilled him.

"Forget all this drone bullshit. Get the dogs out. They'll find them."

60

Scattered rays of sunlight filtered down through the trees' canopy, dappling the ground beneath Lock's feet. Ahead of him, Chance picked her way daintily through a knot of undergrowth that blocked their path. Her breathing was heavy and labored.

"You okay?" he asked her.

"I'm out of shape, is all. Not enough exercise, and the food in prison sucks."

Lock's heart bled for her, as it did for every murderer who complained about prison food. He decided to keep that thought to himself. He was thinking about Carmen. With a little luck her ordeal would be over soon. That was all that mattered to him. Getting her back. Safe and sound. Everyone else, besides Ty, could go hang.

His thoughts returned to Chance, stumbling through the undergrowth. "Back there, what you did to those two people? You proud of that?"

She stopped walking, and turned to face him. "You never did get it, did you?"

"What am I supposed to get exactly?"

"You have to choose a side."

"Then you didn't get me either," he corrected her.

"How's that?" she asked him.

"I'm on my side. Always was."

"You keep telling yourself that, Ryan." She began walking ahead.

Lock dug a hand into his pocket, feeling for the burner phone the kidnappers had left for him. No calls showed on the screen. He scanned the forest around them, and listened for signs of movement. Save for a couple of squirrels chasing each other along a nearby branch, everything was as it should be. "So why now?" he said.

"Why what now?"

"Escaping."

"Saw my opportunity and took it."

Lock lengthened his strides so that he was walking next to her. He kept scanning the area around them. "Not buying it. You could have shanked a prisoner at any time."

Chance pushed away a strand of hair that had fallen across her face. "I could have. So why didn't I?"

"That was my question."

"That monster deserved to die. Couldn't say the same for anyone else inside."

"What about your cellie who killed her two kids?"

"Not even in the same league as that asshole."

"So, come on, you expect me to believe that Browell walking in was the trigger?"

"Let's just say that a lot of things came together, and it was kind of now or never."

"I'm starting to believe you," said Lock.

"Believe whatever you want to believe, just like the rest of them."

"And roping me into it?"

"You were just a happy coincidence."

"What about Carmen? Getting her involved wasn't a coincidence, and don't try to persuade me otherwise."

She stopped walking, and flicked another strand of stray hair from her eyes. "It was her bad luck to be dating you. You're kind of a jinx when it comes to the ladies, aren't you, Ryan?"

Lock had been waiting for a dig about what had happened to Carrie. He was surprised it had taken Chance so long to bring it up. He refused to take the bait.

But Chance wouldn't let it go so easily. "Your best friend killing your fiancée."

"That was an accident."

"You see, Ryan, that's what happens when you take on a toad as a partner."

Lock grabbed her elbow.

She laughed. "Touch a nerve, did I?"

"Just keep walking."

Chance tilted her head back and laughed. Lock chastised himself for reacting. He should have known better. But, as much as he liked to think otherwise, Carrie's death still haunted him.

"Imagine if this one dies too. Then you're really going to struggle for a date."

"If Carmen doesn't make it, you're not going to be here to worry about my love life. That's a promise."

"You know, I love it when you talk killing. Gets me all hot and bothered."

Lock tuned her out. Ahead, he could glimpse patches of blue sky through the branches. Walking parallel to Chance, he peered past the trees, his eyes slowly adjusting to the increased light.

Chance was still bumping her gums about Lock being the literal kiss of death to women he became romantically involved with. He was starting to wish for the buzzing in his ears to make a dramatic return.

He motioned for Chance to stay where she was, and moved on ahead. Every few steps he threw a glance back over his shoulder to reassure himself that she hadn't made a break for it.

A hundred yards later he hit a tree line that fronted onto a paved road. On the other side there was a fence and open meadow. Beyond, the forest resumed in both directions.

Feeling suddenly exposed, Lock stepped out from the trees, and jumped over a drainage channel. His boots hit the edge of the black-top. He scanned the road in both directions. He spotted what he was looking for almost immediately. A road sign. He jogged the hundred yards down to the sign, then ran back, all the time aware that at any moment someone driving down the road could blow their cover. Even if it wasn't a cop, a lone male out in the middle of nowhere while an active manhunt was taking place would likely warrant a call.

He moved fast back to the trees, hugging the edge of the forest as he went back to Chance. He had taken a risk in leaving her. But she had remained where she was. Now she eyed him carefully as he pulled out the burner phone and powered it up.

As soon as it switched on, the screen lit up with alerts for more than a dozen missed calls. Each call had no number displayed. Lock moved to the phone's contact list. One number had been pre-programmed.

He called it, and waited for someone to answer. It didn't take long. They were clearly eager to speak with him. That alone told him that the balance of power had tilted in his favor.

"Why the hell you have the phone turned off?"

Lock took a breath. "You know they can track cell-phone signals, right?"

"It's a burner. No one knows it exists."

"I wouldn't bet money on that."

"Okay. Well, you ready to take some directions and get to the RV point?"

"We're on foot. You come to us."

There was some mumbled discussion in the background. The kidnapper came back on the line. "Okay, where you at?"

Lock gave a location as best he could, using a description of the surroundings and the details from the road sign. When he finished he asked if the man at the other end had got it all.

"Yeah. We'll find you."

"Okay, let me speak to Carmen."

"We ain't got time for that now."

"Fine," said Lock. "Then get here as fast as you can. You let Carmen walk into the woods, and I'll give you Chance."

"How do I know you'll let us have Chance?"

"Because, unlike you, I'm a man of my word."

61

Struggling for breath, Ty leaped over a tree trunk. On the other side, a steep slope fell down to a stream. Adjusting his feet so that he was side on to the slope, he leaned back and skated toward the stream.

Behind him, he could hear what he'd guessed was a bloodhound dragging its handler through the thick forest. Every so often he would hear it baying. From the volume, it was getting closer too. Five more minutes and it would be right on top of him. Along with several dozen assorted marshals, Feds and cops.

The baying came again. Yeah, it was definitely closer.

Ty looked down at his boots. They were caked with mud.

He stepped into the stream, and started walking. A few yards down, he almost lost his footing on a particularly slippery moss-covered rock.

Steadying himself, he kept wading downstream.

He could hear men shouting close by. He pressed on, his pants legs and boots soaked.

The bank grew steeper on either side. Ahead he could see a rush of water. The current was growing stronger, pushing against the back of his calves. He put out a hand to steady himself against the bank.

The dog bayed again. This time it sounded a little more distant. He couldn't be sure, it might have been wishful thinking on his part, but the animal sounded more frustrated than excited.

Ty pressed on, struggling to stay on his feet as the stream began to widen. Finally, another fifty yards downstream, he waded over to the opposite bank, and climbed out.

From mid-thigh down he was soaked. He quickly checked his weapon to make sure it was dry. His legs and one side of his body throbbed with pain.

Ty struck out again through the woods, keeping a steady pace, as the water dripped down his pants and into his boots. The sound of the dog, and the men with it, fell away until he couldn't hear them anymore.

62

Lock tied off the gag he'd placed around Chance's mouth. She shook her head violently from side to side. Her eyes and nostrils flared with rage. "Now, that's the woman I recognize."

She settled a little. She lolled her head from side to side, indicating that she wanted to speak. He reached across and pulled the gag from her mouth, careful not to let any of his fingers get within easy biting range.

"What?"

"Why are you doing this?"

"Exchange protocol. I don't want you giving away our position to your buddies. Don't worry, I'm sure they'll remove it when I hand you over. *After* I have Carmen."

To his surprise, Chance seemed to accept his explanation. "Okay, just don't make it too tight. I don't want to throw up."

"Can't make any promises," Lock told her, pulling the piece of fabric back up.

He guided her slowly behind a pine tree. They were about fifty yards from the side of the road, far enough away that he would be almost impossible to spot. But close enough that he would be able to watch the kidnappers. Or that was what he hoped. Trading Carmen for Chance would require concealment. And, he hoped, kidnappers that had no interest in sticking around when the deal was done.

63

The red and black SUVs turned slowly off the road. They picked a path slowly through the trees until they came to a rise. Brake lights flared as they came to a stop at the top of the rise.

The front passenger door was flung open. Padre appeared. He walked to a spot where the tree line revealed an open vista of the rest of the forest. Another man joined him. He handed Padre a pair of binoculars.

Padre brought them up to his face, thumbed the wheel to adjust focus, and scanned the area below. He watched as a pickup truck drove down a road at the edge of the trees.

He thumbed the focus wheel again. This time Rance came into view, sitting behind the wheel of the truck. Next to him, sandwiched between Rance and Point, was the lady lawyer. She was blindfolded.

Padre shook his head. He'd told them not to blindfold her. They had disregarded his request. *Stupid.* Worse than that, *careless.*

A woman wedged between two guys in the front of a pickup may or may not look suspicious to some average Joe. But put a blindfold on her? That was guaranteed to prompt a call to someone.

In any case, what did it matter what she saw?

He handed the binoculars back and turned to the others.

"It's a half-klick to the RV on foot. That's how we'll do it. Slow and quiet. Drivers, you meet us back down there, but stay clear of the road until it's all done."

64

Lock watched from his position within the fringe of trees as a pickup truck that had been fitted with a cap, a large fiberglass box that enclosed the truck's flat bed, came to a stop. His eyes darted back to Chance. She had stayed put. Good news for everyone.

Chance had already been informed that if she made a break for it before the time came, or in any way tried to reveal their position, he would shoot her. He had meant it. Because of that, she had believed him. If it came to it, he was prepared to kill her and rush the truck to get Carmen.

He caught a glimpse of a blindfolded Carmen inside the cab, a woman still trapped in an unfolding nightmare. Lock closed his eyes for a second. He thanked God that she was alive.

He opened his eyes again, packing away his relief and the mixture of lingering fear and naked rage that had come with seeing the woman he loved. There would be time enough for relief and thanks when the exchange was concluded. Right now he had a task to complete. The dangerous part had arrived, the minutes and seconds closest to the finish line.

Point got out of the truck. Lock watched him scanning the trees. He stayed close to the vehicle. Rance lowered his window and the two men exchanged a few words.

Edging away from Chance, Lock took up a position behind another broad pine tree he had already scoped out. Point walked away from the truck, toward the tree line.

When he was in position, Lock cupped his hands, and placed them like a megaphone around his mouth. "Send Carmen out of the truck and into the woods. As soon as she's clear you can have Vaden."

Both Point and Rance whiplashed round, their heads on a swivel as they tried to place Lock in the dense green and brown canopy. He stayed where he was, his back to the tree, just enough of an angle to watch them.

Point drew a handgun from his holster. He kept it angled down and away from him, aiming the barrel into the blacktop. From inside the truck cap came a deep, baritone barking.

Point screamed at the dog inside, "Shut the hell up!" then asked Lock, "How can we know to trust you?"

Lock faded back behind the tree a fraction as the dog's barking fell away to a low, throaty growl. "Because I could have shot you by now. Listen, let's not drag this out. I'm a hell of a lot more trustworthy than you assholes. Even with your limited intellectual capacity, you must realize that."

He waited a beat before taking a fresh peek. Point was walking to the truck.

He holstered his weapon while he grabbed the handle, opened the door, and helped Carmen out of the cab. She was a little shaky on her feet. Not uncommon in kidnap victims.

Rance stayed where he was, the truck's engine idling. He peered into the woods. He seemed on edge. Lock didn't blame him.

Point pulled a hunting knife from a sheath on his belt. He used it to sever the plastic cuffs that were secured around Carmen's wrists. She stood in front of him and blinked as sunlight broke through the trees.

"Okay, go," Point told her.

She seemed uncertain. Behavior that Lock had also seen before. Even after a short time, people began to cling to captivity. They adjusted. It became the known. Being set free was the unknown. Anyone who had watched an animal hesitate when a cage door was opened had seen the same thing.

Lock held his breath. He couldn't afford to break cover to go help her. This was one part of the exchange that Carmen had to do on her own. He willed her to move.

Another few seconds ticked past. Finally, Carmen took a single step away from the truck.

Attagirl, Lock said to himself. *Keep moving. Come on. Fifty more steps and this will all be over.*

She hesitated. His heart sank. She looked like she was about to keel over any second.

Then she took another step. The second was followed quickly by a third, and a fourth. Eventually she stepped off the road and onto the verge.

Point watched her go. Whatever was inside of the truck stirred again and began its ferocious barking. It shifted its weight against the side of the truck cap. It was a large dog, and it was restless. Lock double-checked that his SIG was ready to fire.

Carmen cleared the tree line. But she was headed in the opposite direction, away from him.

"Carmen!"

He watched her stop and look over in his general direction.

"Turn left and keep walking back."

She changed direction.

"Okay, good. Keep walking."

"Now, you send me Chance," Point shouted over to him.

"Okay, give me a second, I'll send her out," Lock said, stalling for time. He didn't want Point to get antsy but he wanted Carmen with him before he gave the two men what they had come for and lost his bargaining chip.

"Send her out now, or I'm coming in."

"Okay, okay. You got it."

Staying low to the ground, Lock ran back in a low crouch toward Chance. Her hands were cuffed and the gag was in her mouth. Her buddies could deal with both of those.

He held her where she was as Carmen got closer. When Carmen was within ten yards, Lock removed the blindfold from Chance's eyes. She squinted and blinked as her eyes adjusted to the light.

Grabbing Chance by the shoulder, he guided her out from behind the tree. Carmen could see them now. The two women's eyes met briefly before Carmen started to run toward Lock. He pointed out the road to Chance.

"It's been real," he said, giving her a gentle push in the direction of the road.

She said something but the words were muffled by the gag. She started walking. Lock turned back to Carmen. He holstered his weapon, put his arms out and took her hands in his. They stayed like that for a few seconds, looking at each other.

"I'm sorry," he said.

She managed a half-smile. "Can we just get out of here?"

She was right. Apologies, along with everything else, could wait.

"This way," said Lock, guiding her by the hand back into the woods.

He would stay within the forest, but close to the road, until they had gone. Then he would use the burner phone they had given him to call in the cavalry. With any luck the Feds, and whoever else was out there, could scoop up Chance and her two buddies before they even made it to the freeway.

Carmen squeezed his hand as he led her between trees and across the forest floor. On the road behind them he could hear Chance talking to the two men in the truck.

Lock froze as he heard a baying sound. A dog. But not the one locked inside the back of the truck. This sound was coming from somewhere else.

"Wait here," he told Carmen.

Releasing her hand, he jogged a few yards back toward the road. He stopped and listened. The baying came again. A tracking dog. A bloodhound or some variant thereof.

Maybe he wouldn't have to make the call after all. By the sound of it, the cavalry was headed straight for them.

oint also heard the baying. Like Lock, he knew what it meant. The posse was here, and they had a four-legged location device heading in their direction.

After the briefest of hugs with Chance, he helped her climb up into the cab next to Rance. No mean feat given that her hands were still cuffed.

"Let's get the hell out of here," she urged.

"We will. Just gimme a second."

He walked to the back of the truck, dropped the tail gate, and quickly stepped to one side. Before he could lift up the top of the cap, the Ridgeback had squeezed through the gap.

Point reached into his pocket. He dug out a dried liver treat, the beast's favorite. It jammed its muzzle into his hand. He reached down and unclipped the muzzle, freeing the dog's jaws and open palming it the treat.

The tracking dog bayed. The Ridgeback's ears twitched.

"You hear that?" Point said to the dog.

The question was redundant. All that was needed was the command.

"Go get it."

For most dogs 'get' signified a fetch or a retrieval. Not for the Ridgeback. For the Ridgeback it meant seek and destroy.

The Ridgeback took off, disappearing into the woods, heading straight for the sound of the baying.

Point opened the cab door, and climbed in next to Chance. He slammed a hand onto the dash. Rance put the truck into Drive and stomped on the gas pedal. They took off down the road.

Jammed in between them, Chance smiled quietly to herself. She already knew what was coming next for the men sitting either side of her.

LOCK TENSED as he heard the dog crashing through the brush. Without hesitating, he grabbed Carmen around the waist, and pushed her behind a Douglas Fir. There was a branch about six feet from the base of the tree.

"I'm going to give you a boost," he said, kneeling down, and entwining his fingers to form a makeshift stirrup.

She placed her foot in his hands and grabbed his broad shoulders for support.

"Okay, on three. One. Two. Three."

He lifted her toward the branch. She grabbed it and hauled herself up.

"What about you?" she asked him.

Lock drew his SIG. He had decided that shooting the dog would be a last resort. He didn't believe in harming animals. He wasn't about to start now. Unless there was absolutely no alternative.

He saw the dog break cover a hundred yards behind him. It was a Rhodesian Ridgeback. Too big to be anything other than a male.

It was heading straight for them. Lock took up a shooting stance and raised his gun. He tracked the dog as it bounded toward him.

He took a deep breath in though his nose and exhaled slowly through his mouth. He would rather shoot a human being who was threatening him than a dog.

His finger moved to the trigger as the dog closed in.

Behind him came the baying sound. The Ridgeback slowed, and switched direction, moving away from them. Lock tracked it through the iron sights of his SIG.

It disappeared through the trees. He lowered the gun and let out a deep sigh of relief.

He looked up to Carmen, still folded over the tree branch, arms and legs dangling.

"It's safe," he told her.

From behind him, a man's voice. Deep and filled with menace.

"You sure about that?"

Lock spun round to find himself facing a bear of a man with a huge beard. He was dressed in camo and sporting a rifle. Raising his SIG to the man's chest, Lock placed himself in front of Carmen as she eased herself to the ground.

One by one, more men emerged from the trees. All dressed in camouflage gear and heavily armed.

Without being asked, Lock lowered the barrel of the SIG. "I'm guessing you boys aren't with the government," he said.

The man with the beard smiled. "Good guess."

Lock counted off the men that he could see. Eleven in total. The two kidnappers weren't among them.

The man with the beard glanced back over his shoulder in the direction that the Ridgeback had gone. "We should probably get out of here."

"What about the dog?" one of the men with him asked.

"He's working. Best leave him." The man turned toward Lock and Carmen. "But you two lovebirds, you're coming with us."

66

Their hands and feet cuffed, Lock sat facing Carmen. "Sorry," he said. "This wasn't the reunion I had in mind."

She forced a smile that collapsed at the edges. "Me either." She swallowed hard. "So what do you think happens now?"

He had a good idea of what was going to happen but he wasn't about to share it. The power of terrorism, and he had no doubt that the description fit Chance and her motley crew, lay in its ability to capture the darkest recesses of a person's imagination. Terrorists conjured nightmares. They brought them to life. Even though being knocked down and killed by a careless driver had the same result as being beheaded by a jihadi, the latter scared people a hell of a lot more, even though it was thousands of times less likely.

"I think," Lock said finally, "that we take the first chance that presents itself to get the hell away from them. Maybe I can distract one long enough for you to make a break for it."

The look on Carmen's face told him she wasn't buying it. Neither did he. But it beat the hell out of admitting that what probably lay ahead of them was a bloody, painful and slow death, filled with who knew what kind of degradation and torment.

"I don't know if I could run, even if I had the chance."

"Well, I'll think of something. But you have to promise me one thing."

"What's that?"

"That you don't lose hope."

"Easier said than done, Ryan."

"I know. But you have to try."

Carmen forced another frayed smile. "I'll do my best."

"Half the cops in California are going to be out looking for these guys," Lock added. "Plus the Feds, and the United States marshals. All we need to do is hang in there long enough."

"Who are you trying to convince? Me or yourself?"

There was no point in lying. "You want the truth?" he asked her.

She nodded. She did. At least that part of her hadn't changed, Lock thought.

"Both of us."

Lock tried to pull his hands apart. The edge of the plastic cuffs dug into his wrists. Then he remembered something obvious that did make him feel better. There weren't just several thousand law-enforcement officers looking for them. There was also Ty.

67

Ty paced toward the edge of the holding pen. He pressed his forehead against the bars. A wave of muscle rolled all the way down to the cuffs cinched around his wrists as he flexed his arms.

"Hey, can someone take these cuffs off?" He paused, waiting for the duty officer to look up from his desk. "If it's not too much trouble."

The officer slowly pushed his chair back, got to his feet, and wandered over to him. Ty thrust his hands through the bars. Taking his time, the officer slowly removed the cuffs.

Ty pulled his hands back through the bars, and rubbed his wrists. "Any chance I can speak with someone about getting out of here?"

"I'll see what I can do," the officer said, walking slowly back to his desk. He lifted the phone, and had a brief conversation that Ty didn't catch. He put the phone down and came back. "You're going to have to wait, Mr. Johnson. We're stretched pretty thin right now."

Ty stared up at the ceiling for a moment, trying to stay calm. "Because of this manhunt?"

"That's correct."

"And that's why I need to get out of here. To help find these assholes."

The duty officer offered an apologetic shrug. "I'm sorry, but I can't release you until someone's spoken to you."

"And they don't have time to speak to me because they're looking for these guys?"

"That's pretty much it."

Ty took a deep breath, slowly exhaled, and stalked back to the bench he'd been sitting on. He took a seat, a couple of other prisoners shuffling down to make room for him.

68

If Lock had learned anything over the years, it was that, more often than not, life served up setbacks. What mattered wasn't so much how they happened (that could be saved for later) but how you dealt with them. He had promised Carmen he would get her home safe, and he still would. Or he'd die trying. And, right now, it was looking like he'd be able to make good on his promise sooner than anticipated.

The pickup truck was slowing down. He could hear chatter from the double cab. Finally, it stopped.

Carmen looked at him. Before she could say anything, the back opened, and the guy with the beard, the leader, poked his head inside. "We got ourselves a roadblock up ahead. I hear anything from either of you, and I'll put a bullet in you both. Understood?"

Lock nodded. Carmen followed his lead.

"Good."

The back of the pickup shut again, plunging them into gloom again. The cab door slammed as the guy with the beard got back in. The vehicle started to move.

"What do you think we should do?" Carmen whispered.

Lock had already thought it over. The cops manning the roadblock would be armed. So were their captors. Carmen and he were unarmed, trussed like a couple of turkeys. The plastic ankle restraints meant they couldn't even make a run for it, assuming they could get out.

"We do what we just told him we'd do."

"But this might be our last chance to get away from these lunatics."

It was possible, thought Lock. But unlikely. "If they'd wanted to they could have killed us back there," he told her. "I would have, if I was them."

Carmen shot him a wry look. "That's comforting."

"I'm just saying. Hostages are an added complication. If we're alive, they have a reason to keep us that way. At least for now."

She didn't look reassured. But there wasn't any time to add anything to what he'd already said. The truck was rolling to a stop again. Lock could hear a voice through a PA system ordering the driver and passengers to keep their hands where they could be seen.

69

A long with the other four men in the double-cab pickup truck, Padre placed his hands on the dashboard, and waited for further instruction from one of the four California Highway Patrol cops manning the roadblock.

"Okay, driver, toss the keys out of the window onto the ground. Then keep your hands where I can see them."

The driver glanced at Padre. Padre's left hand dropped from the dash. He fumbled in his front pants pocket, dug out a set of keys, and palmed them off to the driver.

"Passenger, keep your hands where they are visible!"

Padre shrugged and put his hands back on the dash. "Go ahead," he told the driver. "Just like we planned for."

Stifling a giggle, the driver left the truck's key fob in the ignition, took Padre's keys and tossed them as far as he could from the truck.

One of the CHP officers began to move out from the protection of his vehicle door. His colleagues, guns trained on the truck, provided cover.

Padre, smirking, watched the cop walk toward the keys. When the cop was within a few yards of picking up the keys, Padre's hand reached down to his webbing.

"Passenger! Keep your hands where————"

Padre's hand came back from the webbing. His fingers wrapped round a grey-black grenade. He removed the pin. His left hand kept pressure on the safety lever as he grasped the grenade with his right. Carefully, he passed it to the driver as the cop on the PA went ballistic.

Padre put his hands back on the dash, waggling his fingers in the air for effect, making clear he wasn't holding anything. The driver repeated his key toss. The grenade sailed through the open window. It arced high over the approaching cop's head.

The grenade landed with a dull thud two feet beyond the keys. The occupants of the pickup ducked beneath the dashboard. They squirmed behind seats and into the footwells as the cops opened up on the truck.

The driver fired the engine, and threw the vehicle into reverse. The cop nearest the grenade, finally realizing what he was looking at, began to scramble back toward his patrol car.

The grenade exploded as the pickup's driver reversed as fast as he could. The blast wave from the explosion lifted the retreating police officer up into the air. Shrapnel ripped through his lower legs, shearing through his right ankle and separating foot from leg. His screams were primal and raw.

The pickup stopped. The doors popped open. The driver stayed at the wheel as the other occupants, Padre included, split for either side of the narrow road and threw themselves into drainage culverts. Shouldering their rifles, they opened up on the remaining three cops.

After the first burst of gunfire, Padre tapped the shoulder of the man nearest to him. The man sprayed covering fire toward the two CHP patrol cars as Padre ran down the culvert to get a better angle.

The cops struggled to return fire. One reached for a shotgun in the front of his vehicle. As he lifted it out, Padre popped up almost parallel to him. Before the cop could bring the shotgun to bear, Padre unleased a targeted three-round burst that sent the cop tumbling back into his vehicle, blood pouring from a head wound.

The surviving two cops were back up behind the furthermost

patrol car. One raised his hand in a gesture of surrender. That only intensified the incoming fire. Padre was joined by one of his buddies. Together they started toward the two cops. One pinned them down with covering fire while the other advanced. Then they switched.

Less than a minute later, Padre called a halt. A few more rounds popped off. Finally, the guns fell silent. Padre walked across to the patrol cars. Three officers were dead. One was crawling down the road on his hands and knees, bleeding heavily from his stomach, trying to escape the bloodbath.

Padre calmly drew his Glock from the holster on his hip. The cop turned as Padre's shadow fell over him. "Come on. I have a wife. Kids."

Padre raised the Glock and pointed it at the officer's face. "I hear you," he said, squeezing the trigger.

Padre took a step back as the cop slumped, dead, onto the road. "Damn shame," he said to himself. With no sense of urgency, he strode back past the two patrol cars and the three other dead officers. The pickup drove to meet him. Padre climbed back into the cab.

As the door swung shut, the driver buried the gas pedal. The truck took off, swerving round the patrol cars. Soon, the scene of the massacre was a distant dot behind them.

70

Their faces pressed to the truck bed, Lock managed to reach his hands out toward Carmen. The tips of his fingers found hers. She was shaking uncontrollably. He didn't blame her. Terror was the natural reaction to their predicament. After what had seemed like an eternity, but could only have been four or five minutes, the shooting had stopped, and the truck moved off at speed.

The sudden acceleration sent them in opposite directions. Lock's fingertips parted from Carmen's.

"Hey," he called. "You hear me?"

Her voice came back to him, muffled, like he was sitting at the bottom of a swimming pool. The ringing in his ears was back with a vengeance.

"Yes," she said.

"We're still alive."

She didn't reply. He rolled over onto his side so that he could see her. She was curled up into a fetal ball. It was the first time he'd seen her like that. She had survived the kidnapping and come out the other side. But the fire fight at the road block seemed to have tipped her over the edge. Now he had to find a way to pull her back.

"Carmen, I need you to listen to me."

Her eyes opened. It was a start. At least she was capable of a response.

"You're tough. Coming this far proves that."

She looked at him. Her eyes focused. Another good sign. She was still present. Her body might have folded in on itself but her mind hadn't, not yet anyway.

"These guys could have killed us by now but they haven't. Even back there at the roadblock."

She was still looking at him. He could only hope he was getting through.

"We could be dead. But we're not. That means we have hope we'll come out of this. But I need you to hang tough. Can you do that?"

Her eyes flecked with tears, she gave the most minimal of nods.

"Good," said Lock. "Now, if we can figure out why they've kept us alive maybe that will help us get out of this."

He had made the connection only as he'd said it, but it made sense. Perhaps the only thing that did. They weren't alive on a whim. These weren't people who spared other human beings out of the goodness of their hearts. Carmen and he were alive for a reason. And, Lock guessed, that reason was because this crew of killers weren't finished with them. Not yet anyway.

71

"You know that I could do whatever the hell I want to her, right?"

Lock shifted uneasily in the hard wooden seat, his hands secured behind him, as Chance paced back and forth in front of him. Carmen was seated against the far wall of the office. A glass panel that ran the length of the opposite wall revealed the warehouse floor beneath.

Chance had changed out of her orange prison scrubs into jeans, sneakers, and a black T-shirt emblazoned with a Stormfront logo. Lock knew from previous research that Stormfront was a major neo-Nazi/white nationalist internet forum. He imagined that right now Chance's escape, and the subsequent mayhem, would be the number-one trending topic of discussion on that particular portal.

"You can do what you want with both of us," said Lock, ceding ground. There was no point in antagonizing Chance or any of her buddies. Not right now anyway.

"Damn straight I can," said Chance, pulling a small hunting knife from the back pocket of her denims and prowling over toward Carmen where she placed the tip under Carmen's chin.

Lock did his best to remain stony-faced. Any reaction from him might hype Chance up even more. And she didn't need any more hyping.

Carmen broke the silence, fixing Chance with an even gaze. "I was on your side."

It was enough to distract Chance from whatever she was going to do with the knife. She dropped her hand back to her side. "That's what I thought. Then I saw that picture of you with this sack of shit over here."

"It was a coincidence. Nothing more," said Lock. "I had no idea Carmen's legal firm was representing you, and even if I had, what difference would it have made?"

Chance stalked her way back to Lock. The blade caught a shaft of light and twinkled in front of his eyes as she brought it up to his face. "You expect me to believe that?"

"I'm not asking you to believe anything, but it's the truth," Lock replied flatly. He felt a lot calmer with the knife at his own throat rather than at Carmen's.

He tilted his head back so that he made eye contact with Chance. "What is it you want from us?"

Chance smiled. "Not us. You. It's what I want from you." Her eyes slid over to Carmen. "She's just here to make sure that you'll do it."

Lock didn't greet the news with any sense of reassurance. The way she had said it left him in no doubt that whatever Chance wanted it wasn't going to be good.

72

L ock stared at the photographs laid out on the table in front of him. Standing in a semi-circle around him were Chance, along with the bearded man he'd heard called Padre, and a handful of others – he'd recognized a voice as belonging to one of Carmen's original kidnappers. He could tell that, besides briefing him in the mission they wanted him to complete in exchange for Carmen's safe release, they were mostly here to savor his reaction.

"This will be a piece of a cake for a man like you," said Padre, jabbing a skull-ringed finger at a photograph that showed the main entrance to the Temple Emanuel synagogue in Beverly Hills.

Padre was correct. For a man such as Lock, walking into a public place with minimal security and murdering innocent unarmed men, women and children wouldn't be difficult. Nor would it have proven difficult for anyone with even a modicum of training. Terrorism of this type didn't take skill or courage so much as a complete absence of humanity or morals.

Trying to stay cool, Lock glanced up at Chance and Padre. "If it's so easy then why don't you do it?"

Chance shot him a sugary smile. "What? And take all the fun out of watching you do it?"

Lock had to hand it to her. There was a twisted simplicity in what she wanted him to do. He had been expecting she had wanted him taken, with Carmen, so that they could make him suffer. If the authorities, or Ty, didn't get to them in time, he'd figured a long bout of physical torture for both of them, followed by a single bullet at the back of the ear. This, though, was on a whole other level.

Chance might wish Lock dead, but she obviously wanted to take more than his life. She wanted to tarnish his memory, along with everything he'd ever stood for. His being murdered by a bunch of neo-Nazis out to settle an old score was one thing. His being convicted and imprisoned for the slaughter of innocent people at worship was something else entirely.

At the same time, he knew that refusal would carry a penalty. The only question was what form it would take.

"And what if I say no?" Lock asked his captors, as he glanced up from the photo-montage of the synagogue and surrounding area.

The smirks that greeted his question told him that this was something they had already given thought to. Padre delivered the answer. "Me, some of the boys and your lady-love go in a room and have some fun. Don't worry, you'll have a front-row seat. And once we're done running that train on her, we'll really set to work showing her some tough love."

Lock stared at him and didn't break eye contact. He had a feeling that Padre wasn't given to idle threats. Then again neither was Lock.

"That answer your question?" Padre asked him.

"It does," said Lock.

The immediate choice was obvious. He had to buy time until he could figure something else out. Saying no now wouldn't do that. It would seal Carmen's fate. But he had to sell it to them. They knew what they were asking him to do went against everything in him. That was why he had to make a yes that came with conditions.

Lock made a show of taking a deep breath, followed by a slow exhale. His hand touched the edge of one of the pictures. He counted to five before looking up at his captors.

"Friday prayers?" Lock asked. "That's when it'll busiest, right?"

Padre nodded.

"I'll need a number."

That question was met with puzzled expressions.

"A number?" Chance asked.

"I'm not going to go inside and stay shooting until the cops show and I take a bullet myself. I'll do this, but it can't be a suicide mission. I need an exit strategy, which means that you have to provide me with a number."

More blank expressions.

"How many do you want to die?" Lock said.

Padre and Chance traded a look. This was seemingly one question that hadn't been anticipated.

"And make it realistic," Lock added. "Something achievable that'll give me time to get away. Now that I ask, what are you giving me to do the job? It's going to be tougher with a handgun than a rifle. Ideally, I'll need both. And I'll need to know what security is like. You have done proper surveillance, right?"

Judging by their expressions, the scatter of questions seemed to be selling them the idea that Lock was prepared to commit the atrocity to save Carmen. He had shifted into operational mode, at least as far as they could tell. This was a problem to be solved. His only worry now was that he had acceded to their request too readily.

Chance must have thought the same. "That quick, huh?"

"You say that like you gave me a choice here," Lock said, hoping that his answer would play to Padre's ego and how convinced he'd been by the threats he'd made.

"There's always a choice, Ryan," Chance said.

"Not this time," Lock replied.

"Would you give us a moment?" said Padre, his sudden bout of politeness unnerving Lock.

Padre put an arm around Chance and steered her out of the room, leaving Lock with the rest of the motley crew. Less than a minute later, they were back. This time Padre was going to do the talking.

"Okay, here's the deal. The synagogue has one armed guard. Two on Fridays. If you like, we can assist with neutralizing them. We'll give you whatever you feel you need."

Lock decided to stick to his script. "What I'll need will depend on the number of people you want me to kill."

Padre looked at Chance. She offered a go-ahead-and-tell-him shrug. It was obvious that during their discussion outside the room they had arrived at a number.

"Twelve. Doesn't matter if they're male or female, young or old," Padre informed him.

"No. Younger and female. The old ones are gonna be dead soon anyway, and women breed," Chance cut in.

For a moment Lock found himself caught by the raw craziness of the conversation that was taking place. The tone of the discussion was so matter-of-fact. They talked about slaughtering innocent people the way most others would discuss the weekly grocery list. All Lock wanted was for the talk to be over so he could figure out what the hell he was going to do with the time he'd hoped he'd bought himself.

"I'll do what I can," he said. "But once the shooting starts, picking out individual targets can get tricky. This kind of operation isn't what you'd call an exact science."

"Not just shooting," said Padre, his fingers closing around a grenade attached to his webbing. "You can carry a few of these babies too."

"What? Throw a couple into a kindergarten as I leave?" said Lock, unable to damp down the sarcasm in his voice.

"There's no kindergarten," one of Padre's cadre of men observed.

Chance hadn't missed the shift in Lock's tone. "You sure you'll be able to do this?"

73

"They want you to do what?" Carmen whispered, the two of them sitting alone in the room where they were being held, so close that their faces were almost touching.

They were operating on the assumption that the kidnappers were listening in on their conversation. Or, at the very least, attempting to.

Lock repeated what he'd just told her.

"They're even sicker than I thought. So what do we do?"

"Play along until I can think of something. I mean, I'm not going to kill innocent people."

He waited for her to flinch. His refusal would mean her death as well as his. From her reaction he could see that the thought didn't trouble her, if it had even occurred in the first place. "Good," she said. "I'm glad. I couldn't live if I knew that I was only still here because other people had died."

Her words were of cold comfort to Lock. He wasn't sure he could bear the idea of losing Carmen because of his actions, or inaction, no matter how weak the connection. It had happened to him once, and almost destroyed him. He wasn't sure he could face something like that again in his life. But maybe he'd have to.

"Let's just hope we all survive this," he said, his words lacking conviction.

"This might be nothing, but I think I might know why Chance did this," Carmen said.

"Not to get back at me?"

"That was probably just a bonus, but there's something else."

"Just when I was starting to feel flattered," Lock said.

Carmen threatened a smile, which had been the idea. To Lock's mind, finding laughter in the dark could be a life-saver. The darkest times were often accompanied by bitter irony, which frequently came with an element of humor.

"So what do you think is?"

"She has a child. Or, rather, she had."

Lock's face froze.

Of course.

As soon as Carmen said the word "child", it all came flooding back. When he and Ty had stopped Chance in San Francisco, she had been pregnant. Being pregnant had been one of the main reasons she had managed to get away with causing as much chaos as she had. She had used it as cloak and shield.

After San Francisco, and once the media storm had died down, Lock hadn't given too much thought to Chance. She had been buried inside the prison system for life without parole. He remembered reading something about her having given birth, but that was about it. He'd had sporadic death threats from white supremacist and neo-Nazi groups, but he regarded them as regular people regarded junk email, and treated them in pretty much the same manner, by careful filtering.

"He was taken from her shortly after he was born and placed for adoption," Carmen continued.

"How long did he stay with his mom?"

"I'm not sure. It's usually pretty quick in a case like that where the mother has no chance of being released. A couple of weeks, maybe."

For the first time Lock felt a twinge of compassion. Chance had been fostered after her father had gone to prison. To see her own son taken from her must have been heart-wrenching. "Was she allowed any kind of contact?" he asked.

Carmen shook her head. "She tried, but no dice."

"And you think that was what this escape was about?"

"I don't know, but a son you had to give up is a pretty powerful motivator."

"So where is he?"

"I don't know," said Carmen. "I'm pretty sure he was adopted by a family in California. But I don't know where exactly. Mike would know. He was busy filing some kind of appeal that would have allowed her to find out."

"And did she?" Lock asked.

"I'm not sure, I doubt it. But if she couldn't get the information through the regular channels there would be other ways."

"Like pay someone?"

"Or hack into the adoption records somehow," Carmen added.

Lock flashed back to how adept the kidnappers had been at encrypting their messages, at least until they'd slipped up. He didn't know a lot about that world, but from what he'd seen he guessed they could do something as simple as access a sealed adoption record. Even if they couldn't hack into the computer system, they had the contacts to find a civil servant who would be amenable to a bribe in return for the name of the family who had adopted the baby.

Raising his cuffed hands, Lock rubbed at his chin.

"What?" Carmen said to him.

"This is it. This is our leverage."

"Her son?"

He nodded. "We find him before they do and we'll have something to use against her."

Carmen grimaced. Lock knew how it sounded. He was talking about using an innocent child as a bargaining chip. But maybe there was a way to do it that meant no one else had to get hurt.

"You not forgetting something?" Carmen said, raising her cuffed hands.

"A minor detail. You hang tight."

He walked to the door, and knocked against it with his forehead. A few moments later, a solitary shaven-headed, heavily tattooed guard opened it. Even cuffed, he would have been easy for Lock to overpower, but the others were still close by, and he didn't want to place Carmen in further jeopardy. Not now he had the start of an idea as to how he could dig them out of the hole they were in.

"I'm ready to go do this," Lock told the guard. He leaned in to kiss Carmen's cheek, aware that, if he couldn't make his plan work, this might be the last time he'd see her.

"Be safe," she said to him.

"You too."

He turned and walked out, leaving Carmen in the room. The guard closed the door and turned the key. Lock shuffled down the corridor, the ankle restraints hindering his movement.

74

After ten yards they stopped outside another locked door. The guard opened it, and motioned for Lock to step inside. Padre was sitting alone at a long wooden table. He got up as Lock entered, unsheathed a hunting knife, bent down and used it to sever the white plastic ankle restraints. "Take a seat," he said to Lock.

Lock held up his cuffed hands. "What about these?"

"They stay on until we get to the safe house," Padre growled.

"We?"

"Yeah. I'm going to be your partner for this gig."

At first Lock didn't say anything. This added a whole other level of difficulty. "I'd rather work as a lone operator," he said finally.

Padre smirked. "I'm sure you would. But that ain't happening. Too risky."

"You have Carmen as insurance."

"True enough, but that might not be enough to stop you doing something stupid."

Lock tried again: "Listen, I appreciate the help, but I'll be more effective on my own. And, no offence, but you don't exactly blend into the surroundings."

Padre's smile grew wider. "We both know that ain't true, or you wouldn't have a partner. He don't exactly *blend* either."

"That's different. I've known Tyrone a long time. I know I can trust him. There's an understanding between us. That kind of thing doesn't happen overnight."

Padre seemed to give this some thought. "True."

"So what do you say?" Lock pressed. "Let me take care of this myself."

Padre sheathed his hunting knife. "How dumb do you think I am?"

"You really want me to answer that?"

"Funny guy." Padre leaned in, grabbing Lock's collar. "Case you have any ideas about backing out, or trying something, I ain't letting you out of my sight until you're done."

75

Blindfolded and cuffed, Lock lay alone in the back of the pickup truck. He estimated they'd been driving for around forty minutes. Judging by the noise, and the start-stop nature of the journey, he estimated that the first ten had been on surface streets before they had made it onto a freeway. Now they were back on surface streets.

The truck began to slow. Lock listened hard, but making out all but the most obvious of noises was impossible with the constant ringing in his ears. Along with everything else, it was beginning to grind away at him. He was exhausted, mentally and physically. He had to find a way to push through it. He had no other choice.

Finally, the truck came to a stop. He heard the cab doors open and close. He counted them off. Three door slams would mean a minimum of three people riding up front, Padre and two others. He guessed the rest of the gang were still with Chance and Carmen.

He'd spent the ride turning over in his mind what he had to do. Padre, Chance and the others might not have realized it but their threats against Carmen served only to make his life easier in some respects. Without a risk to her he might have been caught in two minds, torn by the morality of the choices he'd have to make. That was no longer the case. By threatening the woman he loved, they had only strengthened his resolve. When the time came, he would offer them the same quarter they had given him. None.

The back of the truck opened. Hands grabbed his feet and dragged him over the truck bed and out. He struggled to stay upright. The same hands grabbed his wrists, cuffed in front of him, and guided him forward.

"Watch the step," Padre told him.

Lock lifted his foot and tentatively put it down. He followed with his other foot. Padre pushed him forward.

A dozen more steps and someone reached round and pulled down his blindfold. Lock closed his eyes, opening them slowly, allowing himself time to adjust to the light. In front of him was a large television screen. Behind him was a couch and two reclining chairs. Bare floorboards ran to white-painted walls. A bulb swung overhead. It looked like a crack house after a hasty clean-up. The odor of stale bodies and feces was such that Lock would have happily traded his sense of smell for his hearing.

"Don't worry," said Padre. "We ain't staying more than a night." He clapped a hand on Lock's shoulder. "Tomorrow's game day, buddy."

"Now that we're here, you mind taking these off?" Lock said, holding up his hands.

"In a little while."

Lock couldn't summon the energy to argue. There were other more pressing matters to deal with. Such as . . .

"Chance has a son," he said, framing it more as a statement than a question.

Padre's look of studied self-assurance evaporated. "Say what?"

"That's why she decided to get out. So she could go to him. I was just a bonus."

"I don't know what the hell you're talking about," Padre countered, his expression at odds with his dismissal.

"Sure you don't," said Lock.

He had his answer in the way Padre's eyes had darted from his to the floor and back again. Carmen's hunch had been right. Lock was sure of it.

"What's this got to do with you, anyway? And how come you're so interested?"

"It doesn't. I just like to understand what drives people. That's all," Lock told him.

"All that drives us are the Fourteen Words."

"Chance too?"

"Her too."

Padre backhanded a stream of sweat from his forehead. His eyes were wide, and not just with annoyance at Lock's probing. He looked like he'd had a bump of something, most likely speed, on the drive over. That would make him less predictable, but also less focused.

"Listen, can I get some water?" Lock asked. "If it's not too much trouble."

"Sure," Padre said, and stalked off.

Through the doorway, Lock counted two others. With Padre that made three. They were all armed, or at least Lock had to assume they were. Still, three was a manageable number. Especially in such close quarters. All he needed was to have the cuffs off.

He watched as Padre disappeared into the back of the house and one of the others wandered in to stand guard.

Lock smiled at the guy, a scrawny mass of pimples and white power tattoos. "Nice place you have here," he said, taking in the squalid surroundings with a sweep of his head. "Who was your decorator?"

76

Under the watchful gaze of United States Marshal Petrovsky, Ty picked his possessions out of the deep blue tray as a correctional officer ticked each one off against her list. As Ty lifted his SIG Sauer P229, Petrovsky leaned over the counter toward the officer.

"That permitted?"

With a theatrical sigh, she cranked her neck up from her paperwork. She shot Petrovsky a death stare that had no doubt been perfected over the years and now managed to convey an acidic disdain. "No. I'm releasing it to him because it's completely illegal."

Petrovsky's jaw tightened. "Just checking."

Ty's smile was cut short as he lifted the next item from the tray and tried to hastily jam it into his front pocket.

"Pack of Trojan condoms," said the CO, making a tick against her list. She glanced up at Ty and gave him a searching look. "Magnum size. Really?"

"Better safe than sorry," said Ty, his massive shoulders offering a bashful shrug. He grabbed his cell phone. The CO moved down the list, her gaze floating back to Ty for a moment.

"Apologies for breaking up this special moment, but I'm going to need a word with you before you leave," said Petrovsky.

"I'm listening."

"Good. Because what I'm about to tell you is deadly serious."

Stuffing his cell phone into the rear pocket of his jeans, Ty turned back to the marshal. "Go ahead."

"Stay out of my manhunt."

"That it?" Ty asked him.

"You're not going to interfere?"

Ty stepped toward Petrovsky. The US marshal was tall, but Ty had several inches and at least fifty pounds of extra muscle. Petrovsky was no shrinking violet, but Ty's aura was enough to wilt the most testosterone-fueled of men.

"I just spent the last six hours in here on some bullshit charge that won't even make it to court while Ryan and Carmen are out there, facing who knows what. And I'm the guy you're warning?"

Petrovsky's face flushed.

"I'll stay out of your way, and you stay out of mine. How's that?"

"You've been warned," said Petrovsky, doing a swift about-turn and heading for the exit as Ty scooped up the last of his belongings from the tray. The correctional officer handed him a pen and flipped the form around so that it was facing him. "Sign here."

Ty hastily scrawled his name, and followed the retreating Petrovsky toward the exit. Outside, Petrovsky had joined a small knot of other marshals and law-enforcement officers.

Ty pushed his way past them and out through the gate. As he walked, he retrieved his phone, and tried to call Lock. A Hail Mary pass if ever there was one. It went to voicemail. No surprise. Ty was going to have to do this the hard way, and hope he wasn't already too late.

77

C hance stalked into the room, a Glock holstered on her hip. She was carrying a TV tray loaded with sandwiches, a bag of potato chips, and a bottle of water. She placed it on a table in front of Carmen.

"Thank you," Carmen told her.

Chance reached down to free Carmen's hands. She caught her eyes drifting toward the Glock. "Don't get any stupid ideas," she cautioned her.

"I won't if you won't," Carmen said, trying to keep her tone light.

From nowhere, Chance drew back her hand and delivered an open-palm slap across Carmen's face. The force was enough to twist Carmen's neck around thirty degrees.

Chance put her hands on her hips. "What? You think you're smarter than me or something?"

Carmen didn't respond. She wasn't sure there was anything she could say that would pacify Chance. From having access to the woman's prison records, she knew that her client was prone to sudden bouts of rage. Rage that, more often than not, took the form of physical violence. Even though Carmen saw Chance as a victim, she was also a perpetrator. A violent, unstable one, her white supremacist beliefs a thin justification for the darkness inside her.

"You might be a lawyer, but you're still a beaner," Chance continued.

"It's not going to happen," Carmen said.

"What? What's not going to happen?"

"You seeing your son. Not if you go on like this. Look, let me try to help you. I can speak to the authorities. Agree to a deal that if you hand yourself in you can maybe have some kind of visitation. If he wants to see you."

Halfway through, Carmen realized she had made a terrible mistake. But it was already too late. The words were out there.

Chance took a step back. Her right hand slid to the butt of the Glock. She peeled back the leather guard from the holster, and began to draw the weapon.

"Did you tell him about my boy?" Chance asked, the gun clearing the holster.

"Tell who?"

"Your boyfriend. Who else?"

"No, of course not. I'm bound by attorney-client . . ."

Chance pressed the tip of the Glock's barrel against Carmen's lips. Carmen clenched her jaw, her teeth clamping together. Chance kept pushing, forcing the gun into Carmen's mouth, her eyes wild with rage.

"I'm going to take this gun out of your mouth in a second. And I want the truth. Lie to me and I'll blow your head clean off."

Carmen began to choke as the barrel probed deeper into her mouth, pushing against her tongue and moving to the back of her throat. A second later, Chance pulled it out.

"Well? Did you?"

78

Lock chewed slowly, then swallowed the last bite of food. He looked up at his lanky captor. "Can I get some water?"

The man reached down for the bottle, slowly twisted the cap and raised it to Lock's lips. Lock moved his head fractionally so that the water spilled down his chin, dribbling onto his shirt. "Damn. Sorry," he said. "That was my fault."

"No problem." The guy was studying him. Waiting for Lock to ask him to remove the cuffs. Then he would know Lock was up to something.

"Can I have some more?"

The guy put the bottle to Lock's lips again. This time Lock kept his head steady. The guy tipped the bottle back a little further. Lock kept drinking. Like a man dying of thirst. He drank until the bottle was empty. The guy took it away.

"Thanks. Guess I was thirstier than I thought," he said, matter-of-fact.

"You want anything more to eat?"

Lock shook his head. "No. Feeling a little queasy to tell the truth."

A few more seconds passed in silence. The guy started to pick up. Lock squirmed in his seat.

"Sorry about this, but I need to hit the head."

The guard sighed. "You need the john?"

"Yeah, and quick, or I'm going to piss in my pants."

"Okay."

Lock stood. The guy followed him into the bathroom. Lock struggled to lower his zip so that he could pee. He didn't say anything. Instead he held up his cuffed hands. "Kinda tricky. You couldn't . . ." He was looking down at his crotch.

"You want me to pull it out for you?"

"I don't want you to, no. But I can't get it out otherwise and I don't want to piss in my pants either, so here we are."

Lock made another show of trying to lower his zip and free himself, with no luck.

The skinny guard sighed again. This wasn't what he'd signed up for. Pulling another man's junk so he could take a leak. He pulled a set of cuff keys from his pocket. "Don't try anything, okay?"

"You're the one with the gun. What am I going to do?" Lock said, holding out his hands toward him.

79

P adre snatched up his cell phone from the passenger seat. He tapped the answer icon. At the other end of the line, Chance was hysterical. He could barely make out what she was saying.

"Hey, calm down, will you? I can't hardly understand you."

Padre spun the wheel, and turned into the street at the end of which was the safe house. He slowed as a neighbor backed out of his driveway.

"He knows! He knows!" Chance kept screaming.

Padre bit down on his bottom lip. Chance was prone to getting herself all het up. Usually over nothing. He loved the woman. Worshipped her. But she was hard work at times. Always making a mountain out of a molehill.

"Who knows what?"

"What do you mean who? Lock. He knows. He knows about Jackson. That beaner bitch told him. She wasn't supposed to. What with her being my lawyer and everything, but she did."

Padre choked back a laugh. Somehow he doubted that client-attorney confidentiality was still in play if you kidnapped your lawyer and put her through the kind of shit they had. What was

Chance going to do? Make a complaint to the California State Bar?

"So what? So he knows? There's nothing he can do about it."

The nose of the truck eased across the sidewalk and into the driveway. Padre pressed down on the brake pedal and came to a stop behind one of the other vehicles, a stolen Camry that he planned to use for the attack. The side door into the house was open.

Sloppy, he thought. He'd told the guys to keep it closed and secured at all times. The last thing they needed was some curious neighbor wandering inside uninvited.

Chance was still hyperventilating. "Just chill, will you?" Padre said, climbing out of the cab.

He pushed open the door and shouted for the guys. There was no response. The sole of his right boot slipped out from under him. He looked down to see blood smeared across the linoleum floor. It trailed back into the house, thick and copper red.

"I'll call you back," he said.

Chance started up hollering again but he killed the call, pocketed his cell phone and drew his gun, staying tight to the door frame as he pushed toward the hallway and saw a pair of legs protruding from one of the rooms.

Padre raised his gun, pushing it out ahead of him, his finger on the trigger. "Rance?"

No answer.

Padre kicked against the boot sole. No reaction. He stepped into the doorway, sweeping the room with his gun. Only when he knew the room was clear did he glance down.

The dead body was a kid named Wylam. New to the movement. Not the brightest star in the sky. Padre should never have left him with such an important task. But he'd figured that having Rance in the house as back-up would be enough. Problem with that was Rance had a habit of slacking off when his buddy Point wasn't there. That must have been what happened here.

"Rance!" Padre called out again.

Still no response.

Padre knelt down next to Wylam. He'd been shot twice. Once in the chest and once in the head. Both bullets had hit dead center. No prizes for guessing who'd fired them.

The sound of footfalls. Padre stilled, dialing into the sound. Sounded like it was coming from the basement.

Padre smiled. If Lock thought he was going to play hide and seek in a basement, he had another think coming.

Reaching up to the webbing underneath his jacket, Padre's hand closed around a grenade. Chance would be pissed that he'd killed Lock but that was too bad. He'd never liked this whole idea of using Lock. It carried way too much risk, as had just been proven.

There was revenge, and then there was being plain dumb. Allowing a man like Lock to keep breathing when it was easier to kill him was dumb.

With the grenade in one hand and his gun in the other, Padre stepped out into the corridor. Measuring each step, he moved slowly toward the basement door.

80

His mouth covered with a thick binding of grey duct tape, his hands cuffed to a rack of metal shelves that were secured to the wall, Rance tried desperately to free himself. His shouts and screams were muffled by the tape. He thrashed one way and then the other. He kicked out at the shelves, trying to topple them from the wall.

Light spilled down the steps leading into the basement as the door opened. Rance redoubled his efforts to free himself. Straining as far as he could, he tried to see who was at the very top of the stairs. He breathed a sigh of relief as he saw the hulking silhouette. Padre. Lock must have fled after he'd overpowered him and brought him down here.

Everything was going to be okay, Rance told himself. Padre would realize he was down here, free him, and then they could go hunt down Lock. Or at least get the hell out of there before the cops arrived.

He began to shout Padre's name, but the duct tape transformed words into guttural, nondescript noises. Then an air-conditioning unit in the opposite corner of the basement started up, drowning him out entirely. No matter. He was safe now.

81

It was too dark down there for Padre to see anything clearly. And he was damned if he was going to shine a torch and give Lock the easiest kill shot of his life. There was only one way to deal with a rat like Lock.

Padre pulled the pin from the grenade, kept the safety lever pressed down. "Burn in hell, asshole." He drew back his left arm and gently tossed the grenade under-arm down into the basement, the safety lever popping up as the grenade released from his grip.

Slamming the basement door shut, he ran as fast as he could down the corridor. Seconds later there was an almighty bang as the grenade exploded, letting loose all hell, and shaking the walls around him.

Padre reached up to his pocket, and pulled out a pack of smokes. He tapped one out, holstered his gun and fumbled for his lighter. He flicked it. The flame appeared. He lit the cigarette and took a long, slow, satisfying drag. The smoke filled his lungs. He exhaled slowly.

Someone was behind him. He could sense them. Instead of turning, he eased his hand into the front of his jeans, feeling for his cell phone. He edged it out, tapping on the last number dialed before easing the phone back into his pocket.

A second later, his suspicions were confirmed as he felt the chilling unmistakable sensation of a gun barrel pressing into the back of his skull.

"Make any sudden moves, and I'll blow away what little brain you have," said Lock.

82

With the SIG still pressed into the base of his skull, Lock hustled Padre outside. Even in a neighborhood this crime-ridden a grenade exploding in a basement was still sufficient to warrant further investigation.

Lock reached round and opened the passenger door for Padre.

"Scoot over, you're driving," he told Padre.

"You're the boss," said Padre, who seemed to have collected himself after the initial shock of realizing that he'd just fragged his buddy Rance in the basement, rather than Lock.

Padre settled behind the wheel. "Where we going?"

"Take me back to the place where you're holding Carmen."

Padre side-glanced him. "Sure thing."

Padre fired up the engine. He threw the truck into reverse, and began to back slowly out of the driveway.

"What's the address?" Lock snapped. He wanted to see if there was any hesitation on Padre's part. There was nothing to stop him driving somewhere else to buy time.

"One forty North Orange Avenue."

Lock conjured up where it was in his mind's eye. It tallied, at least roughly, with the kind of distance they'd driven before. Padre had reeled it off without pause. If it was a lie it was a credible one that had been expertly delivered.

Padre got to the end of the street. He pulled up to a stop sign. An LAPD cruiser was heading in the opposite direction, toward the house. No doubt to investigate.

"Take a right," Lock instructed him.

"No problem," Padre said, spinning the wheel, and heading in the opposite direction as the cop car sped past them. "I don't want to be pulled over any more than you do."

Lock didn't reply. Padre had a point. They had at least one aim in common. To get to the other safe house without incident.

83

C ell phone in hand, Chance flew out of the bathroom. She'd been in the shower when Padre's call had come in. Thank goodness she had looked over at the sink when she had or she would have missed the screen lighting up with the incoming call. Turning off the water, she had stepped out of the shower and picked up the phone. She'd listened long enough to hear Padre give Lock her location. The rest she had pieced together. Somehow Lock must have gotten the drop on Padre. It was only a matter of time before he, the cops or both would arrive to try to rescue his damsel in distress.

Throwing on clothes over her still damp body, Chance shouted to the others. She flung on a holster, motored through into the room where Carmen was being held, and lifted her to her feet. She began to hustle her outside as the others grabbed their gear.

Two vehicles were parked at the side of the house. Chance would take Carmen and one of her men – he could keep an eye on Carmen while she drove. The lighter they traveled, the less likely it was that she'd be stopped.

"What's going on? Where are we going?" Carmen asked, as Chance opened the rear door of a nondescript red Nissan sedan.

"We're going to take a little trip to the beach," Chance said, slamming the door, and hot-footing it around the car to the driver's door.

84

L ock reached over and cuffed Padre's left hand to the steering wheel of the truck. He reached down toward Padre's pants pocket.

"Woah! You ain't my type, dude," Padre protested, as Lock plucked the cell phone from his pocket.

Lock tapped the screen and pulled up the last number called: Chance's, seven minutes before, for the past six minutes and forty seconds. He had only noticed it when Padre had reached down to terminate it – he had seen the screen lit and realized what had happened.

Lock pocketed Padre's cell, and raised the gun in his hand so that the barrel was pressed hard into Padre's temple. "You just made a big mistake," Lock told him.

Padre continued to smirk. "How you figure that?"

"You would only have called Chance if you'd given me the correct address. If you'd lied, or were driving me somewhere else, you had no reason to take a risk like that."

As he spoke, Lock watched Padre's jaw tighten and his eyes narrow. It was confirmation that what his theory was fact.

"Either way, it's too late. By the time we get there, she'll be long gone. So will your girl. Too bad, huh?"

"Guess you outsmarted me," Lock told him.

Padre glanced at him. "You're being mighty gracious about it."

"Guess I am," said Lock, pulling back the barrel of the gun, and leaning against the passenger door. "Pull over here."

Padre side-eyed him warily. "What?"

"You heard me."

Padre slowed the truck and pulled over to the curb. They were on a quiet street with barely any through traffic. A wall ran down one side, a chain-link fence on the other, fronting an abandoned lot.

"Switch off the engine, but leave the keys in the ignition."

Padre did as he was told. Lock leaned over and unlocked the cuffs, the gun back at Padre's head in case he made any sudden move to fight or flee.

"Okay. Now get out. Nice and slow."

The smirk had returned to Padre's face. He clearly couldn't believe his luck. Lock was not only admitting defeat, he was giving him his freedom.

Padre opened the door. Lock slid over the driver's seat. Needing no further encouragement, Padre stepped away from the truck. He walked toward the back. Lock followed him out through the open door.

Padre was walking slowly down the street. He turned as he heard Lock get out.

"You forgot something," Lock said, holding up Padre's cell phone.

Padre eyed him warily, the way he might regard an aggressive dog that had stopped baring its teeth and begun to wag its tail.

"You sure?" Padre asked.

Lock ignored the question. "Here, take it," he said, extending his arm to full stretch.

Padre took three more steps as a truck with gardening equipment and a couple of day laborers sitting sleepily in back drove around them.

Lock waited until the truck was out of sight. The street was silent. He raised the gun, aiming at Padre's face.

Padre turned to run, his hands coming up to his face as he twisted. Lock pulled the trigger.

The bullet peeled Padre's jaw from his face. Blood puffed out in a broad spray. Padre screamed, the sound muffled by his splintered jaw bone. Lock fired for a second time, this time catching Padre flush in the throat.

Padre fell, mortally wounded, but not yet dead. A hand reached up toward Lock in a gesture of supplication, pleading no doubt for Lock to deliver a third and final shot to end his suffering.

Lock tucked the gun away. His fingers tapped across Padre's cellphone screen, calling up Ty's number. As he waited for his partner to answer, Lock got back behind the wheel of the truck.

In the side mirror, Lock watched as Padre, blood pouring from his neck and face, or what remained of them, crawled, fingers digging into the road, toward the back of the truck. He collapsed, rolling over on to his side, his hands clutching at his throat.

The truck's engine turned over. Lock pulled away, leaving the dying man alone in the street behind him.

85

"Jackson, can you please stop kicking the back of the seat?"

Alicia whirled round to confront Jackson who was swinging his legs back and forth in back of their Suburban. His eyes were glued to the screen of the games console that Jim had let him have for the drive back from Phoenix.

"Feet off the seat," she scolded.

"Sorry, Mom," he said, moving his feet and going straight back to his game.

They had been spending time with Alicia's mom. At least, that was what they had told Jackson, but the truth was that Alicia had been spooked by the news about Freya Vaden, especially after the cops had swung by to make sure they were all okay.

Despite her husband's having shrugged it off, the cops had been really interested when she had described the man she'd seen staring at Jackson a few weeks before. Especially when she'd told them she'd seen him a few times after that: once down by the pier when she was with Jackson, then outside his school, although the guy had disappeared pretty quickly on both occasions when he'd seen her staring at him.

The two officers had traded a look while she'd described him. When she'd asked if they knew who it was, they'd clammed up.

So, Alicia had figured there was no harm in a road trip that would get them out of Manhattan Beach for a while. But now Jackson had school, and Jim was insistent that he couldn't miss another week. They'd had a huge row about it, but he had prevailed. So here they were, heading home, with Alicia hoping that Jim was right about her overreacting.

She glanced at him now. He took a hand off the wheel and patted her leg.

"It'll be fine, honey. I promise you."

"How can you promise that?" Alicia said, lowering her voice to a whisper. "She hasn't been caught yet. Nor has that guy who was hanging around."

Jim shot her the patronizing look he seemed to have perfected. "Only a matter of time. Anyway, the cops said they'd make sure that a patrol swung by the house regularly. We're probably on the safest street in Manhattan Beach right now."

86

L ock stopped the truck a half-block short of the address. He scanned the street before getting out. No one was paying him or the vehicle any kind of attention. It was one of those neighborhoods where people knew better than to take too much of an interest in what anyone else was doing.

He got out and walked quickly toward the warehouse. The area outside was empty. He went to the back, alert for movement from inside. When he reached the door, he pulled it open slowly. Broken glass crunched under his feet as he walked inside. He stopped for a moment, and listened, the Glock aimed at the floor.

Bringing the gun up in a two-handed grip, he moved to the open door and onto the warehouse floor. It was dark and the place smelled strongly of cigarette smoke. An overflowing ashtray sat on a small workbench next to an old couch that was held together with duct tape.

Lock walked across to a flight of metal stairs that led up to a mezzanine level with offices. The stairs clanked under his feet. He reached the top and moved down a gangway.

He came to an office and stopped. He pushed through the door and inside. Bending down, he lifted up a T-shirt. It was the one

Carmen had been wearing when he had last seen her. He could still smell her on the fabric.

He got to his feet and exhaled. No blood. No bodies. A hasty exit. They had fled, and taken Carmen with them. She was alive, at least for now. He had an idea why she hadn't been killed. Chance still needed her, and Lock could make an educated guess as to why that was.

He pulled Padre's cell phone from his pocket and tapped Ty's number again. This time his partner answered almost immediately, hitting Lock with a rapid-fire blaze of questions. Lock assured him that he was okay, and brought him up to speed.

"I'm on my way over there to get you," said Ty.

"No need. I'm good. Listen, how close are you to downtown?"

"Close. Maybe ten minutes," Ty answered.

"I have a job for you."

87

Mike Mazarovitch opened the door of his BMW, eased himself into the driver's seat that automatically adjusted its position to suit his frame, and tossed his briefcase over onto the plush leather upholstery of the passenger seat. As he sat back, he was suddenly aware of a hard piece of metal pressing into the back of his head. His heart pounding against his chest, Mike's eyes flicked to the rearview mirror, taking in the black man who was holding a gun to his head.

"Look, man, take my wallet. The car too if you want. It's no big deal. I'm insured."

Ty smiled. "You think I'm mugging you? Or jacking your ride? That's kind of racially insensitive, don't you think?"

Mike had heard the words, but he didn't follow. "What?"

"A black man sticks a gun in your face and you automatically assume he's just a stick-up man after your wallet and your whip?"

Mike started to half turn in his seat. "No, I mean, well, yeah, if someone puts a gun to my head. I don't see what the color of your skin has to do with it."

Ty's hand clamped down hard on his shoulder. "The son that Freya Vaden gave up for adoption. Where is he?"

Mike's expression shifted from raw fear through relief and settled somewhere near defiance. "I can't tell you that. There's such a thing as attorney-client—"

Ty's hand moved from Mike's shoulder. He shifted forward so that he was parallel to the man. He pressed the gun into his face. "You knew what this was about all along, didn't you, Mike?"

Mike didn't answer.

Ty shifted the gun into his open palm and smashed it hard into Mike's face. His nose broke with a crack. Blood poured out of his nostrils and ran in two streams across his lips and down his chin. He reached a hand up to his nose. Ty grabbed it and shoved it back down, twisting Mike's wrist back on itself for good measure.

"This isn't a game," Ty told him. "People are hurt. People are dead. So when I ask you again in a second to tell me what I want to know, you are going to tell me, or your life is going to get a lot worse. You feel me?"

Mike nodded. Ty released his wrist. Mike pulled out a handker-chief and used it to staunch the flow of blood from his nose.

"Now," said Ty. "Where can I find the folks who adopted Freya Vaden's son?"

~

LESS THAN A MINUTE LATER, the rear passenger door of the BMW opened. Ty got out. He stuck his head back into the cabin for a moment. Mike was still tending his broken nose.

"By the way," said Ty, "call the cops or don't. It's up to you. But seeing as they have some of their own dead, you might want to think about the kind of welcome you'll get."

Mike glanced around, still dazed by what had just gone down. But his eyes signaled that he knew exactly what Ty was getting at. His calling this in would likely cause more problems than it would resolve. "You'll leave me alone if I don't say anything?" he asked.

Ty's eyes made a final pass over the interior. "Good job you got the leather seats, huh? Easier to wipe down. Blood's a bitch to get out of fabric."

"I guess."

Ty eased himself out, tapping on the car's roof as he made to close the door. "Safe home now."

"Ty, what you got for me?" Lock asked, Padre's cell phone in one hand, the other holding the truck's steering wheel.

"Manhattan Beach."

"Great. Text me the address."

"You think we should call the cops?" Ty asked.

Lock had already considered it. "Not yet. Not while she has Carmen. It's too risky."

"Okay, brother, I'll keep it on the down low. You want me to meet you there?"

"Yeah. Call me when you're there, but don't go near the address. Don't want anyone else calling the cops." Lock knew that Ty's presence in white-bread Manhattan Beach would draw more suspicion than his own.

So did Ty. "I hear you," he said.

Carmen sat in the front passenger seat of the red Nissan, her hands and feet secured, while Chance drove, wearing mirrored Aviator-style sunglasses, her hair tied up and covered with a baseball cap. Carmen had been surprised that Chance had ditched the others until Chance had explained to one of them that two females in a car were less likely to arouse suspicion.

Up ahead, Carmen spotted a sign for the next freeway interchange. Chance made a sudden lane change. The truck she'd just cut off blasted its air horn in reproach. Chance threw an arm out of the window, raising a single finger to flip off the driver. Steadying the Nissan, she hit the gas pedal, accelerating away as they passed directly under the sign that read "Manhattan Beach".

Hunched over the steering wheel, Lock scoped out a parking spot next to a partially demolished home, the front of which was surrounded by chain-link fence, aimed at keeping any curious neighborhood kids out. Manhattan Beach was the land of the scraper, a phenomenon where people bought a perfectly good existing house, often for millions of dollars, bulldozed and replaced it with one of their design.

With the truck tucked into the curb, Lock counted down the houses to the one he was looking for. The driveway was empty, but the place had a garage so an empty space out front didn't necessarily indicate that no one was home. He would just have to risk it.

He got out of the truck, and took a quick look at himself in the side mirror. He was a mess, bloodied, bruised, and just plain dirty. Maybe he'd been wrong: a tall, imposing African-American ex-marine would have blended better into the background than he would. But Ty wasn't here yet.

Walking purposefully toward the Hallis residence, Lock watched for signs of movement. Apart from a lone jogger halfway down the block, the street seemed quiet. But he had walked into plenty of unpleasant surprises where the same could have been said. The cops, or people infinitely worse, might be lying in wait, with no interest in advertising their presence.

Lock made it to the driveway and kept moving. Loitering outside was not a good look. He headed down to a gate next to the garage. It wasn't secured. He pushed it open and walked down a path. He came to another gate. On the other side was the backyard. This gate was padlocked. Lock took a few steps back, made a run, grabbed onto the top and hauled himself over.

Dropping down on the other side, he took a moment to scope out the yard. It was smaller than he would have assumed from the street. A trampoline sat in the middle of a small lawn. A smoker barbecue stood off to one side along with some patio furniture—a bench, two chairs and a picnic table.

Mounted just under the roof, an alarm box matched the one out front. From the make Lock knew that it wasn't a dummy. He'd had the same system installed in a client's property. It was good. Not entirely tamper-proof, no system was, but robust enough that entering without setting it off would take time and tools he didn't have right now.

He took a step back, working out his next move. Time wasn't on his side so there was only one. As long as he was quick, his method of entry could do double duty.

He walked to the back door, and used the butt of the Glock to smash through the glass. The alarm began to wail.

For the first time Lock was grateful for his recent bout of tinnitus, muffling the noise. He reached through and, using the key that had been carelessly left in the lock, opened the door.

He stepped inside, moving quickly through the house with the Glock drawn as an extra precaution.

No one was home.

He moved upstairs. The third door he pushed open with the toe of his boot was the one he needed. He stepped into the boy's room, holstered the Glock and pulled out Padre's cell phone.

91

C hance stood on the brakes. The red Nissan shuddered to a halt, Carmen almost faceplanting into the dash before the seatbelt locking mechanism kicked in. Up ahead, several Manhattan Beach Police Department patrol cars covered the entrance to the block they had been heading for.

Thankfully for Chance, if not Carmen, the two officers who were in the street were facing the other way and had missed the emergency stop.

Chance slapped a hand against the steering wheel and cursed. As she tried to assess her next move, her cell phone rang.

It was Padre. About time too.

She tapped the green answer icon. "Make it good because this whole deal is a shit show."

"No kidding," said Lock.

"You did this?" Chance asked.

"Did what? What's the problem?"

Chance wasn't about to give up her location that easy to Lock. "Never mind what my problem is."

"Let me speak with Carmen."

Chance threw the Nissan into reverse and began to back into a nearby driveway so she could turn around and get out of there. "Sure. And make it count because it's going to be the last time you ever do."

Lock didn't hesitate so much as a second. "No, it won't. Because if it is, neither you nor anyone else will ever see your son alive again."

Chance didn't believe him. But what was with all the cops on the block where her son lived? No, she told herself, there was no way Lock would do something like that. Her boy was innocent in all this. Lock knew that, and he wouldn't harm someone who was innocent.

∿

LOCK CRADLED Padre's cell phone between his shoulder and ear. A woman with a shopping cart pushed past him as she went to her car. Lock moved out of her way, leaning against the side of the truck as he counted Chance's seconds of silence. The more seconds, the more likely it was that he had placed doubt in her mind.

After four had elapsed, she came back with "Horseshit."

"You really think I'd have anything to lose if you kill the woman I love? You know I wouldn't. If that wasn't the case, you wouldn't have taken her in the first place. Think about it for a second."

"He's a child. You wouldn't kill a child."

"You think that?"

"Yeah, that's what I think."

"Then you don't really know me," Lock told her, lifting the phone away and slowly exhaling. She wasn't buying it. And if she didn't buy it, Carmen was as good as dead. Which was why he'd used his time inside the house wisely.

"You're bluffing."

"Am I?" said Lock, pulling up the photos icon on the cell phone, tapping on a video and sending it to Chance's cell.

"Take a look at what I just sent you. I already took him out of his house. Why else do you think the cops are there? You know as well as I do that I'm already looking at time inside, where I won't last long. Like I said, I've got nothing to lose if you kill Carmen. But you want to make a trade, that's a different matter. We both get what we want and no one has to suffer."

~

CHANCE OPENED the text that had just arrived. She hit the triangle to play the video, and watched.

It showed, judging by the posters and decor, a young boy's bedroom. The shades were pulled down. Someone lay under the bedcovers. It looked like a child, but she couldn't be sure. The video had been shot in such a way that it didn't show anything but a child-sized lump under the sheets.

The video quickly moved to a family photograph on top of a chest of drawers. Chance's heart quickened as she looked at the picture of her son with the two smug, self-satisfied assholes who had taken him from her.

"Could be anyone in that bed," she told Lock.

"Correct. It could. But is it a risk worth taking? That's what you have to settle on. And if you doubt me, ask yourself why most of the Manhattan Beach Police Department just rolled up on the house."

92

J im Hallis stepped out of the house and over the broken glass littering the patio outside the back door. Alicia was still in the car with Jackson, along with what looked like half of the Manhattan Beach Police Department. The other half appeared to be with him. They looked at him now for a verdict.

Jim mustered an apologetic shrug. "Nothing's been taken. Not as far as I can see anyway."

He could only assume the cops already knew this: they had insisted on going inside first when he'd called in the break-in a few minutes before, immediately after they had arrived home.

A couple of the older cops walked over and stood by the trampoline. They conferred for a moment before heading back to Jim.

"Okay, Mr. Hallis, if you want to bring your wife and son back inside we can arrange for a locksmith. Or you may wish to go stay with relatives for a while."

That would be Alicia's choice, which was why Jim wasn't going to mention it. He shook his head. "No, we just got back from staying with family. We'll stick it out here."

The two cops exchanged a look. "Okay. Well, when we leave we're going to have a unit parked at the end of the block for the rest of the day and through tonight. We'll speak with you again in the morning."

Jim put a hand out and shook the officers'. That was the upside to living in a place like this, with the size of the property taxes around here. When things went bad you could count on people to help you out. "I really appreciate it, Officer."

~

TWO BLOCKS AWAY, over on Pine, Lock was parked next to another scraper site blocked off by fencing. He watched as the Manhattan Beach Police Department cruisers peeled away from the scene, only one remaining on active watch.

One unit wasn't a number that gave him comfort. Chance and her buddies were more than capable of taking on a single cop in a car.

To save Carmen, Lock had raised the stakes, or at least raised Chance's emotional temperature. He could hope that she didn't do something reckless. But hoping for the best was rarely a workable strategy.

He had bluffed that he possessed what she wanted. But it was a bluff that could be blown out of the water at any moment. He needed, somehow, to pull an ace from the pack, and there was only one left in the deck.

93

Chance grabbed a handful of Carmen's hair and pulled her head back. She brought up a knife blade so that it danced shakily in front of Carmen's eyes. "This was your idea, wasn't it?" she said.

Carmen tried to clear her mind. That was easier said than done. A glint of light reflected off the blade, and threatened to send her mind spinning in circles. She took a deep breath.

Her reaction would seal her fate one way or the other. She had to persuade Chance that Lock was serious, while at the same time not enraging her so much that she lost control. She knew in her heart that Lock wasn't capable of killing a child, but she couldn't say so to Chance.

"I would never have told Ryan to hurt your son. I swear."

"Like your word's worth anything. You told him about my son. You had to have. That was why you were asking me all those questions before. Then Lock starting asking Padre the same questions. But it all started with you."

Carmen decided on a change of tack. "You kill me, and your son's dead. And it'll be on you."

Chance blinked. The words seemed to have found their target. A threat seemed to be more credible to Chance than any amount of pleading. Given the woman's background, that shouldn't have surprised Carmen as much as it had.

"You think he'd do it?" Chance asked.

There was only one answer that would keep Carmen alive. "You've pushed him to the edge," she told Chance, praying it wasn't true.

94

Alicia Hallis stood by the living-room window, looking out onto the street. Jim came up behind her, and put a hand on her shoulder. She shrugged it off. "We should have stayed where we were. Coming back was a dumb idea."

Jim took a deep breath. This was an argument that seemingly had no end. "This is our home. More importantly, it's Jackson's home. We can't stay away forever."

Alicia whirled round to face him. "Who said anything about forever? Just until that lunatic is caught and put back in her cage."

A voice from the doorway. Jackson had emerged from his room and was standing there watching them. "What are you guys arguing about?"

"We're not arguing, sweetie," said Alicia.

"We were just talking," Jim added.

Jackson folded his arms. "What's going on? Why were all those police cars here?"

Jim crossed to his son and offered the same shoulder squeeze that Alicia had just rebuffed. Jackson was a little more accepting, scooching in closer to his dad as Jim wrapped him up in a hug. "Nothing for you to worry about," said Jim.

"Then can I go see Morgan?"

Morgan was one of Jackson's school friends. He lived four doors down. The two boys had been tight since kindergarten. They spent most days after school hanging out together. Jackson hadn't seen Morgan, apart from at school or soccer practice, since the whole thing had started.

"No!" said Alicia, her voice high and sharp.

Jim felt Jackson push away from him. He took off for the hallway. A second later they could hear him running up the stairs and back to his room.

Jim shot Alicia a see-what-you-did look. She glared back at him.

"Why do I always have to be the bad guy with him?" she asked her husband as, outside in their backyard, a pair of legs swung over the fence and a figure, shaded by the cover of some shrubbery, jumped down, made a quick check that no one had seen them and headed straight for the still-to-be-repaired back door that was wide open.

95

Staying low, Ryan Lock raced toward the back door, and went into the kitchen. He moved with care, trying to stay light on his feet, and minimize any noise. Not being able to hear himself only added an extra level of difficulty to the task.

In the kitchen, he heard someone walking down the hallway toward him. Lock moved to the door that led into the hallway, and ducked to the blind side.

As Jim Hallis rolled on through the door, Lock shifted behind him, throwing an open palm over his mouth, and pressing two fingers into the side of his neck with pressure to create enough pain to show the man that he was serious. "I'm not here to hurt you, or your son. But I need to talk to you and your wife," Lock said, as softly as he could while still being heard.

Gauging the noise he made wasn't something he had thought about since his hearing had taken a beating. But it was now.

He watched for Jim Hallis's reaction, and prayed that his wife, and Jackson for that matter, stayed where they were for the next few seconds. The red flush seemed to go from Jim's face.

"You understand that I just want to talk?" Lock said.

Jim nodded.

Lock eased the pressure on his neck a notch. "If I take my hand away I want you to stay quiet and walk me into the living room to meet your wife. You can tell her I'm the guy who's come to fix your door. Then we explain what I just told you. Can you do that for me?" Another nod. Lock relaxed his fingers a little further, easing the pressure and the pain. "If you shout, or hit a panic alarm, or in any way try to alert anyone before I have finished speaking to you, I can't guarantee your safety. Do you also understand that?"

A final nod. Lock dropped his hands from Jim, but stayed close enough that he could reassert physical control if he needed to.

"Who are you?" Jim said, side-eyeing him.

"Right now, I'm the repairman. Let's go."

Lock stayed behind him. He pulled his shirt from his pants so that it flapped out at the bottom, partly concealing the gun on his hip. He allowed Jim to walk a few steps ahead of him into the living room, where Alicia had turned on a local news channel.

"Honey, this guy's come to fix the door."

Alicia turned and immediately froze, eyes wide. She wasn't buying it. Not for a second.

Lock didn't blame her. He didn't look like a repairman, unless, of course, they'd just gone ten rounds in a boxing ring and been hit by a truck.

Alicia made a sudden dash for a panic alarm that lay on the coffee table. Pushing off with his back foot, Lock raced her to it, beating her with only inches to spare.

He stepped back, pulled the Glock and raised it toward them. "Sit down. I'm not here to hurt you, but I need to speak with you."

96

L ock picked up a throw cushion from the couch, placed the Glock underneath it along with the panic alarm, and put the cushion back where it had been. Jim and Alicia sat together on the couch opposite. Jim had an arm around his wife, and she wasn't pushing him away.

Glancing down at the cushion that concealed his gun, Lock said, "I don't want your son to be alarmed if he walks in on us."

"Who are you?" Alicia asked him. "And what do you want?"

He told them, as quickly, clearly and succinctly as he could. He skipped past most of the ancient history about how he had come to cross paths with Chance's father and then her. He began with the part he had played in Chance's capture, figuring that would explain why, at least in part, he'd become entangled in the mess.

To their credit, Alicia and Jim Hallis listened to him in silence, only twice interrupting to ask him to clarify something. Finally, when he was done, Alicia asked, "So what do you want from us, Mr. Lock?"

Lock took a deep breath. He had given this a lot of thought. It wasn't an ideal solution. Far from it. It was borderline nuts. But it was the only way he could think of that Carmen could be released safely.

"I want you to allow Freya Vaden to see her son."

Jim shifted uncomfortably next to his wife as Alicia reared up. "Absolutely out of the question."

Lock's chin dropped to his chest. That was the answer he had been expecting. It was the answer he would have given, had the roles been reversed. It was the only answer a parent who loved their child would give. Yet it couldn't be the final answer. Not if this whole nightmare was to be brought to an end without any more bloodshed or pain.

"They meet for an hour. Freya gets to see her son. That's it. It's over."

"How can you say that?" Alicia said. "You can't give that kind of guarantee. You think seeing Jackson will satisfy her? What if she tries to take him with her?"

"I've thought about that," said Lock. "I think I can arrange this in such a way that there's no risk of that happening. Freya sees him, then goes back to jail and we go on with our lives."

"And what about Jackson? That's going to mess with his head in ways you can't even begin to imagine," said Jim Hallis.

"It'll be hard," said Lock. "What I'm asking isn't easy for anyone. But kids are a lot more robust than we like to think. If he doesn't know the truth about where he came from, and he finds out later, and that you concealed it from him for all those years, that won't play well either."

Alicia could barely keep the acid from her tone. "You just told us you were some kind of super-charged bodyguard. Now you're a child psychologist too?"

"I think what my wife's saying is that, no matter how you try to dress this up, it's no good for us or our son. So that means the answer's no."

Lock's hand dug under the cushion. His hands closed around the butt of the Glock.

"You said you only wanted to talk," said Jim.

"I did. I do. But just as you want to protect your son, I want to protect Carmen. That's what I came here to do, and that's what I'm doing. If it means some extra therapy sessions, that's a damn shame, but what can I tell you? The world's not a fair place."

Lock stood, the Glock in his hand. "Now, let's go get your son."

Alicia stood up. Hands on her hips, her chin jutted out, she stared defiantly at Lock. "You're not taking him anywhere with you!"

Lock took three quick steps toward her. When he was at arms' length from her, he stopped. He raised the Glock. "I'm sorry. I really am. Now you can both come with me and we can all make sure he stays safe, or I can tie you up and take him out of here by force. Your choice."

"That's not a choice," Alicia said, intimidated by the gun in her face, her hands and voice trembling.

Lock stared at her, taking no pleasure in any of this. "Welcome to my world."

97

The Glock tucked out of sight, with the help of a windbreaker Jim Hallis had lent him, Ryan Lock climbed into the back of the Hallis family car with Jackson. His parents rode up front. Having taken their cell phones, Lock had waited outside as Jim and Alicia had done their best to explain to Jackson that his birth mother wanted to meet him. Jackson had seemed puzzled, bordering on bewildered, but happy to go along with it.

Lock had already gleaned from Jim that they had never kept the existence of Jackson's mother a secret from him. He knew he was adopted. He knew his birth mother was in prison, and that was why she couldn't keep him. But they had left the other lurid details for later.

Now, as they turned out of the driveway and headed in the opposite direction from the Manhattan Beach Police Department cruiser parked at the other end of their block, Jackson was suddenly curious. "Did my birth mom get out of jail?" he asked.

As Jim and Alicia froze, Lock stepped in. "She's out for a little while, but she has to go back."

"How come?"

Now it was Lock's turn to struggle. Thankfully, Alicia was there to make the catch for him. "It's like a vacation she's having. And one of the things she wanted to do was to see you."

Lock had to hand it to her. That was better than the answer he'd been putting together.

"Okay," said Jackson, apparently satisfied. "Can we get ice cream after?" he asked, a moment later.

As his parents assured him that they could, Lock packed down a fresh wave of self-loathing for what he was doing. Placing three completely innocent people in harm's way to save Carmen. But, he told himself, he was there to keep them safe.

He could have handed the whole thing off to the cops. They could have tracked Chance down. They had the resources, not to mention the motivation. But their motivation had given him pause. These things could easily go wrong, especially when the main drive was Chance's recapture. A hostage could be killed, either by Chance, one of her cronies, or simply in the cross-fire.

No, it was better this way. If things went south it would be his burden to carry. If he handed it off and Carmen died, he would always have a question hanging over his decision.

This was his puzzle to solve.

98

At the end of the Manhattan Beach pier, a fisherman cast his line, and glanced over at Ty Johnson, who was struggling to make sense of the fishing tackle he had hastily assembled from a pawn shop in Hawthorne.

"Might want to think about putting some bait on the end of that hook," the fisherman side-mouthed.

Ty flushed, looking down at the bare hook tied to the end of his line. At least Lock wasn't here to witness his moment of humiliation.

The fisherman dug into a large plastic bucket of iced bait, and tossed Ty some. He caught it with one hand. "Thanks. I'm kind of new to this."

"No kidding."

~

Lock scoped out the area as Jim Hallis pulled into a parking spot a block short of the entrance to the pier. Everything looked normal. The place was busy without being crowded, which was close to the ideal situation for something like this.

The risk to Jackson from Chance was close to zero, at least in terms of physical harm. What Lock worried about was an attempted abduction, and the immediate fall-out from it if Jim or Alicia rushed to intervene. There was no question in Lock's mind that Chance would not hesitate to drop either of them if she had to. Given that, as she saw it, they had her son, she might try to harm them as a simple act of revenge.

Lock glanced at Jackson. "You ready?"

Jackson gave an embarrassed shrug. "Sure."

"Good. Now, remember that I'm going to be close by the whole time so if you change your mind you can," Lock reassured him.

Lock knew that curiosity had gotten the better of Jackson, and he felt slightly ashamed of himself again. He placed his fingers on the door handle.

"I'm going to step out to make this call. Won't take long."

Neither Alicia nor Jim said anything.

Lock got out and immediately walked to the back of the vehicle. If they had a sudden change of heart and decided to flee, they'd have to back over him to get away.

He pulled out Padre's cell phone and made the call. The answer was immediate.

"We're here," he said.

CHANCE'S EYES were out on stalks as she placed a hand in the small of Carmen's back and guided her down the pier. The sun was a pink-orange blush on the distant horizon and the ocean was calm. Down below, a line of surfers patiently waited their turn and a couple of people walked their dogs on the beach.

An elderly man waddled past them in khaki shorts and T-shirt. Chance checked him out for signs of a gun or a radio. She had the feeling that at any moment someone could grab her, then cops and Feds would come flying in from all directions.

She was prepared for that. She had pretty much made her peace with the idea that Lock had set her up. That was what she would have done if their situations had been reversed. Her only hope was that first she would get to see her son. If she didn't? If it was a matter of complete betrayal? Well, she would make good on her threat to kill the woman next to her.

～

JACKSON CLAMBERED out of the back of the car. He was holding his skateboard. He'd insisted on bringing it with him.

"You good?" Lock asked.

Jackson didn't say anything. He walked onto the sidewalk, threw down his board, hopped on and began to skate in the direction of the entrance to the pier.

Alicia shouted after him: "Jackson!"

He turned, giving her a what-now look that was more thirteen- than eight-year-old. He stopped, expertly flipping up his board and catching it one-handed.

"Wait for us," Alicia said to him.

Lock whirled round to look at her. *Us?*

That had not been the agreement. He was to walk Jackson down to meet with Chance. She would release Carmen and have an hour to spend with Jackson before he went back to his parents. Having either Alicia, Jim or both of them could only lead to any number of dangerous complications. It was all kinds of a bad idea.

Lock had to head it off, and fast. Chance was waiting. They didn't show soon, she would get antsy, and the whole thing could fall apart.

"I go alone with him. That was the agreement," Lock said, as Jim joined his wife on the sidewalk.

"Agreement?" Alicia snorted. "You had a freaking gun on us."

Lock stepped toward her. Thankfully, Jackson was wrapped up in checking his board. "And I still do," said. "So keep your voice down."

Jim looked scared. Lock wasn't sure what was terrifying the man more— Lock, the gun, or his wife. On balance, thought Lock, it was more than likely his wife.

"Tell you what," said Lock. "Walk behind, but keep your distance and be cool. You flip out and we could all get hurt."

Jim nudged his wife to accept the offer. She shot him a look of disgust but finally, she said, "Okay."

Lock jogged to catch up with Jackson. Alicia and Jim Hallis waited, and when Lock and their son were twenty yards ahead, they fell in behind them.

99

Alicia Hallis watched Ryan Lock walk onto the pier with her son. She turned to her husband. "We should call the cops," she said, digging into her purse for her cell phone.

Jim placed his hand on top of hers and held it. She started to twist away from him. "I already did," he told her.

She looked at him with fresh eyes. She had pretty much already decided that if anything happened to Jackson their marriage would be over. His casual attitude had always grated on her, and when he hadn't stood up to someone coming into their home it had only reinforced her view of him. "When?" she asked him.

"Back at the house. When I went to the bathroom. He was so focused on what you were doing that I figured I had the best shot."

Alicia looked around. If Jim had called the cops then it kind of begged an obvious question. "So where are they?"

He didn't know. Usually there would be at least a patrol car near the pier. But right now there wasn't so much as a cop in sight.

"What did they say when you spoke to them?"

Here Alicia came again with the criticism, he thought. He was the one who'd risked getting shot and he was still going to get it in the neck.

"They didn't. I texted the number they gave us."

Alicia glared at him. "You sent a text?"

"I thought that if I was overheard talking to someone . . ."

Alicia pulled her cell phone from her bag. Lock wasn't looking at them. No one was. No one was going to stop her.

❧

STAN PETROVSKY STOOD, one foot on the rear bumper of the patrol car that was parked, along with a half-dozen others, just out of sight of the pier. He put a hand up to his earpiece, pressing it in, and trying to focus on the stream of updates that were coming in from the members of the Arrest Response Team.

Ten yards away, the Manhattan Beach chief of police stood with a couple of her senior officers. Bitching, no doubt, about Petrovsky's call.

The local cops had wanted to apprehend Lock and the Hallis family en route to the pier. Petrovsky had had different ideas. If they did that they could kiss goodbye to recapturing Chance, at least for the time being.

Needless to say there had been massive resistance and pushback against Petrovsky's desire to wait. But he had an ace up his sleeve: the lawyer who was being held hostage. He had argued that, assuming she was still alive, they would be placing her in mortal danger.

His real motive, though, was his desire to take Chance and as many of her remaining crew as they could get. Dead or alive. It didn't matter which.

A fresh message crackled in Petrovsky's ear.

"I got a visual on Vaden. She's just rolled up."

Petrovsky keyed his radio. "Okay, hold your position. I'm on the move."

❧

LOCK STOOD with his back to a railing as Jackson circled a bench on his board. An elderly lady sitting on the bench reading her Kindle shot him an irritated look as he clacked past her. "Can't you read the signs? There's no skating on the pier."

Smiling to himself, Lock nodded to Jackson to knock it off. Jackson lifted up his board with a mumbled "Sorry," and walked over to stand with Lock.

The lady grumbled something that Lock didn't catch through the hum in his ears, and went back to her reading, completely oblivious to what was about to go down.

Walking slowly toward them were Carmen and Chance. A few steps behind came two men in their twenties who, judging by their ghostly white skin and shaved heads, had to be two of Chance's motley crew.

Lock pushed off the railing as Chance approached, and the two guys moved in to flank Carmen.

"Stay here," Lock told Jackson.

He walked toward Chance. "He only speaks with you as long as he wants to," he said to her.

Chance looked straight through Lock to Jackson. There was a shiver of longing in her eyes that Lock hadn't seen before. He doubted anyone else had either. Her in-your-face bravado had given way to something else.

Looking at the woman standing in front of him, it was hard to imagine that she was capable of such cold-blooded brutality. But she was, and he had to remember that. "You're not taking him with you either," he added. "So don't even think about it."

Her gaze shifted back to him. "I know," she said.

"Now," Lock continued, "tell Dumb and Dumber there to step away from Carmen or I'll blow their heads clean off their necks."

Chance turned and signaled to the two men to step away. Reluctantly, they retreated to the other side of the pier.

Lock stayed where he was as Chance walked past him and spoke to Jackson. He didn't catch what she said but Jackson nodded. Mother and son walked over to the bench and sat down. A few seconds later, the elderly woman got up and scuttled off at speed, throwing anxious glances over her shoulder at Chance as she went.

~

NEAR THE END of the pier, about a hundred yards from where Lock was standing, close to Chance and Jackson, Ty began packing up his collection of fishing gear. The man next to him side-glanced him. "Never going to make much of a fisherman unless you learn to have some patience."

Ty grabbed the last of the gear and shoved it into a bag. He snapped the rod clean in two, and shoved that in with the rest of his supplies as the fisherman stared at him, open-mouthed. He felt for the gun tucked into his waistband and headed back up the pier, his long strides eating up the ground.

He closed in on Carmen. She was rooted to the spot and staring at Lock, who was standing a short but respectful distance from Chance and Jackson. Lock would stand guard until either of them was done. That had been the promise he'd made to Jackson's parents.

Carmen smiled when she saw Ty. He reached her, and offered her an arm. "Link my arm, we're getting out of here," Ty told her, throwing a deathly stare toward Chance's two skinhead buddies, who returned the favor but stayed where they were.

"But Ryan?"

"Ryan's going to hang out."

Carmen stopped, forcing Ty to stop too. "That's her son?"

The two skinheads shuffled their feet. Their hands hovered near the beltline of their long shirts.

"Yeah, that's him. Now we need to split," said Ty.

Carmen remained at a dead stop. "I need to make sure he's okay."

She was serious. Ty could see that. It was commendable. Very few people delayed walking to freedom and safety because of their concern for someone else. Ty had always gotten the superficial part of what had attracted Lock to Carmen. Now he got a glimpse of the deeper reason. They were kindred spirits. He leaned in toward her. "Ryan's here for that."

"I know, but—"

Ty cut in: "You see those two assholes with Chance."

Carmen's eyes slid over to them. "Yes."

"They have guns. I have a gun. Ryan has a gun. The less people we have in the mix right now, the safer for everyone. We stick around and we're not making things any better, we're making them worse. You feel me?"

WITH A WAVE OF RELIEF, Lock watched Ty escort Carmen down the pier and toward the street. On the bench, Chance was talking with Jackson. He laughed at something she said. His reaction took Lock aback.

She reached out, took Jackson's hand in hers, and studied his palm. Lock tensed, fearing this might be a prelude to her and the two skinheads across from them trying to take the boy and make a run for it. He shifted his attention back and forth between the men and Chance.

Ty was almost at the other end of the pier with Carmen. They walked toward where Alicia and Jim Hallis were standing.

Just beyond them there was movement as a hulking SUV with blacked-out windows stopped next to the entrance to the pier. The skinheads noticed it too. They called over to Chance.

The SUV rolled up onto the curb, and kept coming. The skinheads were getting antsy. They shifted their weight from foot to foot. Chance ignored them and continued her conversation with Jackson, who seemed oblivious to the fresh ripple of tension.

Behind the first SUV came another. This one dark blue rather than black but with the same heavily tinted windows. It parked across the entrance to the pier.

Out on the Pacific, two inflatables were cutting through the water, heading for the pier. Each carried six men. Even from this distance they looked to Lock like some kind of law enforcement. Under their lifejackets they wore black body armor, and several were sporting helmets.

～

LOCK HELD UP HIS ARMS, palms open to the two skinheads as he walked over to the bench. Chance looked up at him as he reached them.

"Think it might be about time to wrap this up for now," he said, with a nod to the black SUV that was rumbling ominously in their direction.

Chance moved in to hug Jackson, tenderly kissing the top of his head. When she pulled away, Lock saw tears in her eyes. Her lip was trembling. Jackson looked embarrassed.

She and Jackson stood up. She wrapped him in a tight hug. The skinheads were heading over to her, their eyes out on stalks as the boats moved under the pier. Judging by their reaction, Lock was certain that this wasn't their cavalry.

Finally, Chance let Jackson go. Now she was full-on sobbing, her shoulders rising and falling.

Lock motioned that he was going to take Jackson. He shouldn't have felt anything for Chance. Not after what she had put him and, more importantly, Carmen through. But he couldn't help himself. There was humanity in the darkness. There always was when it came to the bond between a mother and her child.

After a few more awkward seconds, Chance nodded to Lock, moving in for one last squeeze before stepping away.

"I'm going to walk you back to your folks," Lock said to the boy.

Placing a hand gently on Jackson's shoulder, Lock walked with him back to where his parents were standing with Ty and Carmen.

～

INSIDE THE BACK seat of the lead SUV, which was crammed with members of the marshal's Arrest Response Team, Petrovsky keyed his radio. "Okay, everyone, hold up until Lock clears us with the boy."

The marshal driving brought the SUV to a gentle stop. Through the front windshield they could see Lock and Jackson less than forty yards away and closing all the time. Beyond them, Chance had been joined by her two-man escort who were growing increasingly agitated as they realized they had no easy escape route.

TEARS ROLLING DOWN HER FACE, Chance watched Jackson retreat into the distance with Lock. Next to her, one guy's face twisted into fury.

"You just gonna let that asshole Lock walk away like this?" he said, reaching down and pulling out his gun.

He brought it up, trying to center Lock in the sights. His hand was shaking. He did his best to focus. He took a breath, adjusting his footing. He readied himself to fire.

100

As the guy began to draw, Ty handed Carmen off to Jim Hallis, and took off back down the pier. The tailgate of the SUV popped open to reveal two armed marshals. One raised his weapon. Ty ignored him, and kept running.

Lock looked up as Ty cleared the SUV.

"Threat, rear!" Ty bellowed.

Grabbing the back of Jackson's collar with his left hand, Lock spun around 180 degrees so that he and Jackson were standing back to back, Lock's body placed between Jackson and the threat.

With his right hand, Lock drew his gun and brought it up to return fire if he had to.

~

As the skinhead's finger fell to the trigger, and Lock pivoted, Chance had already reached for her knife. Her fingers closed around the handle as she drew it out, clasping it in an icepick grip, the blade pointing down from her hand.

Raising her arm, she brought the knife down in a wide slashing arc across the gun arm of the skinhead who was about to take the shot at Lock. The blade sliced diagonally from his elbow halfway down his forearm. The gun dropped, and he fell into a crouch.

He looked up at her. "What you do that for?"

"You ain't that good a shot and that's my son next to him."

Lock had already scooped Jackson into his arms, taken off, and was running past the SUV, headed for cover. Behind him, Ty had taken a knee, his gun pointed, ready to squeeze off covering fire.

At the same time the SUV's doors popped open. It started moving again, three marshals using the open doors as cover as they bore down on Chance.

~

GASPING FOR AIR, Lock held on tight to Jackson as he rounded the rear of the SUV. Using the hulking vehicle as cover, he slowed, and put Jackson back onto his feet. "You okay?" he asked.

The boy nodded, his face bloodless and drawn. Alicia came at them in a rush, throwing her arms around Jackson. Ty placed himself in front of them, his gun still drawn.

"Get them the hell out of here," Lock said to his partner.

"Why? Where are you going?" Ty asked.

"Just do it," said Lock, turning back toward the SUV as it continued to bear down on Chance and the two skinheads.

Ty grabbed Alicia by the arm and hurried her back toward her husband and Carmen. A half-dozen patrol cars were now parked across the entrance to the pier. Ty holstered his weapon and hustled the small group toward them as a couple of uniformed officers rushed to help.

~

LOCK PUT his hands up as a helmeted marshal pointed his weapon directly at him.

"Get the hell out of here," the marshal barked.

Lock stood his ground. "Where's Petrovsky?"

The marshal stared him. "I said, move back."

Beyond the SUV, Lock could see the two skinheads, arms atop their heads, kneeling. Chance stood behind them, on her feet and defiant.

Several marshals barked at her to assume the position. She didn't move. She just stood there. Then, slowly, she turned her back to them, her hands down loose by her sides, the knife lying at her feet.

At first Lock thought she was going to walk down to the end of the pier. Maybe she planned on jumping. Maybe the inflatables hadn't been cops after all, but some of her guys, although he doubted it from the way they had come in and how they were kitted out.

The marshal was still gun-facing him, weapon drawn. Glancing over his shoulder, Lock checked that Ty was getting Jackson and his parents out of the area.

Chance stopped walking. Several marshals had run forward, a couple of them toting heavy Kevlar ballistic shields, and grabbed the two skinheads. They were swiftly cuffed, hauled to their feet and dragged back down the pier as more marshals poured in from behind Lock to fill the gap.

Chance was about twenty yards away from the closest marshal. Lock counted at least a half-dozen guns pointed at her. He looked back to the marshal with the rifle trained on him.

"Let me go speak with her. Or at least get me Petrovsky."

The marshal ignored him.

Lock took a step to one side so that he could get a better view of Chance.

"Stay where you are," the marshal repeated.

Lock stopped where he was. He had a feeling about what would happen next. He could only pray that he was wrong.

A few seconds ticked by. Chance didn't move. Neither did any of the Arrest Team. They repeated their instructions. Chance paid no heed.

～

CHANCE TOOK A DEEP BREATH, filling her lungs as full as she could. Out beyond the end of the pier, at the far edge of the Pacific horizon, the sun was starting to sink, orange giving way to a pink hue.

She closed her eyes, and conjured up the fresh image of Jackson. He was beautiful. Perfect. He would grow up into a tall, handsome, strong man.

She had given him to the world, a perfect gift. She felt a sudden swell of pride.

Opening her eyes, she smiled. She took another breath, tasting the salty air at the very back of her throat.

She didn't have long. The men shouting at her were growing impatient. Soon they would grow tired of waiting and move in. They would place her in shackles and take her back. She would no longer be free. She would be a prisoner, an exhibit, a warning to others like her. They would punish her for their own failures.

There was only one way left to defy them. A final option. A solitary path she could take.

She took one final breath, this time letting the air release from her mouth in a rush. There was no going back.

Now.

~

LOCK COULD ONLY WATCH. One second Chance was standing perfectly still, facing the ocean. The next, she whirled round to face the marshals. As she spun, her right hand dropped to her side, as if she was reaching for something.

Even with the low buzz in his ears, Lock heard each and every shot as a distinct crack.

Five shots.

Three struck her chest, and one the right side of her neck. The final shot smashed into her nose.

Her slight frame lifted off the ground. Her head snapped back. She landed with a thud. She didn't move.

Blood poured from her head and seeped from her chest. Her arms were spread wide, her legs together in a pose of martyrdom.

Lock saw Petrovsky rush toward her body, his gun drawn and pointed at her corpse. For a second it looked like he might fire a final shot but, at the last moment, he seemed to gather himself and his index finger dropped back to the trigger guard.

His throat tightening, Lock struggled to make sense of the sadness that welled inside him. Hands grasped his arms as two marshals rushed in to move him away.

He thought about shrugging them off. He didn't. He allowed them to turn him around, and hustle him back down the pier.

As they reached the entrance, Lock lost patience. He shook them off. They told him to stay back. He complied.

Ty was standing a few feet away, talking with a couple of Manhattan Beach cops. Lock walked over to him. Ty broke away from the cops.

"Jackson?" Lock asked.

Ty seemed to grasp what Lock was asking without him having to spell it out.

"He's gone. Didn't see any of it," said Ty.

Small mercies, thought Lock. No child deserved to witness what they just had. Hearing the news would be bad enough.

"I couldn't stop her," said Lock.

"You wanted to?" Ty asked, his expression somber.

Lock didn't know. He was still processing it all. His reaction as he had watched Chance standing there had surprised him. "Yeah, I think I did."

A patrol car door opened. Carmen got out. She walked toward them. Ty tapped Lock's elbow. "Catch you later." He wandered over to some cops.

Lock went to meet Carmen.

She put her arms out wide and they embraced. He rubbed the small of her back. She buried her face in his chest.

They stayed like that for a long time. Just the two of them. Both glad they had survived.

EPILOGUE

It had been over two weeks and Lock still couldn't manage a full night's sleep. It was a little after three in the morning, and here he was, standing over the sink in Carmen's kitchen, her cat rubbing against his legs. He reached down and scratched behind its ears. It purred appreciatively. He scooped the animal up into his arms. It placed a paw on each of his shoulders, and rubbed it's nose against his neck.

"Ryan."

Carmen stood in the kitchen doorway. "Come back to bed."

"I'll be there in a minute," he said, handing her the cat.

She studied him for a moment. "You did what you thought was right."

"Yes, I did."

She retreated back to her bedroom with the cat. Lock opened a kitchen cabinet, took out a glass and filled it with water from the faucet. He could go back to bed, but he knew that sleep would evade him.

He drank the glass of water, walked into the living room, threw on pants, sneakers, and a sweatshirt. On his way out, he looked in on Carmen. She had fallen back asleep.

Lock left a note for her in the kitchen, and headed out. He took the stairs, and less than a minute later he was sitting in his Audi.

The streets were as close to empty as they ever got in Los Angeles. He headed west towards the coast.

The night was perfect. Warm enough that he could drive with the windows open. Apart from the freeways, the city was still.

He tried to take a moment to savor the most precious gift he had: his freedom. Many people who had done what he had, taking Jackson to meet with his birth mother against his parents' wishes, would be in jail.

His decision haunted him. He knew why he had done it. Faced with the same dilemma he would likely do it again. But that didn't make it right.

Alicia Hallis agreed, even if her husband didn't. She had been pushing hard for Lock to be arrested for kidnapping, among other crimes. Thankfully for Lock, the various law enforcement agencies, and more crucially, the District Attorney's Office, wanted the whole mess forgotten. Lock wasn't the only person who had come away from the experience with his reputation tarnished. Almost no one had emerged looking good.

Shared culpability wasn't something that offered him any comfort. He couldn't shake the look on Alicia and Jim's faces when he had faced them down and hauled them into his nightmare. Insomnia seemed like a minor penance for what he had done.

He was tired, and he was weary. Guilt trailed him everywhere he went. It pressed in on him like heavy air before a thunderstorm.

Watching Li Zheng's parents bury their son hadn't helped. He had attended the funeral, along with Carmen, and Ty. Before they had even sat down a family member had asked them to leave. They had expressed their sorrow, and complied. Both he and Ty had written separate letters to Li Zheng's parents, expressing their regret for what had happened. They received no reply.

Like Alicia Hallis, Lock didn't blame the parents of the young hacker for their anger or where it was aimed. To all of them, Lock must have seemed like some kind of apparition of doom. That was certainly how he had felt these past two weeks.

The only consolation he had was that Carmen had survived. Others, Ty included, had tried to convince Lock that he had saved her. Without his intervention, she would have been killed. Lock saw it differently. If she hadn't met him in the first place, she wouldn't have been abducted.

Deep down, Lock knew that none of his thinking took him anywhere good. It was the nature of his trade that people could be hurt as a consequence of saving others. You could draw your weapon or keep your hands in your pockets, and others would suffer either way.

He thought of the saying about good men doing nothing allowing evil to flourish. It was true back then. It was true now, maybe even more so than before.

He could be accused of any number of misdeeds and bad calls. He felt every one of them deeply. But he had never stood idly by. In the final reckoning, he didn't know if that counted for much. He could only hope that it did.

In the meantime, he knew that somewhere along the line he would have to forgive himself. There would be others along the way who needed help from a man like him. If he allowed guilt to consume him, he would be worthless to them.

Carmen had said as much to him over dinner the previous evening when they'd returned to the restaurant in Santa Monica where this series of horrific events had begun. After most of the meal had passed with Lock brooding and silent, she had decided that enough was enough.

Fixing him with a stare that was two-thirds attorney and one-third girlfriend, she reached across the table, and wound her fingers around his hand.

"You're allowed to make a choice you might not be comfortable with, Ryan. You're not perfect. None of us are. Everyone deserves a second chance. Even you." The last line she delivered with a wry smile. Carmen knew him well enough to know that he was his own hardest critic.

It had taken until now for the meaning behind her words to fully sink in. She was right. He did.